Noble and Blessed

by

Laura Strickland

Hearts of Caledonia, Book Three

Noble and Blessed

Cover Art by *Diana Carlile*

The Wild Rose Press, Inc.
PO Box 708
Adams Basin, NY 14410-0708
Visit us at www.thewildrosepress.com

Publishing History
First Tea Rose Edition, 2019
Print ISBN 978-1-5092-2478-4
Digital ISBN 978-1-5092-2479-1

Hearts of Caledonia, Book Three
Published in the United States of America

"My name," the woman told Tally, "is Alanna, and I am daughter to our chief, Atholl. You will call me Mistress Alanna, aye?"

Tally realized he'd just been traded. Like an axe or perhaps a surplus hound, he'd been given away, without so much as a thought for his preferences. In this new world to which he'd been dragged and driven, he must come when called and stay when bidden, every freedom stolen away.

Worse, he could not tell whether this change might be for good or ill. He detested MacAtholl right down to his marrow, yet this woman represented an unknown, and might prove twice as vicious. The way she watched him jangled his nerves, and screamed danger. Ah, by the goddess, how might he protect himself?

"I see you ha' taken some injuries," she went on. "You ha' been tended by the healer, aye?"

"Yes." His voice came out husky from disuse; her gaze quickened.

"I will afford you time to recover from your wounds and the long journey before you start wi' your duties here. New clothing, I think. Good food and a rest."

"New duties?"

"You belong to me now. You will work here, and live here also."

Heat rushed over Tally in a wave. He, son of one chief and brother to another—a holy man among his own people—must now do this woman's bidding. But no, he hastily assured himself, as he had from the beginning of this terrible ordeal, she did not own him. He belonged only to the god and goddess, those same who gave him life.

Books by Laura Strickland
available from The Wild Rose Press, Inc.

Hearts of Caledonia Series:
Loyal and True, Book One
Valiant and Wise, Book Two
Noble and Blessed, Book Three
Dead Handsome: A Buffalo Steampunk Adventure
Off Kilter: A Buffalo Steampunk Adventure
Sheer Madness: A Buffalo Steampunk Adventure
Steel Kisses: A Buffalo Steampunk Adventure
Tough Prospect: A Buffalo Steampunk Adventure
Devil Black
His Wicked Highland Ways
Honor Bound: A Highland Adventure
The White Gull (part of the Lobster Cove Series)
Forged by Love (sequel to *The White Gull*)
Words and Dreams (sequel to *Forged by Love*)
The Hiring Fair (part of the Help Wanted Series)
Awake on Garland Street
Stars in the Morning (part of the Landmarks Series)
The Guardians of Sherwood Trilogy:
Daughter of Sherwood, Book One
Champion of Sherwood, Book Two
Lord of Sherwood, Book Three
Short Stories:
Mrs. Claus and the Viking Ship
The Tenth Suitor
Christmastime on Donner's Mountain
Ask Me (part of the Candy Hearts Series)

A word about the Picts and the Caledonii

Not a great deal is known about the Picts, certainly not as much as we might wish. They left few written records, which makes research for even a work of romantic fiction challenging. One thing we do know is that they did not call themselves "Picts." That appellation was leveled by the Romans and stemmed from the pictures (tattoos) they wore on their skin, so numerous they were often referred to as "blue men."

The language of the Picts/Caledonii has not survived except in place names and some given names inscribed on stones. Research tells us it was closely related to ancient Welsh, and I have chosen to give my characters names with an ancient Briton/Welsh flavor.

At the time of my story, Celtic clans had moved into western Scotland from Ireland and settled the kingdom of Dal Riada. They steadily encroached upon the north and east of Scotland, a territory once controlled by tribes loosely gathered under the name "Caledonii." Beneath this name there existed sub-tribes, and I have called mine the "Epidii." Bitter conflict arose between the Gaels and the Caledonii as they contested for land. Later, as legend has it, they would be united via marriage under Kenneth MacAlpin.

But predating the marriage of Kenneth MacAlpin, I would like to think there may have been other unions that offered the gift of peace, however hard-won or temporary. This being a work of romantic fiction, I invite you to imagine, along with me, the individuals both Gael and Caledonian who may have passed down to us their knowledge of magic and deep love of place which endure to this day in the place we call Scotland.

Caledonian hearts are loyal and true.
Caledonian hearts are valiant and wise.
Caledonian hearts are noble and blessed.

Chapter One

The region west of Pitlochry, Scotland
Summer 765 AD

A bird flew up from the sodden grass at Taloc map Radoc's feet, dragging his attention from the deep well of his own misery. A hawk it was, brown and richly speckled, with broad, graceful wings. Startled, he stumbled and lifted his head to follow its flight. Spreading its pinions, it beat up and over the green land, light riding on its feathers, and for the first time in days hope touched Tally's heart. If that bird could fly up, strong and free, then perhaps somehow his spirit might escape its bonds.

"Move," one of the Gaels ordered from behind, and pushed his shoulder so hard he nearly fell. He tried to remember how many days they had been walking. Five? Eight, ten? His mind, usually so sharp and agile, seemed to have shut down on him. His existence, once one of joy, had narrowed to the hard, cold path of sheer endurance, to putting one foot in front of the other and answering the demands of those who so constantly rode him and his companions. He, son of one Caledonian chief and brother to another, had become a slave. For the life of him, he could not quite understand how his world could change so swiftly, and so completely.

He did know he numbered but one in a group of ten

Epidii captives, because he had counted them again and again. Four men besides himself, and five women, all known, all dear to him, and all being herded steadily westward by the murderous band of Gaels that had attacked their settlement.

Away from all he knew. Away from all he loved.

Ah, but he could not allow himself to think on that; as he had swiftly learned, endurance permitted no room for the grief that threatened to overwhelm him. The smallest crack in his armor might admit despair so terrible he would not survive it.

And survival, it seemed, had become all.

Better, far better, to worry for his companions, whose welfare mattered more than his own. All frightened, most injured in the fierce battle that had preceded their capture, they wept and prayed and called out to one another, and endured.

Tally could feel them like points of light in his darkness. Since being dragged away in the midst of death and fire, he'd felt each of those bright lights begin to fade. The worst of it was, he could also feel himself fading.

But the bird—the bird flew free.

He could only guess where they might be bound— west, and probably to the realm of Dal Riada, which sprawled like a dark wound on Caledonia's western coast. He feared they might not all make it, driven as they were, like animals. And he could only wonder if they would ever see home again.

Would he be one of those to die? He bore three wounds, all taken in that last battle—one to his left shoulder that had bled steadily for the first day or two of their trek, one to his head that caused bright pain, and one to his side—far less serious—from a sword thrust. The five women captured, all youthful, bore only scrapes and bruises received during their capture. All had been caught while trying to flee the fire when the settlement burned.

The settlement burned.

Had anyone back there survived? His brother, Wick, chief of the Epidii? His sister, Barta, as fierce a warrior as any man, and her dauntless husband, True? Wick's wife, Verica, a courageous fighter in her own right, whom he'd seen take at least one terrible wound?

Oh, blessed goddess, would he ever see any of them again? Would he ever learn what had befallen them?

"Faster, all of you move faster!" A blow, delivered by a leather strap, descended across Tally's back—not the first, it nevertheless knocked him off his plodding stride and caused him to lift his gaze once more from the drenched grass.

His captor—or at least the leader of their captors—stared down at Tally from the back of a stout pony. The elite Gaelic warriors all rode while the captives, like certain of the Gaels' foot soldiers, were forced to walk.

Tally suspected some of the foot men were also, like him, Caledonian slaves, perhaps captured in other raids long ago and now forced to participate in attacks upon their own people. Sickness rose into the back of his throat; he would die before he would allow these men to use him so.

The Gaels' leader, whom Tally had heard the men address as MacAtholl, glared at Tally with an ugly expression.

"Look lively, blue man"—the derogatory term by

which the Gaels addressed the Caledonii—"or I will break you. Understand? Do no' think I canno' do it. If you do no' move fast enough, I will beat you. If you fall, I will slaughter you where you lie."

Tally, who possessed only a rough knowledge of the Gaelic tongue, understood perhaps half the words, and all the sentiment. Since the night of their capture when, through billows of smoke and the cries of their fellow tribesfolk they'd been rounded up and driven off, it had been clear they could expect no mercy.

Tally's lips curled involuntarily. The Gaels called the Caledonii blue men because of the tattoos that covered their skin. Tally himself bore many, the first— denoting his tribe and parentage—bestowed on him soon after his birth.

His most recent markings, on his cheeks, denoted his status as a holy man, for such he had become to his tribe following the death of old Pith. But this Gael would not know that, and Tally was not about to tell him.

Yet, as the only representative of the chief's house, should he not assume a role of leadership to this train of straggling captives? Somehow lend them strength, and hope?

"Do no' look at me so," the Gael barked. "Do you, a savage, dare offer me defiance?" He raised the whip once again—a stout length of leather no doubt originally meant for the ponies. It took Tally across the face with a stinging blow that barely missed his eye.

Seething with anger, Tally jerked his gaze to the ground. It would do his fellow Epidii no good if he got himself beaten to a bloody pulp. Now, if ever, he needed to think of them rather than indulging his own anger.

With a jerk of the rein that attached Tally to the lead pony, and to the rest of the tribesfolk, they moved on.

****

"Are you all right, Master Tally?" The whispered query broke through the dark fog of exhaustion and pain that held Tally in its grip, like the precursor of death. His body hurt—feet, legs, back, face—but not half so intensely as his spirit, which felt as if it had been dragged by force behind the Gaels' ponies these many days.

With difficulty he stirred and focused on the person beside him.

Sometime after nightfall, the Gaels had halted the party, and the ragged band of Epidii captives had tumbled down where they stood. Some few, Tally suspected, would not be able to arise again without assistance.

He numbered them as he had over and over again. The men: Melis, Camon, Cemedd, and Agarex; the women: Tamia, Cinid, Anneth, Gwydd, and Elenyda. All, he realized with a little shock, were young like him.

All, he supposed, valuable commodities.

She who spoke to him was called Tamia. Perhaps seven years his junior, she'd never been part of his circle, but he knew her family well. A quiet, respectable young woman, who'd always kept to herself, she did not deserve this fate. Ah, and who among them did deserve it?

He slewed around until he faced her in the near dark. The Gaels busied themselves tending their ponies and building a camp; their other stock, so it seemed, might wait.

Tally could barely see Tamia's face in the gloom, but fear shone in her eyes, as it would in those of a frightened hound.

She touched his shoulder with her bound hands. "Your face—he struck you there."

"Yes." It had stopped bleeding some time ago while they walked on. Everything happened, so it seemed, while they walked. Wounds closed over, or worsened. They relieved themselves right there in the trail, just like the ponies. Their spirits shriveled and died.

"It is but one stripe," he whispered. "I will do well enough." A lie, and the faint tightening of her lips showed she heard it as such.

"Master Taloc, what will happen to us?"

Nothing good. But Tally did not want to say that. The Caledonian tribes had been under attack from their Gaelic neighbors all Tally's life. In his experience, tribesfolk captured by the Gaels and taken away had never returned. That knowledge weighed on his heart like a stone.

Never to see his beloved forest again, or the hills beyond—the places where his ancestors lay. Never to see the tower he'd first glimpsed in a holy Vision and determined to raise as a symbol of Caledonian strength and resistance.

He knew not what lay to the west in the kingdom of Dal Riada, but he could guess. And what he guessed, he could not bear to share with this frightened girl.

Others of the captives were gathering, sliding closer across the ground, as their bonds permitted. Pale faces gleamed in the gloom; gazes sought Tally's for reassurance. All so young—he, at a mere score of years and four, must be among the eldest of them.

The young men had tried to fight when seized and, like Tally, bore wounds and injuries. The girls had fared only slightly better, and Tally knew in his heart that when they reached their journey's end, their fates might well be worst of all.

The nearest of the young men, named Camon, repeated Tamia's question in a rough whisper. "What will happen to us?"

"Will they mistreat us terribly?" another of the girls, Cinid, interposed before Tally could answer.

"I hope not." As gently as possible, Tally told her, "No more than they would abuse their ponies. We have become commodities—objects of value." Did they not understand that? Tally's heart ached for them, and for himself.

"Commodities." Tamia repeated it, and her gaze lifted to his. "We will be sold or traded."

"Yes."

She began to weep. "I will never see my mother again."

"Hush," one of the young men, Cemedd, told her. "Master Taloc, there must be something we can do to break free."

With regret, Tally shook his head. "All this distance, I have been pondering it. I do not see a way, not here and now. They all go armed; we are not. They keep us exhausted and barely watered for a reason, so we have no strength to resist."

"Well, I have the strength," Cemedd declared, and surged to his feet. The action pulled at their bonds, so closely were they tied to one another by their common string, and overset one of the women.

"No, Cemedd—have some sense," Tally hissed, just before Cemedd cried out.

"Here! Accursed Gaels, list to me. We need water and food."

A number of the Gaels' heads turned. A strong party they were, though not so many in number as before they'd attacked the Epidii—Tally's tribe had done plenty of damage.

Not enough, though. Not nearly enough.

Now they exchanged glances, and the leader, MacAtholl, strode toward the group of captives. A tall man, quick rather than broad, with shaggy, fair hair and canny eyes, he wore an air of arrogance like a second skin, and the very sight of him made Tally's skin crawl.

He strode up to Cemedd and stood toe to toe with him, nearly stepping on Cinid in the process; the girl scuttled as far away from him as she could.

MacAtholl sneered. He eyed Cemedd up and down before he spoke. "I will ha' silence here."

Cemedd had spoken in his own tongue. Since their capture, the Gaels had demonstrated they understood it far better than the Caledonii understood Gaelic. Now though, MacAtholl answered in his own language.

Cemedd, appearing unintimidated, refused to back down. An ugly look contorted his features as he spat into the Gaelic leader's face, "I have said we need water, fool. And food. Will you run us until we die?"

Instead of answering, MacAtholl looked around at his companions, most of whom had drifted up, in the way of men everywhere when a commotion began, to listen.

"Will you hark to the mouth on this one! A right cock rooster, he maun think himself."

The other Gaels grunted and muttered. Cemedd, to give him his due, still did not back off a whit. In spite of bearing a livid wound at one shoulder, and another along his hairline that had bled profusely, and despite being worn, thirsty, and muddy from the many days' journey, he stood with his head high.

A true example of the Caledonii, Tally thought with a flash of mingled pride and chagrin: defiance in the face of overwhelming odds. The idea brought him to his feet, further tugging on his fellows' bonds. The other Epidii males came up more slowly, one by one, pulling the girls to their feet.

"Och," said MacAtholl with a sarcastic edge, "'tis a show of resistance. I suppose it had to come. It usually does." He leaned in and spoke directly into Cemedd's face; they were nearly of a height, the Gael just a bit taller and Cemedd broader, despite his youth. "Do you wish for a chance, blue man, to prove yoursel'?"

"I do," Cemedd replied.

MacAtholl laughed, a chilling sound that had an edge like a whetted knife. Speaking in the Caledonian tongue this time, he pressed, "And are you willing, cock, to fight for your freedom?"

Even in the gloaming, Tally saw hope take hold in Cemedd's eyes.

"I am!"

"Aye, lads," MacAtholl turned to his companions, "an old tradition among fierce warriors of this kind. I mysel' ha' seen such blue men fight before. It seems we will ha' some entertainment this night."

Chapter Two

Tally wanted to holler a warning at young Cemedd—wanted to scream it. *Do not trust them.* For one could never trust a Gael.

That truth should, by now, be bred into the blood and bone of all Caledonii born during Tally's lifetime— and so Cemedd had been. He could have no more than a score of winters, and though he might consider himself a doughty fighter, nothing here was what it seemed.

The certainty made Tally seize hold of Cemedd's arm in a fierce grip. "No, Cemedd, it will not be a fair fight."

MacAtholl laughed again. To Tally he said, "And who are you to intervene? You already have one stripe; do you want more?"

Tally glared into the man's face and said deliberately, "This that you offer him is not a fair combat." He had heard accounts of such contests, one from his own brother, Wick—now chief of the Epidii— and from Wick's wife, Verica. Wick had, himself, engaged in such, and rather than facing a single opponent, he had faced many, one after the other.

Still gripping Cemedd's arm, he asked MacAtholl urgently, "Which of your men will he fight?"

MacAtholl's eyes, pale blue and sharp as a naked blade, scoured Tally's face. "You are too clever by half, are you no'? What are you, your tribe's wise man?"

For an instant it felt like all the breath had been punched out of Tally's body. Dangerous, indeed, to admit he had any importance to his tribe. Or was it?

"Yes," he said.

"You look young for it. I thought the tribes all kept shamans who were old and grizzled. No matter; for the sake o' your gods I will give you a warning. I am willing to accept no defiance from you any more than from this lad, here." He raised his voice. "All o' you maun learn your places, and the sooner, the easier done. Bring him." He jerked his head at Cemedd, and his men went to work releasing the lad from the line that bound the Epidii all together like a string of snagged fish.

A chance to run? But Tally could not think of abandoning these others only to save himself, and some of the girls could barely stand.

To Cemedd he said, "Be wary. And do not accept challenges you cannot—"

Cemedd met his gaze, head high like that of a proud stag. "Do not tell me how to fight. I would rather die battling than live a slave."

Several of the girls began to weep as Cemedd was hauled away and their bonds refastened. A rough circle of Gaels formed almost magically, into the center of which Cemedd was shoved.

He looked so alone there that Tally's throat tightened painfully.

The courage of a Caledonian warrior. The Gaels called his people many things: blue men, vermin, savages, all with a sneer. He found himself praying with all his might that Cemedd might prove them wrong.

"Choose your weapon." MacAtholl strolled into the

circle and faced Cemedd. "With what will you fight?"

"The spear." Cemedd chose without hesitation. It was the Caledonii's weapon of choice and one with which the Gael had little experience.

"Ha! Spoken like a barbarian." MacAtholl made a droll face and called out, "Have we any spears to hand?"

One of his fellows answered, playing along with the game, "Only those we wrested from our defeated opponents."

"Ah, I do no' suppose our fine cock, here, will argue wi' such quality."

Cemedd stared around the circle that enclosed him with no visible fear. Had he meant what he said? Would he truly rather die with a weapon in his hand than live on as a vanquished man? For an instant, Tally embraced the glory of it. But ending one's life would mean never returning home, and since the rope first tightened around his wrists he'd lived only for that.

"And who will you face, young cock?" MacAtholl called out.

Tally caught his breath. He wanted to warn Cemedd again, "Be careful how you speak!" Instead he whispered a hurried and urgent prayer. *Protect him.*

Cemedd lifted his head and his eyes shone. "Any you send," he replied, and Tally believed he'd spoken fatal words, indeed.

But yet the Gaels may have erred. He could feel the other male captives stir around him, crowding close, inspired by Cemedd's show of courage.

Cemedd accepted a spear—probably one that had belonged to a fallen comrade—placed into his hand, and Tamia began to weep.

"He's made his choice," Tally whispered to her, and to the gods. Just like that, the combat began.

As a lesson—which MacAtholl unquestionably intended it to be—it proved most lurid and effective. Cemedd started out well and made a fine showing, but as Tally feared, his attackers gathered around him like wolves and, in very similar fashion, soon closed in for the kill. None of them used a spear; all employed a Gael's preferred weapon, the sword. MacAtholl had, after all, asked Cemedd with what he, not his opponents, wished to fight.

Tricky bastards, Tally thought on a bright flash of consternation. Cemedd's valiance deserved a better answer—the boy, in truth, deserved a better death. Already weakened by his rough journey, his wounds, and the lack of food and water, it did not take long for him to falter.

The little knot of captives was forced to stand and watch while the Gaels cut Cemedd to pieces. They showed no mercy and, indeed, appeared to enjoy what they did. MacAtholl himself did not participate but stood watching from the far side of the circle, a half smile on his face, an eye on the other captives' reactions.

At first the Epidii at Tally's back hollered and shouted encouragement to Cemedd, before protesting the unfairness of the scene. One or two tried to dart forward and offer Cemedd aid but were driven back with hard blows by the Gaels. Before the end, all had fallen silent except the women, who wept heartbrokenly.

Tally wanted to close his eyes, wished desperately to shut away what he saw. But he felt he must honor

Cemedd's courage by witnessing each blow, every slash, and the brave manner in which the young man met his noble death.

When Cemedd lay in a bloodied heap on the ground, MacAtholl pivoted on his heel and called to the captives, "Is there any other among you who will take up the challenge?"

"You cheated!" called Melis, from Tally's back. "He fought not one opponent but five."

MacAtholl glared at him. "You are in my hands now, blue man. I make the rules. Lesson learned?"

Tally did not doubt it was—and the price had been far too high.

****

Tally lay and watched the moon rise, despair in his heart. Despite his bone-deep exhaustion, he could find no sleep. The combat they'd witnessed played over and over in his mind, and he ached for escape. For home.

He tried to pray, as he had all through this terrible journey, to still his mind enough to approach the place of holiness, but with little success. The goddess, usually so real and close to him, felt distant here, and his spirit, earlier lifted by the soaring bird, seemed to have fallen into the dirt along with Cemedd.

Cemedd—who at least now soared free, just like that hawk. Had the bird truly been there, beneath the feet of so many marchers, or had that been another Vision, one perhaps predicting Cemedd's death? The trouble with Visions, as Tally well knew, was the interpretation—so easy in hindsight, so difficult beforehand.

Ah, and here had he been hoping the presence of the hawk held meaning for him. It had entered his mind that he might find a way to send his spirit flying in its wake.

Instead he lay aching, watching the moon rise. An old moon it was, one past the full of its power and fast waning. It rose late in a bulbous crescent and hung above the trees.

In the past, the moon had often whispered to him in the goddess's voice, which sounded very much like that of his dead mother. A full moon had lit the sky when first he glimpsed the Vision of the tower his people had built on the place where their ancestors lived and died. That had been ten years ago, and since the Epidii and their allies raised it, they had been undefeated in their fight against the Gaels.

Until now.

What had changed? Since that battle and the firing of the tower, the magic by which he lived on a daily basis seemed to have deserted him. Had his goddess also abandoned him? If not, why had she allowed all this to happen, allowed Cemedd to die?

He squeezed his eyes shut against the weary light of the moon and reached again for the strength and beauty of what he believed, plumbing the depths of his spirit. What could he do to persuade the goddess back to him, what offer her? At the moment he felt bereft, with so little to give.

Reaching deep, he spoke the prayer, the promise, in his mind. *Goddess, give me the strength I need to survive this and I promise I will live only for you. I will find a way to return home at any cost. Only, please, do not abandon me—*

"Master Taloc?" The whisper came at him out of the dark. For an instant, he thought it an answer to his prayer. Then he realized Tamia, beside him on the line, once more claimed his attention.

He spoke around the emotion clogging his throat. "Yes, Tamia?"

She slid closer to him under cover of the darkness. Tally lifted his head and peered around. Most the Gaels slept, but two men patrolled the outer boundary of the camp. He cared little for any punishment he might incur, but would hate to see this frightened girl disciplined.

Her shoulder bumped his, and he could feel her trembling. Ah, no doubt she wanted reassurance. But how to give it to her? Back home, he often advised members of the tribe, even those beyond his inner circle. That Tally did have a circle could not be denied—since the age of fourteen when his parents were slain and his life fell apart for the first time, the young girls of tribe Epidii, especially, had flocked to him. He could not explain why, save that he possessed a measure of his mother Essa's magic, and for a time had been considered heir to the place of chief. Yet even after his brother, Wick, returned home and took up that role, the young women remained close to him.

He had formed the closest bond with Rekka. She'd been both friend and, later, lover to him, and he'd intended that in time they should wed. But that time had never come; she had perished in a raid before he could ever carry through with his intention. He'd often thought, since, that their relationship had after all been more friendship than love. And part of him wished to hold out for that great love of which he had so many extraordinary examples before him—Barta and True, Wick and Verica, and most of all his parents, whose love for one another had been deep and unwavering.

He turned his head and surveyed Tamia as best he might in the dark. Her auburn hair hung loose and tangled, her filthy face showed streaks from her tears. She looked terrified. He had so little, in his spiritual store, to give her.

In a whisper he could barely hear, she asked, "Master Taloc, what do you think is happening back home? Do you think my family survived that raid?"

Ah, and there lay the heart of it, rightly. Bad enough contemplating their own fates; how much worse not knowing how things lay with the ones they loved.

The attack had come ahead of an approaching storm. The Gaels had waited until thunder crashed and the god threw his lightning spear across the sky to move in with both sword and chariot. They had attacked not the settlement—not at first, anyway—but the tower which, unlike others of the Epidii structures, stood wholly above ground. It being an important symbol as well as the spiritual seat of the tribe, the Epidii had rushed to the defense, all in the dead of night.

The walls of the tower, constructed of stone, would not burn, but the roof did—and had—setting the interior alight. Tally, who'd been inside at the time, at his prayers, had escaped with his life only to run into a scene of terrible carnage. He'd caught glimpses of his brother, Wick, fighting like a madman, Wick's wife, Verica, not far from his side, and of his sister's husband, True. He'd seen Barta, screaming in rage, throwing herself at their enemies. But he had no knowledge of how they had fared after he'd been hauled away, of who had survived and who had died.

Now Tamia raised a wan face to his and asked,

"Do you think they're all dead?"

And he answered, because he believed she deserved the truth, "I do not know."

"My mother and my father! My sisters and my hound pup…"

Tally's throat closed. How could he comfort her, when his pain felt as great as hers?

He covered her bound hands with his. "They put up a brave defense, and many of them may well have survived." She needed to believe that; so did he.

In a voice like dust, she said, "Cemedd put up a brave defense. Where did it get him?"

"Try to rest." Tally did not doubt they had another grueling day of foot travel ahead of them.

"I do not think I can. Master Taloc, what will happen to Cemedd's body?"

What was left of it.

The girl persisted, "He should have a holy burial."

So he should. How many words had Tally spoken over such honored graves?

"It is not his body that matters so much as his spirit." They must cling to that truth.

"And what has happened to his spirit?" she asked.

"Ah, Tamia," he assured her, "it has flown away on the strong wings of a golden bird."

Chapter Three

The kingdom of Dal Riada

"Mistress Alanna, they have returned, and your brother Donhal among them!"

Alanna turned when the cry reached her ears, and the pony she held by its halter took advantage of the opportunity to rear. A stallion, and unaltered, he'd given her nothing but trouble from the moment she took him in hand. Stocky, shaggy, and strong, the roan demonstrated every step of the way that he meant to fight her, resistant to accepting any and all attempts to teach him.

Some horses, as she knew, could not be trained, they could only be broken. And a broken pony, in her opinion, was fit for naught.

She nodded to the messenger, and murmured to the animal, "Och, you rascal." Exchanging a look with her assistant, Labhan, she thrust the pony's lead into the young man's hand for safekeeping.

"I will go see," she said, and turned away to answer the summons.

Her father, Atholl—a chief here in the kingdom of Dal Riada—had been over-anxious for her brother's return from this campaign. In truth Alanna had two brothers, both half a score older than her, born of Atholl's first wife, who had perished in childbirth. So had his second wife only three years after Alanna's birth.

Atholl had not married again, and Alanna had been more or less raised by the males of her family, which perhaps accounted for why she preferred leggings to skirts, and training ponies for the chariots to tending a hearth. It might also account for why she harbored no interest in marrying and risking her life delivering some man's bairn.

Hers had been a rough and harsh upbringing, and no mistake. Donhal—he who had now returned—had been the only one to spend much time with her. His quirky and often irreverent nature paired well with her own, and bonds had forged between them. Both Donhal and Graedh had been busy raiding in the east this summer season, as in many seasons past. Alanna's brothers had long competed for their father's favor. Graedh, the elder, naturally thought he would be chief after Atholl; Donhal, in some ways as much of a rascal as the pony Alanna had just handed over to Labhan, seemed to think he could win his father's favor by outshining Graedh in the east. It all added to the unrest that beset Dal Riada at this time, a kingdom already split into three factions.

Ah, but such competition was what fueled the Gaels' love of life, and the whole clan held its breath waiting to see which of Atholl's sons would better the other. They, like Donhal himself, seemed to feel whoever brought more wealth to the clan through the acquisition of land, goods, and slaves would ultimately win the place of chief. Each son had backers and champions.

Graedh, like their father, was a cold, unyielding

man. At least Donhal, with his frequently bent honor and his dubious sense of humor, might be approached with argument or reason.

She brushed her filthy palms down her tunic—the pony had tossed her to the ground more than once this morning—and took off running in the direction the herald had gone. If a party had returned from the east, they would make for the chief's house, at the center of the settlement.

Others joined her on her way—warriors who had not made up part of this train, wives of the men who had, children and old men with naught better to do, eager to hear the news.

Alongside Alanna came her good friend Fenna, whose husband, Rannadh, had accompanied Donhal away. They exchanged looks, and Alanna lifted a brow.

"Do you ken," Fenna asked, "who it is has returned?"

"Donhal, so the lad who fetched me said."

Fenna, breathless from hurrying, nodded, "I wonder whether Rannadh is wi' him. I confess, I did no' think to see him before the end of the season."

As Alanna knew, because she heard her father and brothers discuss it endlessly, pushing a kingdom eastward through a land such as Alba made no easy proposition. Hills, deep glens, and lochs barred the way, to say nothing of vast stretches of forest. Despite this, the blue men had been forced back and back toward the eastern sea. But they knew those forests, could melt into them almost magically, only to return and put up another fierce fight.

Thus, taking the land in battle was one thing— Alanna defied anyone to match a Gaelic warrior in battle—holding it another. In the past, their warriors had withdrawn at the end of a season's fighting; now they left a small force during the winter to try and hold the ground they'd taken. The strategy seemed to be working and, slowly, the chiefs of Dal Riada moved settlers eastward in the wake of the chariots.

She frowned as she contemplated it and put on a burst of speed, outdistancing her friend. A crowd had already gathered outside her father's hall, but they parted to let her through. She entered the dun, sweaty and disheveled, to find Donhal already with her father, the two men in discussion.

Atholl, a tall, stern man, had lost the sight in one eye during a battle long ago. That, and the pains in his joints, now kept him from entering battle or joining one of the many forays eastward. He held his power not through his own valor but that of his sons, and the fact that his people liked him.

He looked pleased now, so Alanna noted, and he seldom enough showed the younger of his two sons such approval. Donhal, for his part, wore a self-satisfied expression; both of them turned nearly identical pale blue eyes on Alanna when she burst in.

"Ah, Daughter," Atholl greeted her. "The news is good. Your brother has staged a great battle against the stronghold which the blue men have long been keeping safe from us, and is victorious. It may be the break we ha' been seeking, in the east."

"Indeed," Alanna said. "I am impressed." She gave Donhal a searching look, secretly glad such favor had fallen to him rather than the fierce, unapproachable Graedh, who even now still battled in the east.

Donhal grinned at her and winked. "My men bring

the train even now, with wealth and a number of slaves."

Atholl laid a hand on his shoulder. "Let us go see."

They went back out into the blinding sunshine, to stand on the elevated ramp before the door of the hall. From here Alanna had a splendid view both of the settlement and the far-reaching sea beyond. A bonny day, and no mistake, but she knew the approaching party, including the ponies, would be dirty, hungry, and weary.

The ponies held the greatest measure of Alanna's concern. Her father had long and earnestly urged her to take up her proper place in the clan, that of chief's daughter. Atholl would have liked for her to make a beneficial marriage alliance also, but she'd clearly voiced her resistance.

Indeed, as Donhal often said, she'd proved as hard to handle as some of the ponies she trained, and her father still shook his head over her behavior. At least she did not attempt to compete for his favor the way her brothers did—she would be cursed before she so lowered herself.

Now she stood listening as Atholl made a short speech, praising Donhal and extolling the gains made in the east. "Soon," he told the clansfolk, "Dal Riada will stretch all the way across Alba from sea to sea, and we—we will rule Dal Riada."

Before he finished, the crowd began to shuffle and turn. Alanna heard the rattle of chariots and the voices of those calling to the warriors in the train. She narrowed her gaze against the glaring sun.

The whole raiding party had not returned; she saw but a small, if well-armed, squad led by Donhal's right-hand man, Caennan; counting heads, she numbered but ten warriors, a handful of ponies, and only two chariots. That meant Donhal had left most of his party behind in the east, most likely to guard whatever territory he'd seized.

She did not see Fenna's husband, Rannadh, and feared poor Fenna must be disappointed. But the warriors who were there came proudly, their heads thrown back, shoulders set, and with that touch of arrogant confidence they seemed always to carry.

The triumphant conquerors return, Alanna thought, and wrinkled her nose in distaste. She turned her gaze on Donhal and her father standing together, and not for the first time saw the strength of their resemblance. Tall, well-knit bodies, fair hair like hers and—also like hers—pale blue eyes that had often been compared to water ice. And did she, too, resemble them? She could only hope not.

Donhal flicked her another glance as if he felt the weight of her criticism before fixing his gaze on Atholl. "Well, Father, and have I done you proud?"

Atholl nodded. "Nine slaves, and all young."

Alanna inspected the train of clearly spent figures that straggled—and struggled—behind Caennan. A hard journey across the wild breadth of Alba, and no mistake. Most of the warriors carried wounds, showing they'd battled valiantly. So, she saw, did many of the slaves.

Despite their injuries they had made the hard journey on foot and now looked so exhausted they could barely stand. Four males and five females she counted, and felt as much sympathy for them as for the ponies. She detested the practice of seizing slaves, though it endured, widespread in their world. How must it feel, being taken from one's home by force? To have every choice stolen, for the balance of one's existence.

Yet the returning warriors almost always brought slaves. She inspected this batch even as her father and brother began speaking, Atholl very much in the vein of the great chief welcoming his warriors. Several of the female captives, lacking the strength to stand, sank down where they were. All of them drooped with what looked like defeat.

All but one.

He stood foremost in their train—by chance or by choice as their leader?—and held himself with a measure of grim dignity. A livid weal marked his face from one temple to the opposite cheek, barely missing his eye. Despite that, and in spite of the dirt that covered him from head to foot, she could see that he was…

Beautiful.

Odd, perhaps, to apply such a word to a man, and an eastern savage at that, but it fit. Alanna, an honest woman if nothing else, had to profess an attraction to these eastern men. Something about the way they were put together, their coloring, and the tattoos that covered their skin appealed to her.

Indeed, was her current lover, Nenian, not a slave? She'd become acquainted with him back when he'd worked for a time at the pony sheds, and they'd been meeting in secret for over a year. No one save Fenna knew of it—or so Alanna hoped.

This man outshone Nenian the way the moon outshines a rush light. Tall for one of his kind, and unusually slender, he had dark auburn hair that tumbled down his back, a prow of a nose—marked now by that livid welt—pleasingly slanted cheekbones, and lean cheeks, also marked, just above the beard, by tattoos.

He had to be as spent as the others, yet his shoulders remained level, his chin high. If the blue men, or Caledonii, as Nenian claimed they called themselves, had royalty, then surely such this man must be.

Indeed, Alanna must have stared too intently, for he stirred and turned his head as if he felt her attention on him. Their gazes met across the intervening distance, connected, and held.

He saw her. The knowledge started a thrill that passed through Alanna like a spear of lightning. This man—this slave—noticed her, and that one truth became the most important thing in her world.

Ah, and what eyes he had, wide and of a deep color—what color she could not tell from where she stood—yet full of light. Nenian's eyes were hazel and nearly matched his roan-colored hair. This man's looked far darker.

Heat drenched her, and she had to fight for breath. She no longer heard her father's or her brother's voice droning on, nor the appreciative murmurs from the crowd. Her heart pounded deafeningly.

She had to get near him, this man who stood dusty and exhausted yet not beaten. She must get within arm's reach, determine the color of those arresting eyes, trace with her fingers the tattoos that marked his skin.

Nenian had told her the blue designs carried meanings, marked the tribe into which a babe was born, his parentage and status. Declared great deeds.

She wanted to know this man, in more than the physical sense. She needed to follow what happened to him here in Dal Riada after he was claimed or sold, make certain no ill befell him.

Why?

That, she could not tell. She might, aye, cite this wild attraction, but the compulsion argued more than mere attraction.

He suddenly withdrew his gaze from hers, jerked his head around, and stared forward. Throughout the seemingly endless speeches that followed, the boasting and posturing, he did not look at Alanna again.

That did not matter, for her gaze remained fixed on him, and did not waver.

Chapter Four

Whatever Tally imagined might happen at the end of their journey—and his thoughts had been as lurid as they were far-reaching—he'd not expected to be separated so soon from his fellow Epidii tribemates. But so it proved. After being paraded out like the spoils of battle, the ropes that bound them one to the other were unthreaded and removed. The women, detached from the rest of them, were herded away.

"What will befall them?" Melis asked Tally with a combination of anger and woe.

Nothing good. But Tally did not reply. His throat felt too dry and tight for speech. He hoped the women would be given water and a place to rest—at the moment his mind failed to reach beyond that.

The rest of them, only four in number since Cemedd's slaughter, were bullied and driven through the still-gathered onlookers, most of whom stared at them with hard, indifferent eyes.

No one here cared what happened to them. Having spent his life within the confines of a tribe who, trouble or no, looked after one another, that knowledge felt like an additional wound. He and his fellows might have endured the journey; now they must face a future devoid of every comfort they'd ever known.

Save his faith, he reminded himself. Did he not still have that?

Yet at this moment, worn and discouraged, he found it an asset hard to reach.

The settlement through which they were marched, at the very edge of the western sea, proved a grand and overwhelming place. His own people built modest dwellings that blended into the forest, partly underground so as not to be seen.

The Gaels, so it appeared, did just the opposite. They raised buildings on a grand scale and set them square out in the daylight. The very eagles must be able to see this place from afar, like a scab on tender skin.

He should have expected nothing less from these folk, with their loud clothing and constant posturing. Braggarts, his sister, Barta, always called them, and this settlement did indeed brag aloud, from the stone wall that surrounded it to the large roundhouse where they'd been herded like so many beasts. He wondered how many people lived here. These Gaels must breed like vermin—no wonder they were always greedy for more land.

Now, late in the afternoon and with weariness dragging at him like a sack of rocks hung around his neck, he found himself parted also from his remaining Epidii tribemates, all save Camon. The others were driven away into the teeming distance. A Gaelic warrior with a drawn sword forced Tally and Camon in still another direction, past a large roundhouse to a small stone shed, where he shut them in.

Darkness immediately enfolded them. After the bright afternoon sunlight, it smothered Tally like a thick blanket, making it hard to breathe. For an instant he thought he could not bear being shut away so from the air, the sun, and the moon…would this be the thing to break him?

He heard Camon grunt as he stumbled and collapsed onto the floor. Battling the feeling of suffocation, Tally felt his way forward until his hands met the wall—cold stone, rough and unrelenting. A choking sound came from Camon. Did he fight sobs? The young warrior, as Tally knew, had fought bravely during the attack that had ravished their home. But much had occurred since then.

Tally sank down where he stood, turning his back to the wall. What had happened back home since they left? He remembered the cries, the screams—the blood. He remembered the tower, his tower, and all his hopes and dreams in flames.

His throat, still too tight to allow for words, ached unbearably. He'd conceived the notion of that round tower, directed that it be built as a symbol of resistance against the Gaels. To see it destroyed felt as significant as the loss of a loved one.

He would give much to know who still lived back home, where lay his heart. His brother, Wick? Wick's valiant wife, Verica? Their young daughter, whom they so cherished?

What of his sister, Barta, her mate, True, and their triplets, his nieces and nephew? And all the many friends so dear to him, in so many ways. Would he ever see any of them again? Did they all lie dead?

He had no hope of getting word of them, shut away here. He could not question his captors, and anyway, none of them possessed a shred of mercy.

He thought of the woman he'd glimpsed during that endless session through which they'd stood, a welcoming-home ceremony, without a doubt. Her bright gaze had caught at his, claimed his attention like a demand. No mercy there either, but something else, something—

"Master Tally?" Camon croaked out of the darkness.

Tally's lips twisted bitterly. "Master" might be a title of respect afforded him back home, as brother to the chief and the Epidii's shaman. Quite clearly, it no longer applied. "Camon, I am no master to you nor to anyone—not here."

Camon ignored that. "Are we going to die?"

"No." But there were worse things, so Tally suspected, than death.

"How can you be certain?"

"We are too valuable." He forced the words through his throat.

"But Cemedd…"

"Cemedd was a lesson." An expensive one. "If you choose to die here, they will accommodate you."

"Cemedd chose."

"Yes."

"I do not want to live here, Master Tally. Perhaps Cemedd made the right choice."

Perhaps he had. Tally's beliefs, which ran as deeply within him as his blood and his memories, taught him that death brought release, a swift flight over the land and water to a bright home place, from whence one's spirit would eventually return once again to this world.

He thought of the brown bird flying up from his feet, from the depths of his despair, and wondered if death would be like that. Had he caught a glimpse of his own demise?

He had counseled countless grieving and bereaved tribemates, back home. For the departed, death held no fear. Perhaps he should embrace that truth now.

But to give up on life—to surrender the desire for bright mornings and starlit nights, to release all hope of ever again seeing his home hills… No, *no,* for he had promised the goddess he would return home.

"Why have we been separated from the others?"

"I do not know." Something niggled at the back of Tally's mind. "Perhaps we have been claimed."

"But we are free men. Caledonii."

"Caledonii, yes." Free men no longer. "Better rest, Camon, while we may."

"I want water."

So did Tally, with a burning desire that very nearly obscured all else. But their ability to procure for themselves even so simple a requirement had been snatched from them.

"Rest," he said again. "And—"

Without warning, the door of the hut swung open. It came with a creak and an admission of light—Tally squinted his eyes and raised his hand.

Surprise kept him from making a bid for escape, or so he told himself. In truth, he did not know if he had the strength to stand.

A young Gael stood there with an armed warrior at his back. He said nothing but stepped into their tiny enclosure, set down a flask and a bowl of food on the bare stone floor, and as swiftly as that, stepped back out. The door slammed closed, and Tally heard a bar fall into place.

"What—?" Camon asked.

Tally, seeing with his fingers, reached the flask in

an instant. One taste told him it contained water. Sheer willpower allowed him to cease drinking and pass the vessel into Camon's hands. One of the many things his father, as chief, had taught him remained: look after the welfare of your people before your own.

"Ah, by the goddess!" After a long pull, Camon returned the flask to Tally. "You drink also."

Tally did.

"What is in the bowl?"

"Food, no doubt."

Camon fell upon it, edged closer to Tally, and shared. They had walked a great distance with virtually no sustenance. Tally knew his body needed the food, though his stomach protested.

"What will happen to the girls?" Camon worried between gulps.

Whatever their new masters wished. But Tally did not voice that thought, and Camon spoke again.

"Will they be forced? Can we not protect them?"

"I do not see how." The senior of the captives, Tally knew most of the young women would not yet have been tried. The word "rape" appeared in his mind—an ugly term and no mistake.

His own first experience with coupling had occurred nearly ten years ago. After his parents were killed and his brother, Wick, abandoned his place, Tally had rallied the tribe, sought to keep them together, and led with a measure of his mother's wisdom.

He'd had a following then, a group of young women who lent him their support, including his Rekka, who had lent him far more.

After her death, he'd missed her friendship as much as her presence in his bed. Now he knew her fate had been far kinder than capture would have been.

Sudden sorrow overwhelmed him. He reached out in the dark and clasped Camon's arm.

"Rest. Sleep if you can." The only comfort he could give.

Chapter Five

The night drew down, and Alanna sat on by her father's fireside, not quite sure why she stayed. Ever since the great feast in the hall, Atholl and Donhal had been talking of battles fought and won, of conquests in the east and how they would better the other chiefs of Dal Riada in their holdings. She detested such talk, so why did she linger?

Even Donhal's young wife, Ossia, had given up waiting and gone off to her bed, not before giving Donhal a significant look from her deep green eyes. Ossia adored her husband and had missed him while he remained away.

Yet like Alanna herself, Donhal sat on. Alanna could only imagine he sought to impress their father with tales of his prowess. Much as she liked her brother, she knew Donhal for an oftentimes closed-minded braggart with overblown ideas of himself. The fact that most of those ideas had originated with Atholl meant nothing.

Alanna felt near-sickened by Donhal's boasting and his descriptions of the bloodshed in the east, yet she stayed where she sat, chin in hand, while he and her father discussed every detail—a strange compulsion, not explained by the good mead.

Her father, for once well-pleased with his son, raised his near-empty cup to his lips. "And so, Donhal, have you accomplished what I asked of you? Is that troublesome and stubborn pocket of savages who ha' refused to be routed truly defeated at last?"

Donhal contemplated it with rare honesty. He longed to claim that requested victory, yet as Alanna knew, he rarely lied to his father.

"We burned their accursed tower." Donhal's lip curled in disgust. Over these past several years, that tower set in the forest had become a thorn in his side. A powerful symbol, Alanna knew it must be, and rare, since the blue men rarely built such permanent structures.

A dare, Donhal had declared it, a challenge he would meet. For within its shadow had a strong clan of blue men held their ground for half a score of years.

Atholl's pale eyes met those of his son. "Yet it still stands?"

"It still stands, aye, but gutted and ruined. We could, Father, scarcely pull it down stone from stone. The fighting was fierce, and many of their warriors stood to oppose us."

Contrary, Alanna thought, to what Donhal usually said of his opponents. He spoke of the blue men slinking away to disappear into the forest at the end of a fight.

"Dead?" Atholl demanded. "Did you leave their leaders dead?"

"We left many and many of them dead, Father. 'Twas a sound defeat. Who can say if all their leaders perished?"

Atholl grunted. "Until that nest of vermin is soundly routed, we will have no peace on their land." He shifted on his rug. "And then that accursed Mallach will suppose he has reason to challenge me."

Mallach, one of the other two great chiefs who held settlements here in Dal Riada, vied with Atholl and the third chief, called Ronish, just as Donhal and Graedh contested against each other. It had long been accepted that the one who seized the greater holdings in the east would attain dominance.

Donhal leaned toward his father, a gleam in his pale eyes. Lowering his voice, he said, "Only name me as chief after you, Father, and I will assure the bards sing only your praises in the halls of Dal Riada."

"You, chief?" Atholl returned Donhal's look with one of stern offense. "But you are my younger son. What of Graedh?"

"Has he provided you with as much land, as many slaves?"

"Both my sons labor on my behalf. Should I betray one for the sake of the other?"

A bitter look came over Donhal's mobile face, and Alanna wondered if he did not tire of his father's game, pitting him endlessly against his brother. What an ill fate it was, she thought, to long for the impossible. For some reason, that made her think of the beautiful blue man she'd glimpsed earlier, outside the hall. She wondered who had claimed him and where he might be assigned to work.

Would she have the opportunity to see him again, to speak with him, and to learn the exact color of his eyes? Or were her hopes as doomed as Donhal's?

Clearly, both men had forgotten her presence. They eyed one another like wary stags until she spoke.

"Father, what will happen to the new slaves that were brought in?"

Atholl shrugged with some indifference. "The usual, I suppose."

Before Alanna could speak again, Donhal told her, "I have claimed two of them. The others have been granted to the most valiant of my warriors." His cool gaze met hers with some curiosity. "Why do you ask?"

"'Tis just that we could use help at the pony sheds."

Atholl grunted. "You ha' all the help you need."

"Labhan is but an apprentice, still training. And old Marc's fingers are so bent he is slow at his tasks. I need a younger man to help carry the feed and keep hold of a stroppy stallion."

Donhal's gaze bored into hers so intently she wondered, for an instant, if he could see the truth inside her head—knew she'd been sleeping with Nenian, and felt her attraction to the new slave.

But then he asked, with the touch of wry humor that often colored his speech, "Can you pay for one? Those slaves, as you ken, are gey valuable."

"And," she answered as coolly, "you need ponies for your chariots if you wish to continue your campaign in the east. You ken fine my ponies are the best trained in all Alba." She stated it quietly, because she was certain.

"I ha' plans for the two I kept. I need them in the smithy. You see, wee sister, we require weapons even as we need ponies."

"And if those men are no' suited to the smithy? Not everyone is. Why do you no' let me see them in the morning. If one o' them will suit me, we can bargain."

"Bargain, is it?" Donhal set down his mug for the first time all evening. "Right now, I want my bed and what's in it. Any other bargaining will, indeed, have to wait for morning."

Astonishing, Alanna thought, that he'd stopped boasting on himself and currying his father's favor long enough to remember his wife.

With that wary expression still in his eyes, Donhal heaved to his feet and looked at Atholl. "I hope, Father, you are pleased with what I ha' achieved for you."

"Aye," Atholl granted grudgingly. "Though surely, the mere act of defeating blue men makes no great feat."

****

Tally dreamed of fire and screaming. In the grip of exhausted slumber, he stood transported back to his home, watching the attack over again. Figures moved like shadows all around him, flickering in the garish light and insubstantial despite their cries.

But he saw them fall one by one—friends he'd known all his life, folk who meant the world to him. Here, in the dream, he observed details he'd not had time to notice while the attack took place.

A sword slash to his friend Bocar's chest that took him down in a shower of blood. Bocar lay twitching, his eyes staring at the sky.

Tally, no great warrior—for his strength lay in his belief rather than in physical weapons—had leaped to stand over him, had woven a desperate spell of protection. But he'd found his magic, by then, nearly depleted.

Goddess, stand with me. Great god, defend all I love.

Had the god and goddess deserted him at that moment? He did not want to believe it. Yet so many had died; the tower—his great Vision—had burned. He'd seen his sister, Barta, go down beneath a Gael's blade even as her mate, True, launched himself at her attacker in retaliation.

Had either of them survived?

He remembered the bright sear of pain when he took the wound he now bore on his right arm—like lightning. He knew, then, his personal protection had been breached. He could raise no more.

He awoke in the thick dark of the stone shed with tears on his face, his whole body trembling. His spirit cried for home, *home*. He'd never imagined he could ache so, in longing.

He could hear Camor breathing deeply and the faint sounds of movement from outside. Beneath the close-fitting door of their prison, a trickle of light showed.

Morning. What would it bring?

Like a man slain, he lay on his back and tried to imagine. A dangerous business—his mother had always said imagining things fervently enough caused them to happen. He did not want any of the things he now dreaded to come true.

Was that the reason he had lived all his life beneath the shadow of possible attack by the Gaels? Had someone with great magical ability imagined it, his mother perhaps? Yet until her death, his mother had lived a life of deep reverence and love.

If only Tally could achieve such a life… But held captive here, shut away from the air and light, the beauty of the world that lent him strength, he could not see how.

He remembered the cold, merciless eyes of the man

who'd brought them here, recalled the half smile on his
face when he watched Cemedd die.

He recalled, also, the bird flying up from his feet
on strong wings. If only, like that hawk, he might rise.

Beside him, Camon stirred, coming awake with a
groan and a choked cry. Sleep offered some refuge
from this terrible place, yet was far too short-lived.

"Master Tally?"

Tally sat up. His body protested from top to
bottom, as if he'd been soundly thrashed. His wounds
had stiffened during the night, and pulled viciously
when he moved.

"I told you not to call me that," he bade his
companion, as he had before. "Here, I am no one's
master."

"I need to piss."

So did Tally, now that Camon mentioned it. During
the night his eyes had adjusted somewhat to the low
light, and enough now trickled beneath the door to
allow him to see their prison.

"There is a bucket in the corner."

"Are we meant to stay shut in here with our own
stink? Have these Gaels no decency?"

Tally did not want to answer that question.

Camon struggled to rise. He made it as far as his
knees, groaned again and crept away to the corner.

Do not think about it, Tally bade himself. Do not
think on anything ugly or hard, lest it come true.

Did he truly believe in that power? He did not want
to, but lying there with his eyes squeezed tight shut,
found he did.

Let him only see how his belief might save him
now.

Chapter Six

The day dawned clear and soft with a bank of white clouds gathered over the far reaches of the sea. Despite her late night at her father's hearth, Alanna went to work soon after sunrise. The stallion, Fel, would occupy her this day, and given her patience did not run out, would heed her by the end of it.

She found Labhan at the sheds ahead of her; old Marc, who'd been knocked about by more ponies than Alanna could likely count, had trouble with his joints in the mornings and usually showed up some time around noon. Alanna had no quarrel with that; it allowed her free evenings, as the old man lingered to see the ponies well-bedded.

Anyway, she liked these quiet mornings. Labhan never said much, and they worked together amiably enough. Someday, she knew, Labhan wanted to drive the chariots. Good luck to him—competition for those places proved fierce. Alanna, herself no mean hand with the traces, had few illusions she would ever qualify.

Labhan, son of a warrior, had requested to work with Alanna so he might gain knowledge of ponies, not a bad plan when it came to it. While away on campaign, a charioteer often must be prepared to care for his ponies as well as handle them.

They labored in near silence for a time, spreading

fresh straw and hauling water. Lower down the green slope, the settlement stirred and people began to pass by the low stone wall that fronted the exercise yard.

Alanna paid them little mind and scarcely imagined Labhan did, until she saw him freeze momentarily and stare over the wall. A contingent of two warriors and five young women passed—the women all strangers. The new female slaves brought in yesterday, no doubt, for aye, Alanna vaguely recalled glimpsing them in front of her father's hall.

All looked filthy and spent; two wept as they passed. Labhan, as Alanna plainly saw, stared at but one. Slender and fragile, she had a dirty, tear-streaked face, long reddish hair, and huge, grief-haunted eyes.

Labhan leaned on the wall until the party passed.

"Bound for my father's hall, no doubt," Alanna said, "and those their new masters."

Labhan said nothing.

"She is bonny," Alanna offered.

"Who is?"

She jerked her head toward the disappearing train, and Labhan grimaced. "She's a slave and marked by their accursed tattoos." He scowled and lifted a brow. "You may wish to soil yoursel' with such; I do no'."

Liar, Alanna thought but did not say it aloud. They had both been around enslaved Caledonii, as Nenian called them, all their lives. They both spoke the tongue, or a rough approximation of it. An honest man would acknowledge the occasional attraction.

But Labhan's father had raised him in the solid belief that a Gael stood superior to a blue man—or anyone else, when it came to it. Labhan clearly suspected what Alanna got up to with Nenian, and just as clearly disapproved.

Despite that, he leaned on the wall a moment longer, staring after the group. "I wonder what a man would ha' to pay, to own a lass like that."

"You could no' afford her," Alanna assured him. "Though your father likely could. Why no' ask him?"

Labhan turned his head at last; their eyes met. "She will be claimed by one o' the warriors who participated in the campaign."

"Aye, and he will be eager to sell her, if he already has enough servants. A household can only support a certain number o' slaves."

Labhan spat deliberately into the dirt. "We ha' work to do."

"Then bring out Fel. I am determined that, this day, he will listen to me."

Labhan greeted that news with a snort but did as bidden. Alanna thought again about taking on extra help—Labhan grew more lippy by the day. She wondered what had happened to the Caledonian slave she'd seen yesterday. Had he been one of those Donhal had kept? Would he be assigned to the smithy today? And how would he fare in that harsh, brutal environment?

If he proved cooperative and biddable, he would be absorbed into the life of the settlement and do reasonably well. Should he seek to hang onto his identity with any measure of defiance, his new master would break him as some trainers might break a spirited pony.

Alanna had no words to describe what she'd glimpsed in the captive's face yesterday, but she did not want to see that look eradicated. She believed in breaking neither men nor horses—that explained why it took her so long to train animals like Fel. She sought to win the animal as well as command its obedience.

She'd seen both men and horses beaten into submission. In her opinion, it rendered them worthless.

She might purchase that captive. That thought appeared in her mind out of the desire that had lain with her all night. She could. Labhan might not possess the wealth to procure the little lass who'd caught his eye; Alanna, thanks to her hard work and the excellence of her ponies, did.

Labhan led the roan-coated pony from the shed and into the new sunlight. Large for his breed, Fel had fire in his eyes, both of which he now rolled at Alanna.

She smiled. "All right, my beauty. You and I are going to deal with one another. Leave go of him, Labhan."

"Are you sure?" Labhan looked dubious.

"He's going to make a fine battle pony—one of the best I ever ha' trained."

****

For half a day, Tally and Camon remained alone in the stone hut. Though they could hear the sounds of activity going on around them in the settlement, no one came near; no more food or water was offered, and time stretched out impossibly.

A unique kind of torture, Tally thought. Though it gave them time to recover from their long journey, it also gave them an unwelcome amount of time to contemplate their possible fates. He might wish for something to happen, just to break the terrible monotony of being shut away in the dark, and yet still dread what might come.

45

His wounds, and Camon's, badly needed tending. Tally tied up what he could, using strips torn from their clothing, yet the trail had been dirty, and Camon's deep wound, in particular, needed cleansing. Tally's wounds were not beyond bearing; he'd seen his father endure far worse.

They lay on their backs on the packed dirt floor, and Tally sought to distract his companion with conversation, the only tool to hand. But talk always revolved back to two questions: what had become of those back home, and what was to become of them here in this place?

"Do you think my father still lives?" Camon asked more than once. "I saw him take a fearful blow to the head from a Gael's sword. He went down. And my brother—do you think he survives?"

"I pray so," Tally answered each time, narrowing his eyes and thinking about it. A terrible torment indeed, not knowing. Did those he loved now rest beneath the soil he loved equally well? The defeat had been the worst of his lifetime. His fellow Epidii had fought hard. They'd fought to the very death.

Would he ever see them again? The shamans taught that upon death, the spirit left the body, breaking the bond that held it to the flesh, and flew free to the forever lands. There it contemplated the life just past, learned from what had happened, and planned for the soul's future expansion. Eventually, it might stream back to these green hills, this beloved, stony ground. But those who loved were not promised to meet again.

"I want to go home," Camon whispered.

"Yes," Tally returned. So did he, with a longing that surpassed his fear and even his exhaustion.

The door of their prison abruptly opened. Daylight, sharp as any sword, slashed in. Tally and Camon stumbled to their feet and faced two men.

One Tally recognized as the leader of the party who had brought them here, he who'd watched with a smile on his face while Cemedd died. MacAtholl. The other, a warrior and well-armed, stood at MacAtholl's shoulder, his message clear.

Tally wanted to reach for Camor then, to warn him. They needed no more heroics such as Cemedd had displayed. Though death might make a tempting alternative to slavery, it meant they could never go home, not in this lifetime.

MacAtholl gestured roughly. "Out."

Neither Tally or Camon moved. The hut, once a vile prison, now seemed a refuge.

"Move, I say."

The Gael's command of their tongue might be abominable, but Tally could not claim he failed to understand. He jerked to life and stepped out into the sunlight. It washed over him like a blessing, and an astounding sight met his eyes.

From here he could see most of the settlement. Vast and strong, spread wide and patterned with dry-stone walls, it flowed down a sweep of green land to the sea. As he had yesterday, Tally stared in wonder at the broad expanse of the ocean. They had been hauled to the very edge of the world.

Blinking rapidly, he said to MacAtholl, "Where do you take us now?"

"That is no' for you to ask, blue man."

"What will happen to us?"

MacAtholl's gaze met Tally's, cold as water ice.

"You belong to me. What will happen to you is whatever I decide. Best make up your mind to that now and save us all a great deal o' trouble."

As if to emphasize his point, MacAtholl eyed Tally up and down. "I ken fine you were a man of importance in the past—your tribe's shaman, so you say. It does no' matter now; all that is gone. If you wish to survive, you will do my bidding, and that of anyone to whom I may sell or lend you."

Camon made a choking sound.

MacAtholl flicked a look at him. "Consider yoursel' fortunate; you still have your life. Had I no' chosen to bring you here, you would ha' been lying dead wi' the rest of your clan."

Tally struggled with the need to speak, and gave in. "You killed them all?"

"We did—so put any notion of escape awa' from you. There is naught to which you may return. And running will be dealt wi' harshly. Do you understand?"

Tally gave a single nod, his heart bursting. Dared he believe what this man said? Oh, yes, he believed in the promise of harsh punishment. But had everything he loved and valued truly been destroyed?

Or did this man merely attempt to destroy their hope?

"Now," MacAtholl told them, "come wi' me."

Chapter Seven

"Daughter, what brings you here? I rarely see you so early in the day."

Alanna's father spoke from his great chair at the head of the room. The chair, a new innovation, had been brought from the south, and Atholl loved to lounge in it, wearing an expression of smug superiority.

Alanna gestured ruefully to the string of people waiting outside the hall for an audience. "I had to wait my turn; Father, you are no' an easy man to see."

His remaining eye, so like Alanna's own, flicked over her. His hair had also once been blond like hers; now it had faded to silver. Yet he displayed little weakness.

Atholl MacGraedh had battled most his life. A desire for land had brought his father's father over the sea from Erin to seize this rocky shore. Atholl had grown up contesting with his father's neighbors for supremacy and had spent his adult life on the premise of expansion.

Contention, so Alanna reflected now as she tried to marshal her thoughts, thrived here in Dal Riada—between the Gaelic chiefs who held the kingdom and between Atholl's own sons. What would a Gael do with himself, if he weren't fighting for something?

She had little interest in such politics—she merely wished to live her life, train her ponies, and snatch an occasional night with Nenian. Yet she hated to think what would happen after her father passed, for whatever fragile peace they did hold rested in his gnarled hands.

But that would not happen till many years in the future, she assured herself. Despite the silver hair and the pains in his joints, Atholl remained strong of will and intention. As witnessed by the stare he now leveled on her.

"You want something," he accused. "'Tis the only reason you would seek me out in the midst of an audience day." His lip curled. "When you were a wee lass you followed me everywhere. 'Twas like having a tiny shadow."

Alanna smiled. "You would bounce me on your knee while I pretended it was a pony. And sometimes you took me up to the pony sheds."

He shook his head in mock grief. "You were mad for them even then. So, Alanna, go ahead and tell me what it is you want, besides my company."

She perched on a rug near the foot of the carved chair. For the moment, at least, they were alone, the big room empty save for the dust motes dancing in the beam of light that came through the smoke hole.

Abruptly, she told him, "I wondered if you would speak wi' Donhal on my behalf. I wish to buy one of those slaves he's kept. And he will listen to you far more readily than to me."

Atholl's brows flew up. "I told you last night you ha' all the help you need. Ask him for one o' the lasses he brought back, instead. 'Twould do you no harm to tak' a maid. And perhaps begin to dress like a woman. 'Tis past time, as we have discussed, for you to wed."

"You ken fine, Father—for aye, we have discussed it many times—I will never give mysel' to any man. Can you imagine me taking orders from a husband?" Better to seek what she needed from men like Nenian, who had no choice but to take orders from her, instead. "Anyway, as I said, I need no maid, but more help wi' the ponies."

"You never listened to aught I told you," Atholl admitted. "Nor ha' you ever taken the easy path."

"I must ha' got that from you."

He grinned. "A daughter who works, dresses, and drinks like a son. How fortunate am I? But, Alanna, those slaves your brother brought back are his to use, trade, or sell. I will no' involve mysel' in it."

Alanna's heart fell. She saw again the young man standing at the head of the dusty train, and her very spirit quickened. She wanted him in a way she couldn't begin to explain.

"Do you ken which two he kept?"

Atholl shrugged with disinterest.

"But they were males, destined for the smithy?" The question came out more sharply than Alanna intended.

Atholl tipped his head. "So I believe."

"Ah," Alanna breathed the word.

"Daughter, why are you so interested?"

"I am no'. 'Tis merely that old Marc finds his duties more and more difficult."

"You should dismiss him."

"I canno'; I value still his wisdom."

"Then accept a second apprentice. A slave would no' be suitable—these blue men ken naught about ponies, other than how to slaughter and eat them."

"An apprentice would no' stay up at the sheds all night, and that is what I need."

"Then you will ha' to speak wi' your brother. But a slave will no' come cheap."

"No matter, Father. I ha' built up a store o' wealth, wi' my ponies in such high demand. I can pay Donhal's price."

Atholl nodded grudgingly, and Alanna took it for approval of a sort—the reason she had come. If she did gain possession of the beautiful slave, her father would not be able to object.

She left his presence, stepping out with new determination, but her confidence ebbed as she faced the prospect of locating—and persuading—Donhal. Her brother, a man of mischievous and unpredictable spirit, might react in any way. If he'd already bargained the slave in question in some convoluted deal, she might not be able to talk him 'round.

Yet her resolve never flagged as she sought him around the settlement, asking after him everywhere she went. At last one of his warriors said he thought Donhal had taken his new slaves to the healer for tending.

She found him there, standing outside the hut in the bright sunshine, arguing with another clansman. Donhal had the ability to talk on either side of any given subject, often just for the enjoyment of it. Now his companion rolled his eyes at Alanna and used her arrival as an excuse to move off.

"Good morn," she greeted her brother.

He eyed her without much favor and replied with a grunt.

"How does it feel to be home?" she asked.

He bared his teeth, a habit he must imagine made

52

him look fierce. "I enjoyed having a warm and comfortable bed last night, I maun admit. Ossia was happy to see me." His gaze flickered over her once more. "But, Sister, I doubt you come to me out of concern."

"Ah, but I am concerned, Brother. The ponies I trained served you well during the campaign? You were pleased wi' them?"

He unpropped himself from the wall. "They served very well, indeed."

"I am glad. As I said last night, you will be needing more for when you return east."

"I suppose I will. Do you ha' some ready?"

"I will, within the fortnight."

His pale eyes narrowed. "What do you want for them?"

She kept her expression innocent. Despite his great wealth, mostly built up through raiding, Donhal proved notoriously tight-fisted. He would bargain down even the best offer. Yet ponies had considerable value, and Alanna's ponies most of all.

"I thought we might strike a deal."

"Och, aye?"

"As I mentioned to you and Da last night, I am in the market for a slave. I might be willing to swap for one of those you brought in yesterday—a pony for a man."

Donhal spat on the ground. No fool, he—he might be hard-nosed and tight, but no one had ever called him thick.

"I ha' only the two left. They're inside."

"Both of them are males?"

"Aye, getting tended. Would have had another, but

I had to spend him on the trail, a lesson in discipline to the others. I've distributed the rest in payment to the men. You say you want one to labor at the sheds?" He asked curiously. "Why now?"

"I want someone who will obey orders better than Labhan." Alanna's heart began to pound hard. "Are either of these you kept suitable?" If, indeed, this scheme of hers was meant to be, Donhal would have retained the very man she so desired. If not—well, perhaps that would be an answer from the gods.

"Perhaps, but I want these two for the smithy." Donhal insisted on forging his own weapons, and his forge—a dangerous and poorly-run place—ate slaves the way it consumed fuel. No worker ever lasted long there. "These two are the least badly injured of what I brought back."

Alanna pretended to lose interest. "You do no' need more ponies, then."

"A man always needs ponies. But what am I to do for help? The last fellow ruined his own arm. I canno' help but believe he did it on purpose to escape having to work. Lazy bastards, these easterners. And you ha' to keep on at them all the time. Trust me, Sister, you do no' want one."

Alanna shrugged and her gaze probed the open door of the healer's hut; she longed to see inside. She must, indeed, be mad—and Donhal might already have traded away the man who'd caught her eye.

Yet her heart told her he hadn't, that the fellow in question remained inside getting his wounds tended and that she had a chance to bargain for his life.

"Ah, well," she crooned, "then you would no' be interested in Fel."

"Fel?"

"He is only the grand stallion I ha' been training."

Donhal's eyes narrowed again. "Father said you'd been working with some ornery beast, but that he was no' ready."

"He will be, very soon. He's been a handful, 'tis true. Any pony wi' that much spirit takes a heap o' training, and I did no' want to ruin him. But in exchange for the right man, I might be willing to trade."

"Aye?"

"You should come and look at him." And what was she thinking? She, Marc, and Labhan had all labored long over Fel's training; Marc and Labhan would not be happy with her, and she'd need to reward them well out of her own pocket.

"I just might," Donhal agreed.

"Come now. Labhan will be putting him through his paces."

Donhal glanced at the hut. "I will. Only let me collect the men."

He went inside, and Alanna stood in the bright sunshine, cooling her heels and listening to the voice whispering to her inside her head. Very insistent, it was—the same kind of voice she heard when she first laid eyes on a pony and knew, without being able to tell why, she should have it for training.

Rarely had she felt so certain about anything.

A commotion at the door of the hut spun her around. Her brother emerged, followed by two Caledonii.

Alanna's world staggered to a sudden halt before spinning again, wildly.

Chapter Eight

Bright sunlight nearly blinded Tally as he stepped out of the gloomy hut. It reflected off the vast expanse of ocean that stretched beyond the rocky shore and made him narrow his eyes.

Almost, he did not notice the woman who waited beside the path; she swam into his sight slowly out of the glare, and he saw how she stared at him.

In wonder, in recognition.

Surely she'd seen Caledonian tribesmen before. Enough of them inhabited this place. The healer, back inside, kept a Caledonian boy to fetch and carry. And on the way here, Tally had seen any number of his fellows at various tasks.

Surely, he knew this woman, as well—that was, he did not know her, but he must have seen her before. Wracking his weary mind, he captured the errant bit of information: she'd been present yesterday during those endless, tiresome speeches—up on the raised area in front of the chief's house. And she had stared at him then, also, from pale blue eyes.

Her eyes were not her only remarkable feature. Tall and strongly made, she wore the clothing of a man. That, in itself, did not shock him—his sister had dressed like a warrior most of her life, and behaved like one, as did his brother's wife, Verica.

He sobered abruptly, realizing both those women—

if he could believe his new master—must now lie beneath the green sod, back home. His great tower thrown down, his very dreams destroyed.

Still the woman stared, her gaze a demand. Her hair, all braided tight, made a white-gold halo around her head in the sunlight, a color he'd never seen. Her expression looked tight as the braids, and resolute. Confidence and a very potent attractiveness flowed from her in equal measures.

Tally drew a breath. The session inside hadn't been pleasant. The healer and his assistant had treated Tally's wounds, including the slash close by his eye, with thorough haste and little care. Now, dragged back outside, he faced an unimaginable future. Labor of some sort, he did not doubt, and with no time to recover from the grueling journey or his injuries.

The woman disengaged her pale stare from him at last and fixed it on Donhal MacAtholl instead. The two of them began speaking so rapidly in their own tongue Tally had no hope of comprehending much.

Camor looked at him questioningly, and Tally gave a shake of his head. He reckoned their only chance of survival lay in taking their chances as they came, and this made a chance, however brief, to rest.

The two Gaels jabbered on while an odd feeling stole over Tally. Why did he have the conviction they spoke of him? Perhaps because the woman glanced at him repeatedly as she spoke—argued—with MacAtholl.

MacAtholl turned to them abruptly. "Come."

The two Gaels—very nearly of a height—spun shoulder to shoulder and made off; Tally and Camor followed. Back through the settlement they went before turning up the green slope away from the sea. What was this place? Mind dulled by pain and fatigue, Tally could not decide.

A broad field bounded by drystone walls, with several buildings set to one side, came into view. A young Gael led a pony across the field—he paused to eye them.

"What—?" Camor began.

"Hush."

What happened next only confounded Tally further. MacAtholl followed the woman into the field, where he inspected the pony, and the two of them fell into yet another discussion. Even Tally, who knew little about horses, could tell it for a strong and vital creature, eyes full of life and coat gleaming red in the sun.

The discussion went on and on while Tally swayed where he stood and Camor stared away toward the hills as if contemplating flight.

Do not, Tally warned him silently. At least not before our wounds heal.

MacAtholl caressed the neck of the pony, employing surprising gentleness. The lad holding the animal's head did not appear happy.

Abruptly, the discussion ended. MacAtholl, turning, gestured at Tally.

"Come," Tally told Camor, but MacAtholl bellowed in their tongue.

"Just you."

Misgiving swept over Tally in a powerful wave. What was this? Were he and Camor to be separated?

The woman eyed Tally as he hopped the wall and crossed the brilliant green grass. Her stare seemed to measure him from head to toe—the length of his hair, now a tangled mess, the width of his shoulders, and the strength of his arms. The lad who held the pony's head now spoke in her ear, but she did not heed him.

When he reached them, Tally paused. At a loss, he looked from her face to that of MacAtholl, who visibly fought an inner battle.

The woman spoke to Tally. "Do you ha' a name?"

His tongue sounded strange coming from her lips, all mangled, yet he understood the question. He nodded.

"Well, speak it, man," MacAtholl growled and added to the woman, yet in Tally's tongue, "They are thick as quarried stones, Alanna. Are you sure this is what you want?"

"Aye." A note in the woman's voice caught Tally's ear. His gaze flew once more to hers.

MacAtholl complained, "I think you are mad entirely, and making a braw mistake, but who am I to turn down so fine a pony as this? I wish you luck o' him, Sister." He fixed Tally with a glare and said, precisely as a man might speak to a hound, "You—stay here."

As simply as that, he turned his shoulder and left the field. When he reached Camor, who stared in dawning comprehension and protest, he swept him up with a gesture. They went.

"My name," the woman told Tally, "is Alanna, and I am daughter to our chief, Atholl. You will call me Mistress Alanna, aye?"

Tally realized he'd just been traded. Like an axe or perhaps a surplus hound, he'd been given away, without so much as a thought for his preferences. In this new world to which he'd been dragged and driven, he must come when called and stay when bidden, every freedom stolen away.

Worse, he could not tell whether this change might be for good or ill. He detested MacAtholl right down to his marrow, yet this woman represented an unknown, and might prove twice as vicious.

The way she watched him jangled his nerves, and screamed danger. Ah, by the goddess, how might he protect himself?

"I see you ha' taken some injuries," she went on. "You ha' been tended by the healer, aye?"

"Yes." His voice came out husky from disuse; her gaze quickened.

"I will afford you time to recover from your wounds and the long journey before you start wi' your duties here. New clothing, I think. Good food and a rest."

"New duties?"

"You belong to me now. You will work here, and live here also."

Heat rushed over Tally in a wave. He, son of one chief and brother to another—a holy man among his own people—must now do this woman's bidding. But no, he hastily assured himself, as he had from the beginning of this terrible ordeal, she did not own him. He belonged only to the god and goddess, those same who gave him life.

Those who decreed he should continue living now.

He might instead lie lifeless with the rest of his tribe, back in the forest, might have been cut down in the battle like so many others, or have perished when the tower burned. He might have died with Cemedd along the trail. Instead he found himself here with this woman. There must be meaning in it. The goddess did little without intent.

"I know naught of ponies…Mistress."

"You will learn. So long as you are firm and keep a gentle hand wi' them, it will serve."

She hesitated. Those curious, pale eyes—like water in a shallow vessel—inspected him again. "One warning—do no' attempt to run. If you do, your punishment will be lifted out of my hands, understand? And 'twill be most severe."

Against his will, Tally's gaze strayed beyond the field, beyond the settlement and eastward over the hills.

Across the aching distance to home.

Nothing could keep him here, if the opportunity came to flee. To the root of his spirit he knew that one day he would make a bid for escape. But not yet. She was right; he needed to grow stronger. To dig in a while and survive.

For the better part of Caledonia separated him from home. Not an insurmountable distance, no, but so immense it required consideration.

"Do you ha' a name?" the woman persisted.

Tally lifted his head and looked at her thoughtfully. She did not want to know his antecedents—those same inscribed in blue woad on his skin—or the names of the chiefs who had preceded him. To her, he differed little from that pony being led about the field. His heritage he could only hold to him like a cherished strength.

Nevertheless, he spoke proudly when he said, "I am named Taloc."

****

"There is a certain nobility about him," Alanna told her friend, Fenna, as she reclaimed the ale jug. "A fine sense that he canno' be bent or broken. I do no' ken how else to describe it."

Fenna snorted and gave her a bleary stare. With her husband away fighting in the east, she'd left her young babes with his mother to visit at Alanna's fireside. Friends since very young, they frequently confided in one another, even as Alanna did now.

For instance, Alanna knew that Fenna sometimes entertained fantasies about ending her husband's life. And, Alanna believed, Fenna was one of the few people alive who knew she'd been sleeping with Nenian.

Now Fenna paused with her cup halfway to her lips and raised an eyebrow. "Noble? But he is a blue man. Lass, they are savages. I do no' doubt that is why you so enjoy getting one between your legs."

"Nenian is no savage." Before his capture, he'd been a skilled hunter. Now he worked keeping track of supplies for one of the chief's stewards.

"They are all savages. I maun admit, Alanna, I do no' understand the attraction."

Neither, truthfully, did Alanna. Something in the way a Caledonian male was put together just appealed to her. She delighted in tracing the designs on Nenian's skin, in hearing him whisper words in his own tongue while they lay together in the dark. She enjoyed their illicit relationship.

But what she felt when she looked at Taloc surpassed all that and went beyond even her understanding.

"And," Fenna went on, "to trade awa' that fine pony for him! After all the hard work you ha' put into it, to say naught o' the frustration that beast has caused you." She gave Alanna a hard stare. "It will bring trouble, you mark my words."

"Well, but—"

"Do you intend to tak' him to your bed?"

The very prospect sent heat slamming through Alanna's body, head to toe. Did she? "I ha' no' thought that far ahead."

"You ha' no' thought at all. 'Tis shocking, Alanna. I mean, a man might do such a thing—buy a bed slave to keep. A woman? Never."

"I am no' at all certain this man is willing to be kept." Alanna thought of the expression in Taloc's eyes—deep smoke-gray eyes, as she'd finally been able to determine, burning with intelligence and something else she couldn't quite name.

She could barely wait to see him with the dirt of the trail cleaned away and that dark red mane—long enough to slap against his shoulder blades—untangled. She wanted to sit with him, talk to him, learn everything about him.

What, by all the powers, had come over her?

"I wonder what Nenian will say."

"About what?"

"About you taking another slave to your bed, and so displacing him."

"I ha' not said that is what I will do. Anyway, 'tis not up to Nenian whom I choose for my pleasure."

"You are playing wi' fire, lass," Fenna told her. "Men are men—even if they are painted blue. I just hope you do no' burn up like a signal blaze."

"Not me," Alanna vowed. "I am far too careful for that."

Chapter Nine

Tally wakened and lay with his eyes closed, whispering a prayer. Years ago, his mother had taught him this. *Begin the day, Son, as you mean to live it. Gather blessings and cast them ahead of you on your path. It is your thoughts that create the world; make certain they form the one you wish to inhabit.*

Since then, Tally had striven to do just that—gather his intentions at the beginning of each day, find gratitude and a measure of beauty. It had taken him far and sustained him through many a difficulty, including his parents' deaths and the absence, for a time, of his brother, Wick.

But now the magical intending of his days had come apart. Somewhere on the trail, when the days all blurred together in a welter of uncertainty and sheer endurance, when he became convinced the goddess had forsaken him, he'd lost the ability. The only prayers he'd whispered had been desperate ones, like the promise he'd made the goddess to return home at any cost. Lost in the ugliness of his situation, he'd been able to find no beauty.

What about now?

Lying on the narrow pallet he'd been given, eyes still squeezed shut and lashes twitching against his skin, he thought about it.

Even though he'd seldom been able to sense her

presence, the goddess had brought him through that terrible journey, whole. The place where he now lay felt clean and dry, and smelled of hay and horses. He felt clean also, having been provided, last night, with hot water for washing and with fresh clothing. He'd slept most of the night through with only niggling pain from his wounds.

He was blessed.

He strove to believe that thought—a struggle. But no doubt his lot could be much worse. He had no further knowledge of what had happened to his companions, what terrible courses their fates might take. He did not know how to help them, something he, as a member of his chief's house, felt compelled to do. But another morning had come, flooding in on the goddess's pure light. He had a chance, at least, to catch his breath.

He whispered the prayer and, swiftly, gathered magic from the air around him, his fingers moving in an unconscious and complicated pattern. *Safety. Endurance.* He hesitated over the third word of the spell before he spoke, because of its seeming impossibility. *Love.*

His mother had taught him that the world turned upon the strength of love. Without it, there was no beauty, no strength of heart. No reason to live.

These many days on the forced march across Caledonia, he'd not been certain he had any reason to live. Now he felt the magic, his mother's magic, patter down over his skin, joining with the blue patterns that denoted his past, and he took heart. He didn't know what this day might bring, but he vowed it would not steal yet another precious piece of his identity.

He opened his eyes on the interior of the hut. Built entirely above ground—an oddity to him—it stood lit by the streaks of light coming between the rows of wattle, and under the edges of the roof.

The woman—Mistress Alanna, so she called herself—had told him to sleep here, last night, that he would work and live here. Her possession, and subject to such orders.

But he belonged to the goddess, did he not?

He scrambled to his feet and the shower of magic moved with him. His new world looked small, this space barely four paces by five or so, and that full of equipment he could not identify.

His wounds, having stiffened overnight, pulled when he moved; it would yet take a while before he felt fit enough to attempt an escape. But he comforted himself with the thought of it; he no more belonged here than that bird he'd flushed on the trail belonged in a cage.

He wanted—no, needed—to go home. But he could not be rash about it.

He moved to the door, wondering if the old man, Marc, had barred it last night. No, it came open to his touch, swinging back on leather hinges. He looked out and saw—

The sea. It spread before his gaze like a shining blue cloak reflecting the light, one of the most beautiful things he'd ever seen. Almost—almost, the sight made the terrible journey worthwhile.

And what a view he had from up here! This place, with the horses, sat on a level piece of land above the rest of the settlement; he could see it all. The big dwelling where he'd been taken when they first arrived—the chief's hall—and everything else that lay between him and the sea. Smaller buildings, other dwellings, no doubt, and rafts of chariots, another cleared ground to his right, and low stone walls snaking everywhere.

So, this was Dal Riada. All his life he'd heard about it. This put his most lurid imaginings to shame, and would be a difficult prison to escape.

It made no sense he had not been barred in, and that no one watched him now. Did the Gaels trust in his fear of them, or think him too demoralized to run? But ah, someone came up the hill even now.

The young man it was, the one who worked with the ponies—the woman called him Labhan. He'd been asked to help haul the water for Tally's use last night and had glowered over it. A Gael, he did not like acting servant to a Caledonian.

Now he had a scowl fixed to his face and a dangerous look in his eye. Tally straightened where he stood. With the woman away, would Labhan decide to attack? But no, for here she came also, not far behind him.

Tally's lips tightened, and he tensed. Alanna might possess an unusual and singular beauty, but something about her disquieted him. It must be the way she looked at him, with an interest impossible to mistake. No stranger to female attention, he could not convince himself, now, this was anything else.

But the young Epidii women had been his friends, dear to him one and all. This woman held ultimate power over him.

Labhan, seeing him there at the door of the storage hut, swore in his own tongue and said, in Tally's, "Do no' just stand there, you great lump. There is work to be done. I do no' ken what Mistress Alanna was thinking, taking you on."

Nor, Tally suspected, did Labhan realize Mistress Alanna came on his heels. At his words, she quickened her step, leaping up the slope with an impressive show of strength, and intercepted the lad. They stood several moments in heated conversation too quiet for Tally to hear.

Labhan turned and headed off back down the slope. The woman came on, her pale hair gleaming almost white in the morning sun.

"Good morn," she bade Tally when she reached him. "Did you rest well?" Not waiting for an answer, she went on, "I ha' sent Labhan to fetch some breakfast. We always begin work early. Old Marc comes up later and stays to put the ponies to bed."

Tally sifted among the many questions teeming in his mind. "You mean for me to work here, Mistress?"

"I thought I made that clear yesterday. I suppose naught is very clear to you at present. You will need to learn our tongue if you wish to get along. 'Twill be easier for everyone, if you do, and also may prevent misunderstandings."

He would not, so he assured himself, be staying long enough to need knowledge of her tongue. The east called to him like the memory of his mother's voice. But he told her as he had before, "I know nothing about ponies."

She answered also as she had, "You will learn." She treated him to another of those looks; it started at his head, brushed through his hair like the touch of fingers, and trailed multiple paths across his skin.

"Had I no' traded for you, you would have gone to work for my brother in the forge. I can guarantee you would no' ha' enjoyed it, shut awa' from the air and the light. 'Tis a dangerous place, hot and filthy. You will find this much better."

Better? He very much doubted it but bit his tongue and said nothing.

Watching him, her gaze quickened. "You need no' be afraid to speak as you will, to me. The gods know, Marc and Labhan both do. Why should it be any different for you?"

"Marc and Labhan," he spoke the names with great care, "are not slaves."

She shrugged. "You will find me a fair mistress, so long as you keep to a few rules. You will be respectful in front of others—my brother and father, especially. You will work hard and put the welfare of the ponies ahead of your own. They are my wealth and so what feeds you. And"—she fixed him with a pale eye—"as I warned you yesterday, you will no' try and run. I mean that, Taloc. If you do, they will hunt you down and I will be forced to let them punish you. Understand?"

In his mind's eye, a mad scene played out: himself running across a vast open space and the Gaels pursuing him in a phalanx of chariots, weapons gleaming beneath a dull sun. The scope of what punishments they might deliver defied even his ample imagination. Blood. Horror. Pain. These, they always brought.

Yet he knew he would run.

Earnestly, Alanna told him, "Make up your mind to it. You are beginning a new life here and now. That is how you will survive."

And if he wanted his old life? Misted mornings filled with the scent of the forest, up early for prayers, losing himself in communication with the divine. The way it felt when he stood at the top of the tower and surveyed the far distances, holding the very, blessed soul of Caledonia in his hands. Quiet evenings and laughter with friends, those he longed to see again.

This woman and her kind had destroyed his world, quite possibly murdered all he loved. Yet she stood there looking him in the eye, expecting him to accept it.

"Come," she whispered. "'Twill no' be so bad."

That, Tally refused to believe.

Chapter Ten

"Here, lead her 'round once again. You are doing very well wi' her."

Tally turned obediently and the pony with him. Alanna sounded pleased with his progress. He had no doubt she was. Ten days had passed since she bought him from her brother, and so far he'd proved nothing but obedient.

Now, though, late in the afternoon, he felt restless and short on patience. A wind had sprung up from the sea, and clouds closed in overhead like a heavy blanket.

Days began very early indeed at the pony sheds, and work continued all day, unrelenting. Tally, ordinarily very self-disciplined, did not mind that so much, despite the many things he must learn to do, and the attitudes of his fellow workers. It might be worse. He might be one of the other Caledonii he'd glimpsed from a distance, being driven like beasts.

Alanna treated him no worse than she treated her other helpers, perhaps better. Labhan and Marc might not welcome him here, but clearly she did, showing approval of the tasks he accomplished, all with that undercurrent he could not hope to miss.

But now the rain approached. He loved rain, the sound, smell, and magic of it. Back home, on such an evening, he might abandon his work and huddle up in the tower with his friends for laughter and discussion.

Longing seized him to do just that. But he didn't know if those folk had lived or died.

"She likes you." Alanna sounded well pleased; the pony, a chunky beauty with a hide so pale that—like Alanna's hair—it looked nearly white in the dimming light, had proved uncooperative with everyone but Tally. Animals did like him; they always had, and he'd fostered an affinity with this one easily, partly out of concern.

He'd seen Labhan beat her when he thought Alanna was not looking, and old Marc bound her feet in punishment. Why wouldn't she prefer Tally?

At Alanna's words, Labhan made a sound of disgust from across the way where he sat on the stone wall watching them.

He called to Alanna, "I am going home, before the sky opens and I get drenched."

"Aye," Alanna agreed. "It is going to storm something fierce. Go ahead; I will see you come morning, unless there is a deluge. You also, Marc. Taloc and I will put the ponies to bed for the night."

The old man stared at her and spat. He said something Tally failed to understand and unpropped himself from the wall. He showed Alanna disrespect on a regular basis, which surprisingly she tolerated. Labhan often let his disrespect show also, though not so plainly. Tally, adept at sensing the emotions of others, felt it clearly and knew Alanna did not miss it either.

Now she raised her head in a show of displeasure. She possessed the natural arrogance of all her kind—it instinctively put Tally's back up, but she took a lot from these two. From Marc, Tally could understand. The old man had true skill at handling the ponies, and at treating them when they took an injury. Her attitude toward Labhan seemed more perplexing.

Now, at her bidding, both men took themselves off. Alanna gestured for Tally to lead the pony in. She watched him—or perhaps the pony—closely as they approached the shed where she stood. Tally went but half-clad, as they usually worked in the summer heat, wearing a pair of leggings and nothing more. The incoming wind pricked out bumps on his bare skin and streamed the length of his hair across his face.

Alanna twitched where she stood. "The two of us will put them inside and then have supper together, eh?"

What could Tally say? That he craved solitude and wanted only for her to follow her men, so he might listen to the rain and remember days gone? Instead he avoided her gaze—too persistent, too searching—and thought wearily of all the animals yet to be bedded down.

"You take Dana on in, Taloc. I will gather the rest."

Tally nodded. As she'd reminded him often during his ten days here—ten aching sunrises and ten endless nights—ponies represented wealth, and his mistress proved a canny woman. She took far better care of these animals than of herself.

He started away, only to catch movement from the corner of his eye. A man approached the wall and claimed Alanna's attention.

Tally kept walking. The man's presence was none of his business, even though he'd seen the same fellow here before, and more than once.

A Caledonian, and thus no doubt a slave. Like him.

The man wore rough clothing and kept his hair tightly braided, but tattoos showed on his arms, neck, and chest. When he and Alanna conversed, Tally sensed a certain measure of intimacy—turning back when he reached Dana's stall, he saw them speaking earnestly. The Caldedonian asked something; Alanna appeared to refuse his request.

Go on and leave with him, Tally begged silently. Allow me some peace, time to pray, time to dig through the layers of these constant demands and perhaps discover who I have become…

But Alanna shook her head sharply even as the first rain drops came, biting hard before the wind. The Caledonian left, and both Tally and Alanna hurried to get the rest of the ponies inside. They were drenched before they finished, and Alanna towed Tally into his tiny sleeping place.

He prayed she might leave even then, but they stood, trapped, while the rain beat so hard on the hut he could barely hear her words when she spoke.

"You are very wet." She ran a finger down his bare arm, gathering the moisture, and a new emotion sprang to life in the place, one Tally had felt from her in the past on the few occasions they were alone.

To his own surprise, his heartbeat quickened. Alanna, though nothing like the women of his own tribe, possessed an allure blended from confidence and pure, unstinting honesty. He would have to be more of a fool than he was to mistake what she wanted now.

And what did he want? To be alone, yes. And perhaps, quite astonishingly, for her to touch him again.

"Have you a cloth?" she persisted. "I will help you dry off."

Tally narrowed his eyes and spread his arms slightly. "I have but what you see." The narrow pallet lay marooned amid the litter of harness and other goods.

She bit her lip. "We shall ha' to do better by you, then."

She stepped away from him and fetched a bit of cloth, likely torn from a pony's blanket. Pausing, she stared Tally directly in the eyes and with one finger reached up to touch the welt left by MacAtholl's whip, on his cheek. "This is healing well. I doubt it will even leave a scar."

Tally stiffened where he stood, all his senses coming to attention. She resumed drying him, employing the cloth on his arms, neck, and chest, her light touch moving ever downward. Her eyes followed her own movements, long golden lashes shielding their expression.

"These markings—they all ha' meanings, do they not? Someday, Taloc, you must tell me about them, share your story wi' me."

He said nothing but quivered slightly under her touch—again, like one of the ponies. Suddenly a Vision slammed into him, complete with sound and touch—the two of them together, wrapped in a passionate embrace, naked save for the wealth of Alanna's pale hair loosed around them. Odd that, for he'd never seen her hair loose—though he suspected it might prove her greatest beauty.

Among others. Working with her every day, he could not miss the lure of her strong, supple body or those incredible, pale eyes.

But, he told himself firmly, not for him.

Gently he took the cloth from her. "I can do that myself."

"Aye, I suppose you can, if you will insist on spoiling my enjoyment."

Tally gazed directly into her eyes. "I am not here for your enjoyment, Mistress." Best to get that out into the open at the outset.

"Are you no'?"

"Definitely not." He shook the wet from his hair and passed the cloth back into her hands. "How do you know that the markings I wear have meaning?"

She tossed her head. "Everyone kens that. Besides, I ha' a...friend who is Caledonian."

An image of the man at the wall sprang into Tally's head. "A friend."

"Aye. Is that so surprising?"

"Can you own a man, keep him by force from going where his heart desires, yet claim to be his friend?"

"I do no' own Nenian. He and I ha' an arrangement, beneficial to both of us." She began drying herself with the cloth. Overhead, thunder rumbled. It had become dark as night inside the hut.

Tally briefly wondered about Nenian's situation, his tribe and former life. Ah, well, a man did as he must to survive.

He wanted to tell Alanna she did not own him either, at least not his spirit, wherein he did his best to dwell. Instead he said gently, "Then I suggest you go and find Nenian. He will no doubt enjoy your company this night."

That made her pause and stare at him. Now, he thought, will come the show of temper. In his time here he'd seen countless others of the Gaels strike out in rage. Anger and retribution both came swiftly to them.

Instead, she said mildly, "I would rather stay here with you, Taloc. Talking. Learning."

And if I would rather be alone? He wanted to shout the words but did not.

She gave him a curious smile. "Would you send me out through that storm to get wet once more, when I am only just feeling dry?"

Deliberately he told her, "I have no right—no right at all—to bid you go or stay. This place belongs to you."

"But that is what I wish to make clear to you, Taloc. You have rights when we are alone together—so do I bestow them on you."

And did she not see the irony in that?

"Ah, and what does that look in your eyes signify, I wonder? Taloc, I cannot help but think you are always judging me, and quite possibly condemning me. I ha' no need to grant you rights, have I? You were someone of privilege among your own people, I do not doubt. An *ard ri*, possibly."

At Tally's quizzical look, she went on, seeking for words. "A high king."

"We have no kings among us. Just tribeschiefs."

"Then"—she stepped closer once more—"you were one of those, if uncommonly young for it."

He said, "Your kind kill us so swiftly, Mistress, there is no opportunity to age." He added, asking the question that had so long been in his mind, "Why must you come pushing and pushing upon us? Why can you not be satisfied with what you have already taken?"

She paused in the act of unbraiding her hair and

gazed into his eyes. "There is not one answer to that, but a hundred. We are an ambitious lot and the sons of chiefs desire land of their own. In my family, there exists competition to see who will become leader after my father's death. Here in Dal Riada, three chiefs also vie together for supremacy. It all depends on what we can take." She shrugged. "Quite apart from that, it is our nature. 'Tis said we came all the way across the vast lands south of the far ocean, seeking for more, and that if we stop searching, we will become bored and perish."

"And when all Caledonia is taken? When it lies burned and shredded beneath the wheels of your chariots, when all the peace—the holy peace!—is flown, will you not be bored then?"

For an instant, she continued gazing into his eyes, as if she viewed what he viewed. Then she caught her breath. "You are a Seer. Och, I should ha' guessed before now."

"I am a Seer, and a holy man." Tally caught her shoulders between his hands. Her damp hair, some of it loosed from its plaits, tumbled over his fingers. "You must see how wrong it is for you to keep me here."

"Like a bird in a cage. I do see." Regret flooded her eyes. "But I can never let you go—'tis no' up to me, Taloc, but to my father. I meant what I said. You maun begin a new life here, make the best of this."

"Never." He shook his head. "I will return home— learn that, if you would learn something of me."

She withdrew from him, breaking the contact of his hands. Her hair still only half loosened, she thrust the cloth at him, went softly to the door, and ducked out into the rain.

Chapter Eleven

Alanna rolled onto her back and laid her arm across her eyes, shielding them from the muddy morning light. The bed, made from nothing more than a couple of hastily-snatched rugs, felt warm and perhaps just a bit over-full of sweaty male. Outside, rain still fell. She could hear it pattering on the roof of the storehouse where she and Nenian had spent the night.

She could not say what had driven her into Nenian's arms after she left Taloc, save that Nenian had stopped by earlier and offered, and seemed piqued when she refused. Something she saw in Taloc's eyes— that deep refusal—might have sent her. Now she lay naked and spent, and filled with regret.

What she and Nenian shared had its place, and its merit. But she was not the sort of woman to use folk, and she'd used Nenian last night. That did not make her happy with herself.

Nenian stirred when she did and buried his face in the crook of her neck. "Good morn." He spoke in her tongue—with an accent, but he'd learned. He'd accepted his place, hadn't he?

She replied with a murmur.

"I am certainly glad, Mistress, you came in search of me last night. Very glad." He caressed her naked breast with his fingers before capturing her hand and guiding it down his body to where he stood erect. "Can you tell?"

"Aye." She wrapped her fingers around him and turned to gaze into his eyes. She liked Nenian's body, liked it very much, and from a physical standpoint they dealt well together. He had a pleasant face, well-shaped and narrow, and hazel eyes specked with green. He'd ridden her hard last night, as if seeking to prove something.

So why did she fail to feel satisfied? This man usually scratched her itch. Not this time.

"Surely," he suggested now, "we can find something to do on such a rainy morning."

He traced a finger from her collarbone to her breast, teased her nipple into a peak, and continued downward. When he reached the triangle of curls between her legs, he plunged his fingers inside. "Shall I show you?"

His face swam before Alanna's eyes, transformed and altered to that of another man. High, noble brow framed by wings of flowing, dark-red hair, twin spirals of blue twining up his cheeks above the ginger beard. Eyes of storm-dark gray in which an entire world might exist.

Her world?

"Tell me you belong to me." Nenian bent his head and placed his lips at her breast, even as his fingers, still inside her, began to caress. Yet Alanna felt no arousal.

"I do not." She caught his hand between both of hers and forced him from her. "I never will."

He raised his head and his eyes met hers; the expression in them changed from hot green to cool and distant.

"That is not what you said, before."

"A woman says much, in the heat of coupling. That does no' foster belonging."

"Ah, so you lied to me? And you call yourself an honest woman."

"I am honest. I ha' been honest wi' you, yet words are just words."

"Words may be promises." His expression altered again, taking on a hint of spite. "You want him, yes? That is it—you want your new pet."

Alanna, having just declared her honesty, could not deny it.

Nenian sat up. "Then why are you here with me? Why not stay there with him?" Nenian began to laugh, low and not very pleasantly. "He would not have you?"

Alanna wanted to strike him then, but she never struck ponies—or slaves.

"So you came to me because you know I cannot get enough of you."

That was about the size of it, Alanna acknowledged. She said, "I am no' proud of it."

"Oh, you should be proud. You have wound me so tight around your finger, I certainly cannot refuse you. You will wind him too, given time, so I do not doubt. What then? Will you have us both?"

"Nay, likely just him." The truth again, but Nenian did not like it. She saw his eyes turn colder.

"Will you not at least let me fight him for the privilege of your bed? I could take him, I think."

Alanna did not doubt it. Before attaining the role of manager at the storehouse, Nenian had labored for a time in the foundry and built solid muscle on top of his supple frame. She asked wryly, "You would battle a fellow Caledonian tribesman?"

He laughed. "I know how much your kind loves contests. I would do this for you, yes."

"He does no' want me, so he has no stake in such a contest." It cost Alanna to admit it, but she'd always spoken plainly with this man.

"He will want you, as I say, given time. Who could help himself?" Nenian kissed her, thrust his tongue deep and, in the same movement, slid inside her. She lay with her eyes wide while he spent himself, only withdrawing at the last instant—as she always insisted—to spill his seed outside her body.

She wanted no Caledonian bairn, no bairn at all.

"There, now. You see what you do to me?"

"Aye, but, Nenian, you and I are no' supposed to mean aught to one another. This is just—just…" She made a helpless gesture with her hands.

"I know that is how it began. But you do mean much to me, Alanna. You do not need him."

He was right; she did not. But och, by all the powers, how she wanted him—even while lying here in another man's bed.

****

"How is the new slave working out for you?"

Alanna slanted a look at her brother, who had stopped by the field in passing and paused to greet her. The day had cleared at last and glimmers of sunlight picked out the yellow in Donhal's hair, and the pale hue of his eyes. So like her—was that why Taloc refused her? He considered Donhal his enemy and Alanna also.

"Very well indeed." She gestured to where Taloc rode one of the ponies across the green grass, a sight she'd just been enjoying full well. "As you can see. And Fel?" Alanna had not seen the pony since she handed him over. "He goes well for you?"

Donhal gave a big smile. "He is a dream. I would ha' ten like him, if you can provide them."

"So you are happy wi' our bargain?"

"Very much so. When will you ha' another pony ready?"

"Within the fortnight. You ken fine I do no' like to rush them."

Donhal grunted. "That is too long. We leave in four days to return east."

"Ah, so soon?"

"I maun keep up wi' Graedh. The powers alone ken what he may accomplish to get ahead o' me. I tell you, Alanna, 'tis hard enough fighting these blue men without contesting wi' my own brother for land."

Alanna repeated what her father always said. "Land is no' conquered till it is held."

"Aye, and these savages ha' a habit of rising up from the ashes like bright sparks. That is why I take more men back wi' me. I want to set up a camp on the site o' their accursed tower—if only to make a point."

With her gaze still on Taloc, Alanna asked, "How far is it, this place wi' the tower where you snatched him?"

"Far." Donhal's eyes grew hazy.

"And what is it like there? Much different from here?"

"Much different, aye. All forest, hills, streams. That tribe had carved itself out a place there—I think several tribes, in truth, must ha' come together, which is rare for them. I could no' let it stand, that tower, could I? Had to show them."

"You killed them all?"

"Not all. Did I no' just say you can never kill them all? They send their women and bairns awa' to hide in the forest and like rodents they come creeping back later on. But we did them a damage this time, burnt their tower and, I think, may have broken their back."

Alanna experienced an unexpected flash of sympathy for the man on the pony. Somehow, she needed to convince him he had nothing to which he might return, back east.

"He rides well for a blue man," Donhal observed. "I did no' ken they possessed any skill for it."

"He could no' ride at all when he got here. But aye, he has an affinity for the ponies. He learns most things quickly and does them well."

Donhal slanted a look at her. "I would no' become too enamored of him, Sister."

"Enamored?"

"Aye, as a man sometimes does, wi' a bed slave."

"I ha' not—"

"There are rumors about you." Now he turned serious. "'Tis said you ha' been sleeping wi' one o' Da's slaves, from the storehouse."

Struggling to keep her expression bland, Alanna returned, "Ah, then I will no' have need o' Taloc in my bed, will I?"

"You may well ha' developed a taste for blue meat."

"Brother! That is a shocking thing to say."

Donhal shrugged. "They may be blue men, but they are men. Do no' let them tak' advantage o' you. And," he nodded toward Taloc, "remember, if that one takes it into his head to run, the men I'm leaving here ha' instructions to go after him and show no mercy."

"Why should he run?" Alanna tried to forget the expression she sometimes caught in Taloc's eyes. "I treat him well."

"Why does a wild animal run? Why does the captured fox batter itself against the cage and break its own limbs? He is wild. Do no' forget it."

Donhal leaned close, his head nearly touching Alanna's. "Though, I can sympathize, Sister. From time to time one of their women does catch my eye. Do no' tell Ossia."

"I will not." Alanna narrowed her eyes at her brother. "But does that no' make you wonder, Donhal?"

"Wonder?"

"If the campaign against these people is right, or even necessary, if there might no' come a point when enough is enough? Do you never get weary of striving to do Father's bidding in the east, of spending yoursel' season after season to best Graedh, when Father never seems satisfied? You ken fine he will give Graedh the place of chief, in the end."

All the mirth fled her brother's face. He turned his eyes on her and in them she saw doubt, perhaps even a measure of sorrow. "Will he?" he asked. "Then I would be better striking out and making a place o' my own, would I not?"

Alanna parted her lips to answer; Donhal did not give her the chance. Instead he turned his shoulder and walked away beneath the bright sun.

Chapter Twelve

"Tell me about your land, the place where you were born." Mistress Alanna requested.

Tally frowned and turned away from the doorway where he stood. The settlement seemed oddly quiet with so many of the warriors gone; they'd departed to return east this very morning, with much ceremony and boasting. Now Tally wondered if this would make a good time for him to try and escape.

Alanna never locked him in at night. Once old Marc left, no one remained to watch him. He supposed there must be a strong guard set around the settlement; the Gaels would not be careless enough to neglect such details. But surely with the help of some magic, he could evade them?

Yet as had become her habit, Alanna remained here at the sheds this evening, even after Marc departed and all their work was done. She'd brought a jug and settled in as if she meant to stay.

He eyed her where she sprawled on his pallet and once more felt that niggling pull of attraction. Alanna made a tempting picture with her hair half tumbled down her back and the laces on her tunic loosened. He could not deny her constant presence acted on his senses and wore on his resistance. Each day he wanted her a little more.

He reminded himself, as he had too many times

before, Mistress Alanna might be an attractive woman but she was a Gael, one who believed she owned him.

"Come, have a drink." She waved the jug. "We will while awa' the evening in talk."

A wry smile curved Tally's lips. "What if I do not wish to talk?" What he wanted was to be away from here—failing that, he'd like to lay hold of her and kiss her till her eyes went wide and she lost that accursed confidence of hers.

He could indulge neither longing. So he crossed to the pallet, took the skin from her and drank.

Honeyed mead it was, nothing like the good heather ale they brewed back home. But it had a kick and might well take the edge off his homesickness.

When he lowered the skin, he saw how she eyed his naked chest, tracing the markings there with her eyes.

Gravely he told her, "I have been meaning to ask after the welfare of those who came here with me. Do you know how they fare?"

She shook her head. "I do no'. But I can find out for you, if you like. Here, sit down. Tell me about them."

Tally sat. The pallet, not large, brought them so close their knees almost touched. He could catch her scent, made up of mingled sunshine, pony, and warm woman.

"There were ten of us altogether when we left home—five men and five women. One was killed on the trail by your brother's men."

"Killed? Och, aye, did no' Donhal say he needed to mak' an example o' one of the men?"

"A lesson, so it was meant to be. He let Cemedd

think he might fight for his freedom, a lie. At least Cemedd had the courage to die rather than surrender his freedom."

"There is no courage in such a death—glory, maybe. But why throw your life away?"

If she did not understand, Tally could not hope to explain it to her.

"Please, Taloc, do no' look at me that way."

"How?"

"As if you think I am stupid."

"I do not think you are stupid. But from where you sit, can you not grasp the fact that perhaps freedom is worth the dying?"

"It is not! What good would it be for you to lie still and cold? You would not be able to feel the warm sun on your back, or the cool breeze—a pony or a woman beneath you. Here," she paused, "you might have all of those."

Tally shook his head. In a hundred ways, at a hundred moments, Alanna had made her desire for him known. Now her gaze engaged his and held.

"What of your friend?" he asked.

"My friend?"

"That Caledonian slave who stopped by the field." He drank again. "I regret to tell you Labhan and Marc both gossip at their work while you are away. Perhaps they think I cannot understand what they say."

"Oh?" She quirked an eyebrow.

"They claim he provides you pleasure."

Alanna flushed with what looked like annoyance.

Before she could speak, Tally went on, "They say you have a weakness for Caledonian men. They have noticed the way you look at me. I do not believe they like it much."

"Och, I do no' care what they like or what they say. 'Tis naught to them."

Tally shrugged. "People will talk."

Her bright gaze fell, an occurrence unusual enough to catch his attention. He had learned one thing of her: she rarely backed down.

"They are jealous of you, Taloc, because you learn so quickly and pick up the things I teach you gey well. You are already able to perform tasks it took Labhan nearly a year to learn. And you ride like the ponies are part of you. Marc says they listen to you."

"Animals tend to favor me, so they always have."

She lay back and pillowed her head on her arms. "I asked you to tell me about Caledonia—your Caledonia."

His Caledonia. The ache started at his toes and pulsed upward. "You would not be interested."

"But I am, in all you ha' to share."

"Why?"

"I canno' say, in truth. Perhaps I just like the sound of your voice."

Was she, indeed, infatuated with him like the young girls who used to follow him back home? And could he use it to his advantage? Dared he? This woman had a measure of influence. He was not in the habit of using people; in fact he'd lived all his life avoiding it.

But now he was captive, and had very few options.

"You cannot expect me to give away all our secrets, how strong our tribe may be and who holds the power, so you might run to your father, the chief, with the information."

"I will no'."

Now he crooked a brow.

"You," she said, "have admitted you're a Seer and I can tell you are of a noble house. High born. A chief, or the son of one."

Tally said nothing.

"Tell me about the tower, the one my brother burned."

Tally twitched. "The tower was a symbol, a mark of the resistance we mounted nearly ten years ago, raised on the site where my parents died."

"Ah, I am sorry. How did they perish?"

"Murdered by your people, in a raid."

She squeezed her eyes shut. "So you built the tower to honor them."

"And we have held our ground all this while. Until now." Tally stared away through the open door, as if he could see the far distances.

"As I ha' told you, my brothers—they are both much older than me and had a different mother—compete wi' each other to impress my father and so push east much harder than ever before. The one who seizes the most land and other riches will likely be named chief after Da, and will control a huge swath of Alba."

"Alba?"

"What you call Caledonia."

"So you say we are the casualties of your father's greed."

"More or less." She lifted the skin from his fingers and drank. "Try not to take it to heart—the eastern tribes are merely in our way. Dal Riada must expand."

"Would you not take it to heart, Mistress, if your

very way of life were being destroyed?"

"I suppose I would, at that." Alanna drank once more and frowned. "But you do no' need to call me that—'mistress'—when we are alone."

"But you are, in fact, my mistress—my owner. I must do as bidden."

"That is where you are wrong."

She leaned forward, still staring him in the eyes, and snaked one hand behind his head. The kiss came with the inevitability of a sunrise, and felt near as blinding. Tally tasted her lips, ripe with honey mead, wild and sweet, and he could feel her spirit just as wild, reaching for his. He tasted the headstrong intensity that made her the woman she was.

That, and so much desire it near blasted his senses.

As a sensitive, Tally did not require much to glean others' emotions. He'd felt the fear and suffering of his companions while on the trail, the harsh dispassion of their captors. From the very first, he'd felt Alanna's interest.

Now, astonishingly, he felt it snag, snare, and fan his own desire.

Ah, and what could he expect? On the few occasions she'd touched him, his body had responded without his permission. Now he had her in his arms, her mouth fused to his, and his blood turned to molten fire.

She moaned deep in her throat and wound her arms around his neck. When he gasped, she slid her tongue into his mouth and pulled him down on top of her. The flask hit the floor and spilled a pool of mead.

Tally, his entire body quivering, fought to regain control, but already Alanna filled him, wooed and seduced him, flooding him with her lust, still more vital than his own. A Gael, he reminded himself desperately—this woman was a Gael. He could not countenance the disloyalty of it.

That thought allowed him to seize Alanna's face between his hands and break the kiss. They stared into each other's eyes, neither of them breathing.

"Taloc—"

"No."

"But, please! I—"

"No."

"Where is the harm in it?"

"Harm?"

"If you want this and I want it also, why no'?"

"Listen to me, listen! Your people have been slaughtering mine, all my life—"

"My people, aye, but not me. I ha' never raised a hand against your folk."

"No, you merely train the ponies for the chariots that cut them apart. You compel me to train them."

"You canno' look at it like that. We all work, we all strive. Here, under my care, I can protect you. We can be together—"

"No."

Tally released her and got to his feet. He took a wild turn in the limited space and fetched up at the open doorway.

She shot to a sitting position behind him and ran her fingers through her hair. "There is no harm in it," she insisted again, "and I can be a help to you—that is what I tried to say. I will find out what has happened to your companions. Give me their names. I will do anything you ask."

He spun and looked at her. Swiftly, he reeled off

the litany of names that had been playing over and over in his head, before adding, "The girls—"

"The girls will ha' been taken into various households."

"And raped?"

Alanna did not duck the question. "Maybe. Householders frequently do use young servants so. 'Tis the novelty o' it, you ken."

He spat. "Is that what attracts you to me, the novelty?"

She shook her head violently. "That has naught to do wi' it. You felt what leaped up between us as clearly as I did. Do no' try and deny it."

Tally wanted to. He longed to declare he could never feel desire for a member of the clan that had repeatedly murdered his people. Honesty forbade it.

She rose from the pallet and came to him, wrapped herself around him, and whispered, "Please, Taloc. I promise to discover the fates and welfare of all your fellows. Only, let us be together tonight. I canno' bear it if—"

She kissed him again and, as readily as that, he caught fire, flame from her flame. He might have been lost then, had a scream not suddenly split the deep quiet of the evening.

It came from outside and did not sound human. It raised the hairs all over Tally's body and froze him where he stood.

"What?"

"That is one of the ponies." Alanna leaped for the door and ducked through into the thick gloaming. Tally followed more slowly, unable to fathom what he might find.

Chapter Thirteen

Alanna stumbled in the gloom outside the hut, even though she ran by instinct rather than intention. The tiny place where Taloc slept stood at one corner of the enclosed field. Other equipment huts studded the space nearby and across the back stood the sheds that housed the ponies. Staring hard, Alanna saw that one of the doors swung open. And there, creeping…

A dark gray shape, low to the ground and barely visible in the soft light.

Alanna's every instinct sat up and began howling. Wolf!

They did not come down from the hills often, but when they did the ponies attracted them like a fresh kill. It was the main reason she shut the ponies in at night. But how had the door got open? After Marc left, she'd made sure to shut them all. Perhaps she'd been so anxious to be alone with Taloc she'd neglected to set the bar securely in the hasps and the wind had blown it open.

No matter now. Experience told her where she saw one hungry wolf there would be a pack.

Taloc came up beside her; his shoulder bumped hers. "What is it?"

"Wolves. See, there? Go back inside. I do no' want you to get hurt."

"But—"

"Or better yet, run down and get help. Go to my father's house."

"And leave you alone?"

She drew a knife from her boot. At that moment, the shape at the door of the box turned its head toward them with a glint of tooth and eye.

All this time, the threatened pony continued to scream its alarm, and the others kicked their enclosures.

Taloc huffed a breath. "Is there another wolf inside with the pony?"

"I do no' ken." Alanna started forward.

"Wait." Taloc put out his hand and caught her arm. The sensation of his skin against hers halted her when nothing else could.

Now she saw his eyes glitter as he tossed his head back and seemed to gather…gather the night. She had no better explanation of it, yet she saw him fill and expand, and felt the power that came to him. Before she could prevent it, he ran forward.

"Taloc!" The name caught in her throat. At that moment the pony, Banna, began kicking her hooves inside, trying to knock either the wattle down or the wolf from the shelter. All the other ponies down the line whinnied in distress.

And the wolf standing outside the black doorway turned to face Taloc.

Alanna's very spirit shrieked with alarm, just like the ponies. Her heart clattered in her chest alarmingly. She would impose herself between them if she must, if she could, but at the moment they faced one another like two warriors, and she feared if she broke the stillness between them, attack—raw and bloody— would ensue.

A sob rose to her throat. She could not stand and watch him die, this man who had, so swiftly, come to mean so much to her.

"Nay." The word broke from her lips. "Nay!"

What she saw next defied belief or understanding. Taloc lifted his hands. There beneath the soft dark of the gathering night, he made a bold silhouette, strong and achingly beautiful, and it took Alanna an instant to realize why—light fell from his hands, showered down like drops of rain to outline him.

The wolf guarding the door gazed at him—Alanna could see it more clearly now—and another appeared behind it in the dark doorway where poor Banna kicked and sought to escape. From around the end of the sheds appeared two more; the ponies inside went mad with fear.

Taloc began to speak, low and steady, a current of words that flowed from him like music. The wolves listened the way tame hounds might, heads cocked. Then, as at an inaudible signal, they all streaked away, a group of silent shadows heading for the hills above the settlement.

Jerking into motion, Alanna ran forward—not, despite her strangling worry, to Banna but to Taloc.

People now came hurrying up the hill, having heard the commotion. Alanna had only moments to seek Taloc's explanation.

She seized his elbow. "What was that? How did you do it? Are you at all hurt?"

"I am not injured. You'd better make sure the pony has not hurt itself."

Aye, so she should. Yet, limp with relief, she discovered she could not let go of Taloc. Instead she searched his face and asked again, "How—?"

His eyes glittered at her in the dim light. At that moment, with his hair hanging loose over his naked shoulders and the patterns of tattoos twining over his skin, he looked so beautiful and otherworldly it stole Alanna's breath.

"I merely bade them go."

"The wolves?" She repeated it stupidly. "You bade them go?"

He smiled faintly. "Yes."

"You are a powerful shaman as well as a Seer." It seemed so evident she felt a fool stating it. But all she had sensed in him since the beginning, his inner strength, his quickness in both learning and healing…aye, it all fit.

These many days she had indeed been keeping a Caledonian holy man prisoner. In a shed.

The first group of new arrivals streamed into the field, Marc hobbling among them. The old man, only half clad, puffed hard from the climb.

But he managed to ask, "What has happened?"

"Wolves. Taloc sent them awa'."

"Taloc did?" Marc started at Taloc in surprise.

"Aye."

Marc spat in the grass and exchanged incredulous looks with the others. "Well, you'd better go calm that pony before she does hersel' a harm."

But Banna refused to be calmed. She would not allow Alanna in her box, nor Marc—both received injuries when they tried. Then Labhan arrived belatedly, with a girl in tow; he managed to free the terrified pony from her box. She ran, wild-eyed, about the field while all the other ponies continued their clamor, and no one could catch or calm her.

"She will hurt hersel', for certain," Marc grumbled. "You will ha' to use the whip."

"Beat a frightened pony into submission? Never," Alanna vowed. She set herself to approach the animal again. Already she had welts on both shins and one thigh, taken inside the box. Since Banna's escape, none could get near enough to her to receive a kick.

Once more, Taloc touched her arm. "Let me try."

"You?" Marc hooted. "The beast barely knows you."

"Nay," Alanna said quickly, "but let him try."

Once again—this time with an audience—Taloc stood and gathered himself. Was Alanna the only one who saw the small shower of magic that settled around him? He and Banna, who stood halted at the far wall with her sides heaving, gazed at one another before Taloc started toward her one step at a time, that steady flow of words once more issuing from him.

"What's he saying?" Labhan demanded uneasily.

"Hush. That's his own tongue." At least, Alanna thought it was, though none of the words sounded familiar.

Banna's ears twitched and reached toward Taloc; she listened. As they watched, the pony calmed. The stream of words turned into a song, soft and beautiful.

So beautiful it made Alanna's heart ache.

Was that the moment she fell in love with Taloc? Later, she never truly knew, for a thousand things made her love him. But if she had to trace it back to one instant, she must choose then even though she'd wanted him from the first time she saw him, filthy and exhausted, outside her father's house. Perhaps she'd fallen deeper in love each time she watched him stride across the field with the sun in his hair, or caught the hint of a smile in his eyes. But now she watched him walk softly to her pony and reach out a hand to her, lay his fingers on the terrified beast's neck, and soothe her. Banna stepped forward and laid her nose against his shoulder, visibly seeking comfort.

Everyone there exclaimed. Alanna felt her world tilt, and old Marc touched her arm, just as if he meant to steady her.

"I may ha' misjudged that lad," he said. "He's a special one. Best hang on to him."

"Och, I mean to," Alanna breathed. "I intend to do my best."

Chapter Fourteen

"The young man you asked about, Camon, he is working in my brother's forge and seems to be doing well enough. I might be able to arrange for you to see him." Alanna hesitated. "Would you welcome that?"

Tally turned his head and looked at her. Three days had passed since the wolf attack, and even he could not deny something in their relationship had changed. Alanna looked at him differently now, sought his opinion more, spoke up for him to her other helpers, though both Labhan and Marc now tended to leave him strictly alone.

Alone with Alanna, for the most part. They cleared off whenever they could, but she often lingered at the sheds in Tally's company. He had precious little time to himself.

And he needed that time, he always had. Mornings on his own in the forest, evenings at the top of the tower. Breathless moments deep in prayer. Now he craved those like air.

At the same time—curiously—his attraction to Alanna grew by leaps and bounds. No man could remain immune to her vitality, the life burgeoning from her, the gleam of desire in those pale eyes, and the honesty of her manner.

She certainly did not attempt to hide her attraction to him. He needed only to crook his finger to have all he wanted from her.

A heady idea, indeed. Unfortunately, what he wanted most was escape. But he'd certainly welcome news of those who'd been brought here with him.

"I would appreciate that, yes," he told her, and her face brightened.

"Fine, then I will arrange for it."

"What of the others?" Tally ran his hands down the back of the pony he was grooming, Banna once again. She remained reluctant to let anyone else handle her.

"The other men, Melis and Agarex, are getting by, Melis the better of the two." Her expression tightened. "Agarex recently rebelled and was disciplined rather severely."

"Disciplined?"

"Beaten and shut awa' on his own for several days."

Tally drew a breath. "How can I help him?" When he made his escape, might he be able to take Agarex with him? Or would that be the sort of error that got him caught?

"I do no' ken. He belongs to the quarry master, a man wi' a hot temper. But he is awa' now, campaigning wi' Donhal. Mayhap I could get you in to see this Agarex also."

Tally nodded. "And…the girls?"

Alanna hesitated. Tally could discern her moods well enough now to tell the news would not be good. "Most are doing all right, taken into households and working as servants. If abuse occurs there, it has drawn no notice. One, by name of Cinid, scalded herself wi' hot water. She is in a bad way."

"Has she seen a healer?"

"Aye, probably. One of the others, Tamia, may have been breeched whilst her new master was home wi' Donhal. But he will be gone awa' again now."

"Breeched?" Tally thought of Tamia's terror when they arrived, how she'd sought reassurance from him. And he had been unable to protect her. "I want to see her."

"Impossible. She belongs to a man—"

"You have just said he is away."

Alanna gave him a long stare. "What does she mean to you, this girl?"

"She is my responsibility, as are these ponies to you." Tally stroked Banna's neck.

"That is all? I will see can I arrange it."

"How long will the warriors be gone? Surely your brother gave you some indication whilst here."

"Until winter, most of them. Och, they might return for supplies and more ponies, or to bring home the wounded. But they will be off again, after."

"You say they mean to maintain a settlement out east, for the winter?" Tally ached to know what happened, back home. Who had survived? Had they abandoned the home place and moved farther east toward the sea?

"Most likely. Taloc"—she walked up to him and looked him full in the eyes—"you would no' try to run, would you, while they are awa'?"

Ah, and could she sense his thoughts and emotions as acutely as he could sense hers?

She pressed, "You maun promise you will no'."

He looked away from her, focused on the pony's mane.

"I mean it," Alanna insisted. "You will be pursued

and recaptured. The punishment you receive will make what Agarex took a mere pittance."

"Some things are worth the risk."

"Taloc, no." She seized his arm, compelling him to look at her. "I mean it. I will ha' your promise."

"I do not make promises I cannot keep."

"You must keep this one." Quick and hard she kissed him, there in the bright sunshine where anyone might see. Desire flared between them, and the pony shied. Tally soothed her with his hands even before he disengaged himself from Alanna's grasp.

"I do not belong here, Alanna."

"You could." Emotion surged in her eyes. Was it longing? "I keep telling you, you can begin a new life, as so many have, here wi' me."

Tally said nothing.

Her fingers bit into his arm, and she huffed a breath. "Be sensible. You are no' a stupid man."

"Sense has little to do with longing."

"Aye, well, I understand that right enough. Tell me you will stay, and I will arrange meetings for you wi' your friends."

"I would be grateful for that," he repeated. But yet he gave her no promises.

****

"Folk are saying you ha' gone soft, Alanna. 'Tis a thing I never thought to hear of you. They say you ha' become besotted wi' that new slave o' yours."

Fenna vigorously stirred up the fire that smoldered in her hearth and shot Alanna a fierce look. Fenna had sought Alanna out and compelled her to come for a visit. Her husband remained off at the fighting with Donhal, and Fenna claimed she needed the distraction.

As if, Alanna thought, her two wee children did not prove distraction enough. Even now, they ran about the place getting into trouble and refusing to be still.

The traitorous thought entered Alanna's mind: had her friend only asked her here for a chance to learn some gossip? But nay, Fenna would not use her so.

She spoke as mildly as she could, "People say much and mean little."

"But the way you indulge him—that gathering this morning proves it. No one else sets up an entertainment for slaves."

"I did no' set up an entertainment for them." But Alanna could see how it might appear so, to members of her clan—this morning, she'd arranged for Taloc to meet with his fellow tribe members, most of them. Cinid remained too badly injured to attend, and Agarex's master had not permitted him to come.

The smile on Taloc's face, as he embraced his fellow tribesfolk, had been reward enough. They'd spoken together in a rush of Caledonian, most of it too rapid for Alanna to understand. But she'd picked up on a few things.

They called him Master Tally—*Tally*, not Taloc. And their respect for him ran deep.

She hoped the meeting would settle his mind, help him resign himself to his place here. But the look in his eyes made her doubt it.

Ah, what more could she do to help him accept his lot? Had keeping her promise to him made no difference?

"Have you had him yet?" Fenna asked it frankly. "Your interest is plain to see, and 'tis whispered you stay late where he sleeps."

Alanna might only wish. So far Taloc had resisted all her subtle, and not so subtle, invitations. And that despite the fact that when they touched, or kissed, she could clearly feel not only her desire but his also.

"Shocking, it is," Fenna added.

"Why? Because I am a woman? Men do it all the time, wi' their house slaves."

"Aye, though if my husband ever so much as looks at one o' our servants, I will knock him senseless." Fenna considered it and concluded, "A master canno' get landed wi' his slave's bairn; you can. Best ha' a care."

"Aye, so." Should such a thing happen, her father would not be pleased. It made a good reason why she'd trained Nenian so carefully. But she no longer desired Nenian, not even a little.

"Fenna"—the words that had these many days been swirling in her mind now came from her, unpreventable—"I think I am in love wi' him."

"With your slave?" Fenna sat up abruptly. "Ah, no, Alanna—you could no' be so foolish."

Alanna said nothing.

Fenna reached out to her impulsively. "'Tis no' like you, to be beguiled by any man. You are the strongest woman I know."

"Aye, but Fenna, he is so—so beautiful."

Fenna tossed her head. "Men are no' beautiful. They are braw and brash, and oft times too charming for their own good. But no' beautiful."

"He is," Alanna insisted. "Ha' you no' looked at him? He is light and magic; he is noble."

"You ha' said that before. But how can a slave be noble?"

"I suppose he must ha' been born that way."

Fenna snorted. "You ha' lost all reason. Best to scratch the itch and get it over with. Then you will see him for what he is—just another man, and a blue man at that."

"I would, if I could." Alanna did not like the helpless feeling she got when near Taloc, yet she'd be cursed if she could keep away. Each look, each touch drew her in more deeply.

What might coupling with him do to her? She would be lost...lost. But all things considered, she was willing to embrace that possibility.

Chapter Fifteen

The storm, blown in from the sea, raged overhead, wild and tumultuous as Alanna's emotions. By the time she returned to the pony sheds, she was drenched to the skin.

Yet in the field, all lay quiet. Taloc had promised to walk the boundary of the wall after he put the ponies to bed. She suspected he also said a wee spell to keep the wolves at bay.

A man of magic, as she'd told Fenna, and wholly enchanting with it.

She ran to the door of his hut and then hesitated. As owner of this place she had no cause to beg admittance. Yet Taloc's dignity demanded it, and she called in a strong voice, hoping to be heard above the rain.

"Taloc? 'Tis I, Alanna. Admit me, for the god's sake."

He came swiftly to the door and opened the wooden panel. Radiance from a single rush light shone behind him, outlining his graceful silhouette. His hair—that mane of his, far more glorious than that of any pony—streamed loose over his shoulders, making her fingers twitch.

Ah, wanting him was a sickness, one for which she had no cure.

"What are you doing out in the rain?" he asked. "I

did no' expect you back here tonight."

She did not bother to answer his question, lest she blurt out all and surrender the last of her self-respect. She was supposed to be the one in control, yet here she came creeping to his door.

So unlike her, she who'd worked hard for her independence and unthinkingly accepted her elevated status. Yet he rendered all that unimportant.

She pushed by him, brushing his arm in passing and letting the contact linger. "I wanted—needed—to see you," she admitted.

"Is somewhat amiss?" he looked concerned. Compassion lay deep in this man, for her ponies, for his fellow slaves. Why not for her?

"Nay, I was visiting wi' my friend, Fenna. Talking, until she put her bairns to bed. I merely wished to stop by here and bid you good night."

"Ah."

She turned and looked into his eyes. Could he not see why she had come, what she so desperately wanted?

She drew a breath. "Nay, I lie—I wanted to be wi' you." There, she had said it plain out. She took a step closer. "You always ha' excuses. Tell me again why we should no' be together this night."

He did not duck her gaze or, this time, her words. When he answered, it was in the Gaelic tongue that he'd picked up so easily. "Nay, Alanna. It would not be wise."

"What is wisdom?" she returned, anguished. "What, in the face of this thing that exists between us?"

He swallowed convulsively. "It would change everything, and change nothing. It would alter how we feel, how we work together, but it would not alter the fact that you own me."

Good reasons, all. But the desire pulsing through Alanna made, to her mind, a better one. "I do no' command you," she whispered, "nor compel you. Not in this. That is why I come asking, Taloc." She stepped still closer, her sodden clothing making contact with his bare chest. "Only let me show you, there is benefit in being here wi' me."

She kissed him, pressing her mouth to his and unleashing the whole of her desire. Not particularly skilled in the art of seduction, she usually spared no time for softness or persuasion. Her past encounters had been direct and to the point; even with Nenian they involved physical pleasure and little more.

This, though, was all about need and not just the physical. As soon as their lips met, Alanna's spirit reached for his, hungry and yearning, as needy as her flesh.

He gave a low sigh and his arms came around her, hard. Ah, and did he succumb to her at last? Alanna parted her lips and invited him in, and there in the poor hut with the rain crashing down, they melded together on a rush of exquisite heat.

Alanna tasted...

His strength, his sweetness, his brightness, all backed by a bed of heat. For days uncounted she'd desired this man; now she saw that, before tasting him so deeply, she'd barely guessed what desire could be.

Light filled her head and exploded outward. Quite clearly she thought, *If I make love with him I will never survive it. Surely, surely I will lose myself. But if I do not make love with him, I will die.*

As if he heard her thoughts, Taloc broke the kiss.

Breathing hard, he rested his forehead against hers.

He said, "If you truly do offer me a choice—"

Panic swept Alanna. He meant to refuse her! She curled her fingers around his wrists and interrupted, "I offer you that and far more. Come, Taloc, where is the harm in it? One night."

She could feel his resistance, just as he must feel her desperation. "It would not be one night, Alanna. You know that and so do I. And I cannot—"

"Do no' say it." Half frantic, she caught his face between her hands and kissed him again.

She did lose herself then, for one searing bright, breathless instant, as he flooded in upon her—his quickness, his intelligence, and his magic. Together, they teetered on a precipice, the depth of the fall terrifying.

She had only to pull him in.

"Here." When the kiss ended, she spoke in a whisper. "You take what you will o' me. You shall be the master here this night, and I the slave."

She let go of him, but only in order to shuck her clothing. Her skin lay wet beneath, but flushed with heat. Unmoving, Taloc watched her, hands dangling at his sides.

He must—he must accept this offer. She had nothing else to give.

And what did he see by the radiance of the rush light as her clothing fell away? Her body might not be delicate, soft and beautiful like those of other women. She bore scars and a few bruises from the day's work; nary a tattoo. But her limbs were strong and supple, her breasts surely full enough to please. And her desire for him raged like the storm outside.

"Now you." She reached for the laces on the front of his leggings, with hands that shook.

A gust of wind shivered the walls of the hut, and the rush light went out.

****

Darkness filled the hut, and a wealth of sensation. In the past, Tally had made love with Rekka many times and with other girls of the tribe a time or two—insistent girls. Never had it been like this. Those joinings were gentle, warm and loving. His desire, for the most part, had remained banked, held by his intellect.

Contact with Alanna, though, threatened to overwhelm him and reduce his control to ashes. She tapped a well of heat inside him he'd never suspected existed.

The instant her bare flesh met the skin of his chest and her mouth once more found his, even before she succeeded in freeing him from his leggings and wrapped her fingers around him, he knew he had no hope of stopping what must happen.

A strong current of raging fire would be easier to halt. The blaze at the tower would. But at this moment he—usually so well-rooted in spirit—ceased to care.

The physical became all. Alanna became all—touching her, tasting her. But was the encounter devoid of spirit? Lines of gleaming brightness unleashed from the roots of his soul to embrace and entangle her. They threaded the darkness, glowing in patterns that echoed a web of magic.

"Taloc." She breathed his name into his open mouth, into his very being, on a moan. Her fingers remained curled around him in bands of sheer heat; his had become buried in her glorious hair, where they moved of their own accord to unwind the plaits. Together they stumbled back and fell onto his pallet.

"Taloc." This time she spoke it out loud. Lying beneath her where she'd landed on top of him, naked, he could feel all of her. "Please."

The word came ready to her lips even though he doubted she was used to begging. Like all her kind, she possessed that thoughtlessly supreme confidence that took, and took.

A spark of mischief made him ask, "What is it you want?"

She groaned and kissed him. Her body, alive and sizzling, cradled his from above. "You. But I want to see you. Curse the light."

He wrapped one arm around her and held tight. Using the other hand, he wove a small pattern with his fingers. The rush light—there beside the pallet—sprang back to life.

All the breath rushed from Alanna's body. She gasped. "Magic."

"Yes."

"You are magic." Devoid of breath, they gazed into one another's eyes. "You ask what I want. I want you. Inside me."

"Yes." He could no more refuse her than still his own heart. It would happen between them here, in this storm-torn night just as if the goddess herself decreed it.

Was that why he'd been brought here in chains? So he could be with this one woman, spend himself in her, defying a lifetime of hatred?

"Please," she beseeched again.

And he said for the third time, "Yes."

As readily as that, as easily as weaving a spell, the barriers fell away, his and hers together, as if they'd never existed. When he spun her beneath him, she opened like a flower seeking the sun—mouth, arms, and legs. He wanted to taste her everywhere, to take his time with it, savor the softness of her breasts, the strength of her limbs, and sample her well of heat. But in the end, need rendered him as helpless as she.

Their joining came swift and sure, both body and spirit, so Tally could not tell one from the other. The strength and sheer heat of it shook him, and the need stole both breath and reason. He'd never suspected the mere act of coupling could take him out of himself, make him more than he'd been.

Even after he emptied his seed inside her, they remained joined. And Alanna—the strong, the indomitable—wept.

She wept.

He felt the tears against his cheek, pressed to hers with blinding intimacy, felt the hitch in her breath, as if it were his own.

"Alanna?" He whispered her name and a little shower of magic settled around them. "Alanna, what is it?"

"Hush. Only let me hold you. I ha' wanted this for so long."

"Not so long." He'd not been in the settlement a month yet.

But she corrected him softly, "All my life."

"Ah." He could not dispute it, could he? For their joining had asked a question and given an answer.

After a lifetime spent warring, peace lay here in her arms.

Chapter Sixteen

"Lass, did you no' hear me? I said 'tis her left hoof. You're after holding up the wrong one."

Marc spoke in a growl, not seeking to hide his impatience. The two of them tended a pony Marc fancied had gone lame, and Alanna found it difficult to concentrate; across the field she could see Taloc exercising another of the horses. She found it impossible to tear her eyes from him.

Four days—four nights—had passed since that first they spent together. She'd passed each of those nights in Taloc's arms. Not sleeping, nay—at least, not much. But she'd well and truly, as Fenna had suggested, scratched her itch.

Trouble was, nothing she'd done, from opening herself to Taloc as to no other man ever before, to pleasing him with her mouth, helped ease her craving for him. Indeed, touching and tasting him merely intensified it.

Perhaps, she thought while watching him move with a grace matching that of the pony he led, sunlight turning his hair to copper fire, she was going mad. For she, who'd always taken pride in her self-control, now could claim none.

Marc made a sound denoting disgust. "Pull your eyes back in your head, lass. Ha' you no pride?"

What had pride to do with it? Should she be

ashamed of the things that ran through her mind when she looked at Taloc? Of the things they'd done together and the way he could set her simmering with a mere glance, quivering with a single touch?

"Careful," Marc warned. "Half the clan kens wha' you get up to wi' him. Your father will no' like it, when it reaches his ears."

That captured Alanna's attention. "Does half the clan truly know?"

"Aye."

She stared into the old man's wizened face. "How?"

"People see things, they talk. Especially when they tak' too much mead."

"Who has talked? You?"

"No' me. Young Labhan."

"Him? But he's scarcely been around." Labhan had curtailed his time with them lately, often arriving late and leaving early.

Marc lifted a brow. "Ha' you asked yoursel' why? 'Tis no' a bonny sight watching a lowly slave wrap the chief's daughter around his fingers."

"Taloc is no' a 'lowly slave.' Surely you can see that."

"See what?"

"How fine he is, how noble."

Marc snorted again and soothed the pony with a horny hand. "When I look at him I see a blue man, perhaps a canny one who is persuading you to things you'd be better leaving alone."

Alanna thought hard about that. So far, she'd merely indulged herself with Taloc, and kept her promises, arranging more meetings with his fellow captives.

"Your father will no' like that you ha' let a slave get the upper hand wi' you." Marc jerked his head at Taloc.

"Taloc has not got the upper hand wi' me. And as for us coupling together"—why call it something other than it was?—"men do it all the time."

"Men canno' get a brat in their bellies," Marc answered, even as Fenna had.

Alanna had no reply to that. For the first time, she considered what she'd neglected each time she and Taloc lay together. With Nenian, she'd insisted he withdraw before spilling his seed. Her passion for Taloc made her want to consume all of him, and she'd not once protested when he gave exactly that to her. Dangerous, aye, but surely naught would come of it.

"'Tis no' decent," Marc grumbled, "the way you follow after him wi' your eyes."

Perhaps not, but Alanna could not help herself. She lived for Taloc's company, for that time when the sun went down, so they might be together. But of course at this season the sun stayed up nearly all night.

"Do no' fash yoursel'," she told Marc. "I ken fine what I am doing."

"Do you, so? And wha' of your other slave?"

"I ha' no other slave."

"Foolish lass! I speak o' that one you used to ha' warming your bed—Nenian is his name. Folk are talking about that also."

Were they? "I am through wi' him."

"Aye? And does he ken that?"

"To be sure." Alanna no longer went to him, or called on him. What else was he to think?

"You might want to mak' it clearer. I, mysel' ha' caught him watching you half a score o' times from beyond this wall."

"Oh, aye?" Alanna's heart fell in dismay. Nenian could not possibly believe he had any claim on her. Their relationship had been about one thing only.

She shrugged a shoulder. "I will aye speak wi' Nenian."

"You'd better do. You are headed for trouble, my girl. Now tend to this pony's hoof—the proper one, I do mean."

****

"I spoke wi' Mistress Cargon today," Alanna whispered into the near darkness. She had just finished loving Taloc, which meant surrendering all her self-control and a good deal of her ability for rational thought, and so had to fumble for the words. Each time she loved him, she acknowledged, she lost still more of herself. Yet her desire for the taste of him had become a raging fire. It made her wonder if magic weren't involved.

Now she should feel sated, but still she wanted more.

"Who is Mistress Cargon?" Taloc's voice sounded low and dusky, and sent a shiver over her skin. Was that desire she heard? Did that mean he, too, wanted more of her?

"She owns Tamia. That is, her husband, Bech, does, but as I ha' said, he is awa' fighting. I ha' been trying to persuade Cargon to let you see Tamia."

Taloc stiffened beneath Alanna's fingers. "Bech is the one who raped her?"

"Aye, well, Cargon did no' admit that outright, but

she did no' deny there had been relations, either. Cargon is wi' child again. Men do tend to use their slaves more heavily during that time."

Indeed, when Alanna had gone to Bech's dwelling, she'd caught a glimpse of the girl—hair tangled, face bruised. She would not tell Taloc that, though.

"What are you thinking?" she asked him. She could feel the thoughts moving in his mind, just as, these days, she could sense his presence in the field without looking 'round.

"Naught."

"Are you in love wi' her, this Tamia?" She'd thought she might try and purchase the slave from Cargon, if it would please him. But she had no use for a female slave. Besides, what if Taloc did have feelings for the lass? Might the girl take him from her?

He jerked beneath her hand. "Nay, only a decent man's concern. I feel responsible for her."

That compassion of his again—Alanna could feel that also, all tangled up with his magic. She often felt it flow out to the ponies, as well as to his fellow Caledonii.

To her? Never. She wondered why. He must be able to feel her helplessness in his presence, how he held her in thrall. Did he not know she was used to being the one in control, the one in demand?

Yet he'd transformed her into a woman who shed her clothes for him when he came through the door of the hut, knelt at his feet, and could not wait to submit herself to his touch.

Without shame.

"Let us speak of something else," she decided, regretting ever mentioning Cargon. "Tell me more about your life back east." She craved details about him almost as much as the feel of his fingers on her flesh.

That called his gaze to hers, misty gray and hesitant. "Why do you always wish to hear of that?"

"I want to know everything about you." She traced the line of his lower lip with a forefinger and hunger for him poured through her. "Mayhap I just like the sound of your voice."

"I still have a poor enough command of your tongue"—he smiled slightly—"and you never fail to butcher mine."

"You ha' very good command of my tongue." To prove it, she kissed him hard. "You can send it anywhere upon your body that you choose."

"Ah, I did not mean that."

"But 'tis true." Still gazing into his eyes, she hid nothing.

He ran his fingers through her hair, an action in which he indulged often, and Alanna's heart began to pound hard; had she been standing rather than lying draped across him, her knees might well have failed her.

She whispered, "You canno' deny that when we couple together the pleasure is…" But she had no word for it.

"Blinding," he supplied. "I never dreamed it could be like this, could take me out of myself in such a way."

"You must ha' been wi' other women."

"Yes. But never like this." He ran his palm down her body to cup her breast; heat poured through her, along with a measure of satisfaction. He admitted he'd never desired anyone as he did her. Perhaps what she offered would be enough to make him content here in

Dal Riada.

Perhaps it would be enough to make him love her.

"When we join," she told him, searching for words she rarely needed, "I feel so much more than the pleasures of the flesh. 'Tis as if your spirit and mine come together, and fly."

"Yes."

"'Tis magic, it must be. You are a shaman, and your touch is enchantment."

He did not deny that either.

She broke the bond of their gaze and slowly traced the patterns that swirled across his skin. "You never told me what all these mean. Are they also magical?"

"One or two of them. That one is for protection. Most just tell the name of my tribe and those of my ancestors."

"A noble line."

Another smile touched his lips. "Yet it has come to this—me, a slave."

"Nay, Taloc, nay—you are no slave to me. No slave, when we are here together like this, but my equal. Can you no' feel that?"

"Yes, Alanna."

"Will that no' make you satisfied?"

"Would you be satisfied if I bound you, stole your will, and took you to the east for the rest of your days, never to see your home or those you love again?"

"Aye, if you were there wi' me." Alanna trembled where she lay. "I will always be happy, in your company."

The truth, stark and naked, but he failed to reply in kind, did not admit her presence might be enough for him, the way his was for her. Panic and denial both joined the fire in Alanna's heart. In an act of protest she kissed him and, when he responded heatedly, she loved him again, absorbed him into her like a woman with no thought for the morrow.

Surely, she thought even as they once more soared together, bodies linked, they were meant to be. And surely, surely, if she loved him enough he would make up his mind to staying for the rest of his life here, with her.

Chapter Seventeen

The little mare that had been worried by the wolves now followed Tally around the field like one of his father's great hounds. He had no need to command her; she sought his company at every opportunity and answered commands in either Gaelic or Caledonian.

In that, she reminded him of Alanna. A chief's daughter, a woman of privilege and purpose, she nevertheless deferred to Tally's wishes when they were alone and sometimes also when they were not.

Fortunately for her, he was not the man to take advantage of that. He'd gratefully allowed her to arrange meetings with those who had been brought here with him, if only so he might determine whether any among them were desperate for rescue. When he left this place—for leave he would—he must decide who, if anyone, to take with him.

Not but that leaving Alanna would prove difficult—no, beyond difficult. At this point, it would be a wrenching blow. He'd come to crave the scent of her, the taste and the feel of her flesh beneath his fingers. He'd never imagined a man could deem it a holy—or a magical—act when entering a woman, yet he did. There were times, lying by her side after coupling, he could not imagine how he might ever leave her.

But he would, and soon. Quite clearly, he needed

to make his move while the weather remained kind enough to allow for travel east—back home—and the bulk of the warriors were still away.

Home.

Longing swept over him, every bit as powerful as what beset him in Alanna's arms. All she had to do was look at him in order to tap into that deep river of passion, the one he'd never suspected existed. Yet he'd made a promise to the goddess, and home called to his bones and to his spirit.

He must go, but when? For days he'd assessed and judged the position of the moon and the movements of the guard. He'd subtly questioned Alanna about their routine and believed the Gaels erred on the side of overconfidence. Here, on their own ground, they feared neither attack nor defiance. Should it be tonight?

The Gaels might well prove careless. As for the moon, he'd prayed to the goddess—she who ruled that body—about it. Instinct argued the light of a full moon might aid travel but it would also aid pursuit. When the goddess withdrew her bright face from the sky and no hint of her could be seen, that must be the best time to slip away.

Tonight.

He narrowed his eyes and, hand resting on the warm flank of the pony, gazed away toward the far hills. What would it do to Alanna when he left? He could not say he didn't care. A man could not join so surely with a woman and fail to bond with her, also, in feeling. He knew Alanna trusted him. His departure would likely leave her crushed, embarrassed, and devastated.

Yet he'd never lied to her about his desire to return

home. She knew how he felt for his people, his tribe, and his lands. How could she imagine she might come to mean more?

He felt a prisoner here, even though she refrained from locking him in—a hawk in a cage. He might be able to live for a while on her kisses, the softness of her breasts, and the heat of her flesh. But eventually his spirit would die.

Tonight, then.

Dared he confide in her? No fool, he knew she cared for him; she'd done all but speak the word *love*. She might, then, assist him, offer him supplies, and even cover his absence for a time.

Then again, she might do everything she could to keep him with her. Tally simply could not tell.

Either way, tonight he would leave. Only one question remained—should he go alone?

He wanted desperately to take Agarex and Tamia, those two who faced the worst existences here, but they would slow him down, and if he didn't make it away, he could help no one.

If he did make it away, if any among his tribe survived and he could search them out, he might then mount a rescue.

Or he might never return, never see this place—or Alanna—again.

At that thought, an ache seized his heart. Yes, he'd grown attached to her; he was a man who grew attached easily, as to the pony beneath his hand. He would miss Alanna but he would not let that stop him.

If he wished to leave this night, he must somehow prevent Alanna from staying to lie with him, as had been her habit of late. But how? He closed his eyes and spoke into the radiant air: Goddess, show me the way.

When he opened his eyes, he saw Labhan starting across the field, leading another of the ponies. The young man shot Tally a suspicious look.

Labhan made no secret of his dislike. Indeed, since Alanna began working—and sleeping—with Tally, Labhan had showed up to work less and less frequently.

One person, at least, would rejoice at Tally's absence.

Labhan called, "Are you intending to work this day, blue man? Or will you waste the good weather daydreaming like a maiden?"

"I was but calming the pony," Tally replied.

"Well, calm this one if you think you can. It belongs to one of the chief's closest companions and has gone off its head."

Tally looked at the pony which, even in Labhan's hold, stamped its hooves and attempted to rear. Almost as big as Fel, it had an angry spark in its eye.

Tally smiled.

****

"Tell me again, and clearly, what happened." Even as Alanna made this demand, she leapt the low stone wall that surrounded the field. When she saw the crumpled figure lying in the green grass—a figure with bright auburn hair—her heart, already up in her throat, began beating so hard it made her dizzy.

She'd just been bringing their breakfast when Labhan came running with the news. Taloc, hurt. How badly he could not say, but the gleam in his eyes reflected a measure of satisfaction.

This looked bad. Taloc lay face down, one pony standing near him in an attitude of concern and another not far away with its shoulder to him.

Alanna pelted to Taloc's side and fell hard onto her knees beside him. The closest pony—Banna—shied away, but Taloc lay still as if...

Dead.

"Nay," she breathed while her whole world rocked violently. "Nay."

In her life, she'd never wanted for much of anything. As the daughter of a chief, she could more or less claim what she needed, just as she'd claimed Taloc. Oh, she'd known moments of frustration and defiance, such as when her father pressured her to wed for the sake of the clan. But, genuine fear?

That found her now for the first time, pure raw fear that turned her stomach and tore at her with sharp claws.

She laid a careful hand on Taloc's bare shoulder. The pattern of tattoos—that which she knew quite well, did not flex beneath her touch. Did he breathe?

All she could hear were her own ragged breaths and those of Labhan who stood behind her. "Tell me," she tossed the demand at him.

"Rohan sent his pony—there you see him—because it's been acting up. I thought since the blue man possessed this grand magic of which you are always bragging—"

Alanna swore savagely. Labhan had wanted to see Taloc fail—more, wanted to see him hurt—ever since he'd arrived here. "If he's dead, I will make your life a misery, so I do vow."

"Your pet is no' dead. Roll him over."

Alanna did, with careful hands. Taloc, clearly unconscious, flopped onto his back and lay with his arms limp. A livid bruise showed on his chest just above the heart, and another rose on his forehead.

No blood. But as Alanna well knew, a kick from a riled pony could stop a man's heart.

She placed the palm of her hand on the darkening skin of Taloc's chest and squeezed her eyes shut, praying. She prayed but seldom, relying more often on her own will and determination than on the intervention of any gods, but fear still held her in its fierce grip.

Over the past many nights, she'd become more than familiar with the rhythm of Taloc's heart. Her fingers sought—and found—it now, low and steady, and she could have wept with relief.

Yet Labhan stood by watching critically. She couldn't, as she wished, throw herself on Taloc and shed tears.

"He is but stunned, I think." Gently, she patted Taloc's cheek and spoke his name. His long, brown lashes fluttered and his eyes came open, hazy and dazed.

"Taloc?" She spoke in her own tongue and then his, "How do you feel?"

"My head—"

"No broken bones?" She felt of his arms. "Can you sit up?"

She assisted him while Labhan stood glowering.

"There, sit a moment while you catch your breath." And she caught hers. Relief, she discovered, felt as staggering as alarm.

"What happened?" she asked a third time.

"The pony kicked out, managed to catch me."

Labhan snorted rudely. "So much for his magical way wi' the ponies."

Taloc shook his head. "Something is hurting him. I could sense it." He closed his eyes for an instant. "Left front hoof. Go look."

"Go," Alanna snapped at Labhan, and he jerked to life.

As soon as he moved off, Alanna caught Taloc's face between her hands, the better to gaze into his eyes. She had to fight down waves of emotion before she could speak; even then, her voice sounded rough and strange. "Are you certain you are no' hurt?"

"Yes. Just sore."

Alanna did not doubt it. "But sound?"

"I think so."

She kissed him, quick and fierce, before Labhan returned. "By the goddess, you frightened me."

A new expression came into his eyes, swirling like the hints of magic she sometimes caught there. "I am sorry. I do not mean to distress you."

"No matter; it was Labhan's fault. What was he thinking, bringing that beast here wi'out talking first to me?"

"Do not blame him."

Once again, Alanna had to struggle for breath. Labhan detested Taloc—and had made no secret of it— yet Taloc asked for leniency on the young man's behalf.

"What sort of man are you, Taloc?" But her own heart answered the question before he could: the man she loved, and the finest she'd ever known.

That realization made her swallow hard. Only a fool would lose her heart to any man, and especially to a Caledonian slave. But she'd never had a chance of resisting Taloc—had been lost at her first sight of him, and everything she'd learned about him since merely

drew her deeper in thrall.

"Here, help me up," he requested.

She did so, both of them swaying a bit in the bright sunlight. Labhan came jogging back to them with a disgusted frown on his face and an object in his hand.

"What is that?" Alanna asked.

Labhan held out his hand, revealing a sharp splinter of wood, marked with blood. "Embedded just above the pony's left front hoof, so deep I could barely see it." He glared at Taloc. "How did you know?"

When Taloc did not answer, he muttered, "'Tis uncanny. I do no' like it."

"Go and find Marc; ask him to examine and cleanse the wound."

When Labhan once more jogged off, she turned back to Taloc. "You will rest for the remainder of the day."

"And have him sneer at me?" Taloc shook his head. "I will carry on. I can rest later tonight."

Disappointment replaced the relief in Alanna's heart. But of course he would need to rest tonight, and when she stayed here with him, neither of them caught much sleep. It would be the first night they'd spent apart, though, since first they coupled together.

She nodded reluctant agreement. Better missing one night in his arms than losing him. Anything—anything—would be better than that.

Chapter Eighteen

Tally left the rush light burning when he slipped away from the hut. If Alanna passed by—and instinct told him she might—she would see the faint line of radiance from beneath the door and think he had fallen asleep, enjoying the healing slumber he required.

He took little with him because he had little to take, just the clothes in which he stood, a few scraps of food, and one of the mead flasks left behind from their last night together, refilled with water.

Then he stood, eyes closed, and prayed. Should he be off to the hills and away on his own? Or should he attempt to take Agarex and Tamia with him? He still had not decided.

No question but he had a far better chance getting clear away if he left straight from the hut. Both Agarex and Tamia would likely be shut inside, and trying to get their attention might well get him caught.

Yet his conscience warred hard with his heart. He thought he heard a voice—not that of his goddess, but his mother.

It is your sacred duty to help those of your tribe.

Enough to tip the scales, the words sent him stealing down the slope rather than up and into the trees.

The settlement lay quiet, and he'd memorized the movements of the guards. But at this time of year, dark

held back long for the gloaming, that misty-gray, half-light so soft on the eyes yet so dangerous to someone like him.

He knew where both Tamia and Agarex were housed; Alanna had taken him past both places. Agarex first, he told himself. And he might need to employ just a little magic.

Above the long hut where Agarex lodged—that belonging to the man who quarried stone—Tally paused. All silent; the only thing that moved was the broad sea, which seemed as restless as Tally's emotions.

Agarex would be sleeping the slumber of the exhausted; the slaves at the quarry labored long and hard. He would not have had much time on his pallet. Tally heard no sound from within the building, which appeared all too similar to the pony sheds he'd just left.

How to get the attention of one man inside, and only one? An overseer dwelt here along with the slaves, presumably to keep the crew from running. After a moment's thought, Tally flattened himself against the side of the building, leaving no silhouette should the guards glance in his direction. Raising both hands, he pulled the dim radiance from the air and wove it into a small glittering spell which, after a whispered prayer, he released.

Then he waited, heart thumping hard in his chest, feeling the magic move away from him toward its target.

What had his mother always said? *If you will the magic, Tally, do so for the right reason and with a calm, pure heart. Always use the light. And go sparingly. Remember, magic will drain you, otherwise.*

Difficult, to maintain a calm heart when terror threatened. Waiting proved equally hard, but he did not have to wait long. Soon he felt a stirring in the gloom; a voice murmured on the other side of the wattle wall and another answered.

Agarex slipped through the rear door.

The young man wore only a pair of tattered leggings; his tattoos gleamed in the low light. He stood blinking at the gloaming like a bewildered beast. Looking for Tally? Perhaps, perhaps not.

Agarex. Tally did not speak the word aloud, but Agarex's head came round. He said, "Master Tally, what—"

"Hush. I am leaving here tonight. Will you come?"

Agarex glanced at the hut. When he moved, Tally saw the pattern of bruises on his back, beneath the tight braid of his hair. Tally could almost hear the thoughts move through his mind—no time for thinking, he warned silently.

Agarex nodded abruptly and moved to Tally's side.

"Wait." Tally gathered more light from the air and cast a spell over the hut, suing sleep for all inside. The best he could do.

Agarex gestured up the slope. Beyond the higher part of the settlement, beyond the pony field, lay the hills that led to freedom.

Tally laid a hand on his friend's arm. "We must bring Tamia."

"Why her?"

"She is being abused in that house."

Agarex gave a hard nod. "I would gladly kill her master; I want to kill them all. Have you a weapon?"

"Hush," Tally bade again. Hate would tip the

balance against them, but he had no hope of explaining that to this man who carried his wounds like livid stains. "Come, watch for the guard."

The dwelling where Tamia was being housed lay at the heart of the settlement. There, Tally and Agarex hovered behind the nearest hut, barely breathing, while a guard passed. Silence ensued, during which Agarex twitched violently.

"Master Tally, we must—"

"I know. Let me summon her."

"Eh?"

"As I did you."

Agarex stilled. Once again, Tally drew radiance, wove it with his fingers. If they were to succeed this night—a mighty if—it would be at the behest of the gloaming and the dark, the hills and the land itself. Not his land—not here—yet he had hope the trees would offer shelter and the goddess guidance.

He heard the breath whoosh from Agarex's lungs when Tamia appeared, looking little more than a thin shadow. The girl's hair hung loose around her; even by the uncertain light, Tally could see she carried the same dull, wounded look in her eyes as Agarex.

Agarex moved forward and took her arm. "We are leaving here, running tonight. Will you come?"

She nodded instantly. Agarex put his arm around her, urging her away, and despite the peril Tally's heart bounded. He should know the goddess would not fail them, nor would the magic. Had capture and confinement so severely damaged his faith that he could doubt?

They moved up the slope and passed the pony sheds, an all-too visible group of three. Here patrolled another guard, and Tally paused, motioning his companions down to the ground in the shelter of the outermost stone wall. Swiftly, he joined them.

"Wait."

Breathless moments passed. They heard the guard move past and then, from below them in the settlement, a shout of anger.

"That will be Rohre, who oversees us," Agarex grunted. "He has discovered my absence."

Tally did not question it. "Run."

They did, Agarex and Tamia in a pair, hands linked, and Tally in the lead, blindly choosing the direction. He could not let himself think about the impossible distance ahead or how swiftly the Gaels might mount a pursuit. He could not let himself think about Alanna or how she might feel when she realized he'd fled her.

Would she be angry? Hurt? He shoved the questions from his mind and reached for belief, for the magic that had got them this far.

Once beneath the cover of the trees, he felt better. The Gaels hunted up here and the ways were mostly clear. He increased his speed, his spirit reaching for the distance, until he heard Agarex call from behind.

"Master Tally, pray wait!"

Looking around, he saw Tamia had collapsed in Agarex's arms. "She cannot run. She is hurt."

Tally could not see Agarex's expression in the gloom beneath the trees but felt his emotions raging.

"Hurt, how?" he gasped.

"I am not certain. They have beaten her or broken her or—" Agarex ran out of breath.

At that moment they heard the sounds of pursuit

from behind, voices, calls, and the baying of a hound. Tally's heart fell like a stone. That had not taken long, not near long enough. Ah, were they lost even before they began?

"Leave me." The words came thin and weak from Tamia. "Leave me and run."

"I will not," Agarex seethed.

"I mean it. Go on without me. It is the only chance."

"What kind of man would I be, to abandon you to those wolves? The goddess alone knows what they will do to you in retaliation." Agarex gathered Tamia up in his arms and grunted at Tally, "Go!"

The ensuing effort proved a valiant one. Agarex, boosting Tamia high in his arms, somehow kept up with Tally as he chose a crooked course through the trees. Tally prayed as he ran, more for the two behind him than for himself. He tried to gather magic and scatter it like confusion behind them, but the ability waned along with his strength. The sounds of pursuit grew closer and closer, and Agarex's breath rasped ever more desperately. At last, their pursuers were so close Tally could catch snatches of their words.

"Surround them! There! Cut them off."

His lungs burned and his heart felt as if it must burst; he could only imagine Agarex's plight. Yet they kept on until Tally caught a flicker of movement ahead of them. Two Gaels with leashed hounds appeared from the trees. Tally recognized them as members of the guard.

This time his heart fell so violently, it tripped him up. He stumbled to a halt, and Agarex, gasping, fell to his knees, Tamia still caught in his arms.

With no moon and the cover of the forest overhead, Tally could barely see the faces of those surrounding them. Somehow, that made it more terrible—a scene from a dark dream. Weaponless, unable to defend those at his back, he turned in a slow circle. Surrounded, and he saw the faint gleam of the hounds' teeth and the glitter of weapons from every side.

One man stepped forward to address them. "Fools! Do you ken wha' we do to slaves that run? Were you no' warned?"

In a voice that did not sound like his own, Tally replied, "It was my idea. Punish me and show these two lenience." Behind him, he could hear Tamia weeping as if brokenhearted. She had suffered more than enough.

"You shall be punished, right enough. All of you. Take them."

Agarex fought when they hauled Tamia from his arms and sought to seize him. Tally, recognizing the hopelessness of the odds, did not. But his spirit cried aloud to the goddess, who until his capture had always taken his part.

How can you let this happen? Why have you not got me away, back to where I belong?

The deep well of belief inside him rippled and closed as tight as the fists that seized him. For an instant he wished he could fly away from it all, just like that bird which had soared up from his feet during their forced march.

But the bird had been duly caught and the bars of the cage had closed.

Chapter Nineteen

Labhan brought the news, coming by the hut Alanna called her own. Sometime since, she'd found it necessary to liberate herself from the chief's dwelling; she'd seldom been so glad as now.

Labhan pounded on her door with the flat of his hand, and she dragged herself up from her pallet, where she'd been sleeping the sleep of the deprived. When she stayed nights with Taloc, they slept little enough.

"What it is?" she demanded of Labhan, who appeared both worried and excited.

"We've had runners. I think one of them's your man, Taloc."

"What?" Alanna could not have heard that right.

"When the hue and cry broke, I went first to the pony sheds. He's gone."

"Gone?" Alanna's heart clenched alarmingly and her throat went dry. "Impossible."

Labhan tossed his head. "You go look for him, then."

"I will." Not bothering to dress, clad only in a long tunic, Alanna stepped outside. "He would no' do that."

"He would, though you do no' want to see it, besotted as you are. I ha' been suspicious from the start. There is somewhat about him—"

I trusted him. Alanna did not say that aloud. Already she was moving, pushing past Labhan and pounding up the hill, certain Taloc would meet her at the door of his hut, hair tumbling over his tattooed shoulders and that inquiring expression in his smoky eyes.

Labhan must be mistaken.

"He's hurt," she gasped as she ran with Labhan at her heels. "Still asleep, no doubt."

"I went inside. He is no' there."

"Who's gone after the runners?"

"Belloch and most of the guards. Three runners, someone said. Two are those wi' whom you arranged cozy meetings for your man."

That tripped Alanna up, and put the first genuine doubt in her mind.

No, no. Though he'd not said it—as she'd not said it—she knew Taloc had feelings for her. That truth lay in his touch, and sometimes in the way he looked at her. No man and woman could join so deeply, so completely—so magically—without there being feelings. He would not abandon her.

"Your father is outraged. I heard him tell Belloch no' to rest till he catches them. You ken fine what will happen then."

She did. Slaves had died from the ensuing punishments.

"I warned him," she breathed as she surveyed the empty hut.

"What will you do?"

"Go after them." Hope she arrived in time. Throw herself between Taloc and Belloch, if need be.

She ran on across the green field and leaped the low stone wall, her heart beating an uneven rhythm, and on into the deepening night.

****

Tamia could not stop weeping, even though her captors struck her repeatedly and ordered her to silence. Tally curled his fingers into fists at every blow she received, but could do little more. As on their previous forced journey, his wrists had been bound and his magic had slipped from his reach.

When he protested verbally on her behalf, saying, "She is frightened and cannot hush," he received a swift blow to the face that felled him where he stood, and a kick for good measure. Hauled up again, he felt blood on his cheek.

Agarex swore steadily, in a low stream that sounded like a growl. His hands too were bound, though the Gaels left Tamia's free. The leader of their pursuers, a man of middling years with an ugly, scarred face, at last muttered to his men, "Bring them. We will let the Chief sort it out."

The chief? Alanna's father. The thought of her burst upon Tally's mind with searing brightness. Granted, she'd been somewhere in the back of his mind all the while, along with a large measure of regret at having deceived her. But now he wondered what she would do, seeing him hauled back this way, bound for punishment.

Would she be angered? Outraged enough to abandon him to his fate?

And what would that fate be? His stomach turned within him at the prospect of pain—not for him so much as these other two, here at his invitation. He should have followed his first instinct and gone on his own.

Their group had scarcely left cover of the forest

when a commotion ahead signaled new arrivals. Suddenly Alanna was there, just as if Tally's thoughts had summoned her, pale as a spirit in the dim light and with her hair hanging loose around her shoulders.

Labhan followed her closely, an expression half alarm, half insipient enjoyment on his face.

"What goes on here?" Alanna demanded, breathless. "Belloch, release my slave at once."

"I will no', Mistress. The Chief has ordered them brought back to him. I mean to do just that."

Alanna shot one look at Tally—just one. Her pale eyes, wide and desperate, touched the blood on his face and measured him swiftly. With anger? Tally could not tell.

"Take the others to my father," she snapped. "I will deal wi' my man."

Labhan snorted, the sound clear even over Tamia's continued weeping.

"The Chief makes decisions on punishment for runaways. Come along wi' us if you would speak for your man." Belloch put a sneering emphasis on the last two words. Did everyone in the settlement know what Tally and Alanna had been doing together?

He supposed so—even back home such gossip would run rife. And as he was jerked into motion, he considered anew his escape from Alanna's point of view.

It must be a blow to her pride, a blatant humiliation. For her to take a slave to her bed and treat him with a measure of favor, only to have him turn around and deceive her, flee from her—it must sting.

Yes, surely she would wash her hands of him now, abandon him to his fate. For she fell into the train behind him and said no more, though he could feel her presence like the blood on his face.

Tamia never left off weeping until they were dragged to a halt in front of the Chief's hall—the same place they'd first been brought upon their arrival—when she went suddenly silent, likely out of terror. Half the settlement must be awake and astir. The Chief himself stood before his door with flaming torches mounted at either side, and a range of elderly warriors at his back.

Tally's throat went tight at the expression on the Chief's face. No mercy there—not for any of them.

Their captors shoved Agarex down on the stones at the Chief's feet. Tamia fell beside him, seeming to lose all the strength in her legs. Hard hands forced Tally to his knees, accompanied by a series of hoots and jeers from the crowd.

The Chief held up his hand; ominous silence fell. Tamia had now gone so quiet Tally wondered if she'd swooned. Everyone else listened avidly.

With deliberation that failed to disguise his anger, the Chief said, "Slaves, hear me and hear me well—you three here and any who may stand listening. You are the property of this settlement, just like any pony or hound. A hound or, indeed, a pony that proves defiant or runs off will be disciplined until it learns its lesson. As will you." He added, "Raise the lass."

Rough hands pulled Tamia to her feet. Tally lifted his head, beginning a fervent prayer in his mind. *Spare her. Spare her, goddess, please. It was all my doing.*

"To whom does this slave belong?"

A woman who must be Cargon, heavily pregnant, stepped forward.

The Chief asked, "Has she been a good and obedient servant up till now?"

The woman answered with a shrug of disdain. "She is slow. Stupid. It surprises me she had the will or the brains to run."

"Her punishment shall be five lashes."

No!

Tamia began to weep again, wild with fright. The Chief, not pausing, motioned Agarex to his feet. Agarex struggled in the grip of his captors, defiant.

"Just kill me!" he shouted in his own tongue. "I will not live this way."

The Chief glared at him. "Fifteen lashes," he pronounced. "But you can spare yoursel' five of those if you say which of you instigated this escape."

Agarex pressed his lips together, going silent. But Tamia stole a telling look at Tally.

Tally felt someone stir behind him. Alanna, it was. She whispered, "No."

The Chief motioned Tally up. Before he could move under his own power, he was hauled there.

"You." The Chief's gaze flashed with anger. "You belong to my daughter."

"He does." Alanna stepped up next to Tally though she did not look at him. Her father ignored her.

Still speaking to Tally, he said, "Did you instigate the escape?"

"I did."

"You will answer me, 'I did, Master.' "

Tally said nothing.

The Chief grunted. "We have, I think, found the knot at the center of the tangle. What is your name, blue man?"

142

"Taloc."

"Taloc, were you no' warned of the punishment for defiance? For running?"

"Yes."

"Then you will accept the consequences. Twenty lashes."

"No." Alanna scarcely breathed the word this time, but Tally heard.

He took a step forward. Even as his stomach somersaulted within him, he said, "Chief, since it was my choice to flee and I involved these others, I ask to take their punishments."

A murmur passed through the crowd. Tally felt Alanna's protest reach out for him, wordless this time.

The Chief raised a brow.

"A not uncourageous offer. But do you ken what you say? 'Tis a total of forty lashes."

"I understand. And I accept."

The Chief pondered it before he snapped, "Nay. This one, here," he gestured at Agarex, "needs to learn discipline. But I will let you, Taloc, assume the lass's punishment. Mistress," he told Cargon, "tak' her home. But not before she watches the others accept the consequences of their disobedience."

Tamia shrank to her mistress's side.

"You two," the Chief ordered, "step forward. And someone bring me a whip. This shall be carried out here and now."

Chapter Twenty

It seemed very much like a dream, one of the deep, dark ones that sometimes came to Tally in the night. Shoved forward to the place where the Chief stood, hands still bound and with Agarex at his side, he felt curiously boneless and separate from his body.

All that would come to a screeching halt, he knew, when the first blow from the lash met his flesh. He watched, swallowing hard, as a crop such as Labhan liked to use on the ponies—though Alanna never did—was passed to the Chief's hand.

"Down," the Chief ordered Agarex, "onto the stones."

In reply, Agarex spat. Tally could feel defiance streaming from him, along with hate. Did he truly wish to die? Yet death by whipping, being flailed apart blow by blow, would be lingering and horrifically painful.

And a man could not die from only fifteen lashes.

Only.

The crowd expanded, out of respect for the whip. Tally and his guards stayed where they were.

Alanna once more stepped forward.

Tally got a look at her face then—his first since she met them in the forest. He expected arrogance and anger. Instead he saw only a rigid tension that might be born of fear.

"Father?"

The Chief turned his attention to her. "What is it?"

"I would ask mercy."

Atholl, holding the whip in his hand, laughed aloud. The torches on either side of him flickered against the darkness and made of his one-eyed face an evil mask. "Mercy?" He gestured at Agarex with the whip. "For him?"

"A slave beaten bloody and raw is of no use."

"A defiant slave is of no use either," Atholl swiftly returned. "And they maun learn their lesson. What if all our slaves decided to run, eh? Or to raise weapons against us? Answer me that."

Alanna shifted where she stood. "But—"

"Out of the way, Daughter. Let us ha' done wi' this business. I want back to my bed."

Alanna stepped away from Agarex, and to Tally's side; he could feel her quivering.

The Chief raised the whip over Agarex's supine form. Bad as this would be, Tally told himself—and he knew it would be bad—he must stay strong, not betray any pain.

As did Agarex remain strong. At the first blow, he bellowed—hollered like a bull—not in pain but in rage. It reminded Tally forcibly of his father, who had bellowed just so at the pain of his injuries, taken beneath a Gaelic chariot.

At the second blow, which brought a livid red welt to his back, Agarex reared up and Tally got a look at his face, stark with hatred. If Chief Atholl thought this would solve anything, he was a fool.

At the fifth blow, Tally closed his eyes and tried to pray. Belief, as he knew, could lift a man above much, and he had to accept much—ten lashes more than what he now witnessed. But his heart, his spirit, had shut down back in the forest. Now the goddess, his one strength, seemed far too distant. Where was she? Would she appear and take the blows meant for him when it was his turn?

Agarex's bellows became grunts and then hard hiccoughs. The Chief delivered his fifteen blows and the crowd became silent. Tally opened his eyes to a gory sight—Agarex collapsed on the stones now splashed with blood, his bare back criss-crossed with stripes and running red.

"Take him away," the Chief said.

Agarex, still conscious, was hauled up by the guards. Hate contorted his features; Tally wondered if the strength of it offered him any protection from the pain.

He, Tally, had been taught not to hate. All his life, his mother had cautioned him against it, saying it was a knife that cut both ways and not worth the cost. But it was difficult not to abominate the Gaels. And Tally wondered if he'd share Agarex's hate before this night ended.

Again, he sent a frantic prayer to the goddess: *Give me strength, and the protection I will need.*

"You—step forward." Atholl gave him a fierce look and gestured to the spattered stones. "Down. Twenty-five blows you will take."

Tally's heart beat frantically up in his throat. His limbs did not seem his own, his life did not. When he turned, he had one glimpse of the staring crowd, and Alanna's face front and center. He lowered himself to the hard ground, wondering what he saw in her eyes.

One thought expanded in his mind: whatever came

next, he must keep hold of his dignity. He must do his people proud.

That thought still possessed his mind when the first blow fell. The lash met his skin in a kiss of fire that curled around his naked back and touched his side. Every part of him jumped to immediate awareness—he knew there would be no escaping the pain of each strike.

One.

Ah, goddess, how could he endure it? That was but one—

The second blow mingled with the pain of the first, compounding it impossibly.

Goddess, where are you?

He heard the whip rise again and braced himself.

The blow never came. Instead, he heard a strangled cry. "No!"

A weight came down upon him from above, crushing him into the stones. For an instant, his mind failed to comprehend what had happened. Then, incredibly, he caught a familiar scent, above that of his own sweat and blood.

The whip, already in motion, came down. Alanna's body jerked above his in response; the crowd gasped and people cried out.

Atholl roared, "Daughter, up from there! Out of the way. He will tak' his punishment. Do no' mak' a fool o' yourself."

So angered did Atholl sound, Tally could barely distinguish the words. Alanna must, yet she did not move from the protective position she'd assumed over Tally.

"Nay, Father. If you insist on carrying out this

punishment—"

"I will so do!"

"I shall tak' his blows for him."

Tally gasped. What was it he heard in her voice? A rough agony, and so much wild emotion he could not identify it.

"No," he cried in turn, and tried to rise up and dislodge her. "This is mine to bear."

"Yours is mine," she breathed into his ear. "Do you no' ken that?"

Tally closed his eyes again, this time against a wave of fierce protest. She would protect him, would she, at her own cost? This woman he called an enemy?

"Get up!" Atholl roared. "Or I shall indeed gi' you his punishment, and twice as hard."

"No," Tally groaned again, and bucked against her weight. Had not those for whom he cared suffered enough this night, because of him?

Alanna must have heard him, but she refused to budge. Indeed, she pressed down harder, trapping him with his bound hands against the stone. Over her shoulder she told her father, "Do as you must."

The crowd now made a din; if Atholl replied, Tally—one ear flat against the stones—heard it not. But he felt the blow when it descended, causing Alanna's body to flex much as it did beneath his when they coupled, only this time in pain instead of pleasure.

She made not a sound. One stroke, two, three…after the fifth, Atholl stayed his hand and called out, "I lose heart for this. Be gone wi' you, Daughter. Tak' your accursed slave home."

Somehow—Tally could not guess how—Alanna arose. He came up after her, scrambling on the stones, in time to see her turn to face her father, head high and eyes glowing with defiance.

"His punishment has been met?"

"It has. Get out o' my sight before I level another. But if you value him, be very certain he does no' do this again. Next time I will no' stay my hand."

Alanna reached out blindly; her fingers found Tally's and meshed with them.

"Why—" Tally began.

"Hush. Come."

The crowd parted for them. Alanna, her step steady, the back of her thin sleeping tunic in shreds, led Tally off through the heart of the settlement and up the slope toward the pony sheds.

His thoughts scrambled as had his limbs on the stones, fighting for words, for reason. His feelings conflicted so violently he did not know whether to thank or chastise her. Gratitude, protest, and another emotion, unnamed, warred violently inside him.

She did not speak either, though her fingers squeezed his—still bound—tremendously tight. The grasp brought his body close to hers; though her demeanor remained strong, he felt her trembling.

When they reached the dry stone wall, she paused. "Let us get these bonds off you." She produced a knife; the twine had cut deep, just like the whip, and Tally flexed his fingers carefully before facing her.

"You should not have got in the way of the whip."

"No?" She cocked her head at him in the dim light.

"It was my punishment to take."

"So you said. I gave you my answer."

"How bad is it?" Tally's own stripes hurt like fire, though they numbered but two. "Let me see." With gentle hands, he turned her around. The whip had made nothing of her thin garment, and blood flowed freely, soaking the tatters.

But her chin jerked up. "Not bad. I would accept far worse, for your sake."

A cry from below interrupted her. Someone came up the slope at a faltering run—a woman, Tally saw. Alanna grunted a breath. "It is my friend, Fenna."

"Alanna?" The woman, whose brown hair tumbled down her back, clutched her skirts in one hand and a sack in the other. "What madness was that?"

"No' madness. I could no' stand and see Taloc tak' that punishment."

Fenna shot Tally a scathing look before she said, "Let us get you inside before you fall where you stand. I ha' brought salves and bandages."

"'Tis best left open." Alanna gulped air. "All wounds are."

"Enough. You proved yoursel' brave, if witless, down below. Come awa' in." To Tally she said, "Bring her, if you would be of any use at all."

"Come," Tally told Alanna softly, and she leaned on his arm heavily, all her strength suddenly gone, knees threatening to buckle.

Courageous she might well be, but not invincible.

Chapter Twenty-One

Fenna insisted on fussing, and Alanna hated it when people fussed. Despite her pain—which now that the moment had passed proved far worse than she could have imagined—she wanted only to be alone with Taloc. His company would provide all the comfort she might need.

Yet once inside the hut, Fenna sent Taloc away to fetch water, despite the fact that he, too, had been lashed and needed tending. And she made him wait outside during the painful process of peeling the shreds of Alanna's tunic from her back and bathing the stripes.

Alanna lay face down on Taloc's pallet, the place where they'd so often made love, with the scent of him all around her, while she strove to endure. The ordeal of tending seemed almost worse than the whipping itself, perhaps because it lasted far longer.

Still worse were the emotions battering Alanna's heart. Those, she could not seem to reconcile. She felt anger toward Taloc at having betrayed her, hurt that he might abandon her so easily…and so much love it stole her breath.

Fenna nagged and complained the whole time she worked over Alanna. "What were you thinking, lass, to tak' his punishment? He is a slave—naught more or less—and should he prove defiant, he maun know what to expect. You are fortunate your father stayed his hand."

"Stayed his hand?" Alanna choked. Her back was afire and she'd taken no more than five lashes.

How might Taloc have endured twenty-five?

"The first blow bit deep. It may leave a scar. The others—he did not use all his strength."

"Where is Taloc?"

"I ha' sent him outside."

What if he ran again? Did she, Alanna, truly mean so little to him that he could leave her without a backward glance?

"Call him in, Fenna."

"When I am finished here."

"Call him in." Alanna reared up from her place at great cost in agony. The two women glared at one another.

Fenna snorted. "If you dare no' trust him to wait outside, lass, he is of no use to you."

"You do no' understand. I told you, I love him."

"Och, I see that you think you do. That much was plain to everyone below. More fool, you."

"He will need tending."

"I will no' waste my medicines on any blue man, especially such a one as that."

"Fenna!" Alanna seized her friend's wrist. "I canno' help how I feel for him." Her love for Taloc was greater than their positions of mistress and slave, bigger than her pain. And larger than her sense of betrayal? Quite likely.

"I want no part of it." Hurriedly, Fenna gathered up her medicines. Alanna strove to rise from the pallet and failed.

"Bide you there," Fenna told her grudgingly. "I

will call him."

She went out, leaving the door of the hut ajar. Through the opening, Alanna could see the pale light of the summer dawning—morning had nearly come. And she heard soft voices—Taloc must be there still.

He had waited.

Relief flooded her, tangling with her other emotions. What to say to him? Alanna bit her lip hard as he entered the hut, moving like a shadow, and hunkered down beside the pallet. She wanted to rage at him, to shout and storm. She wanted to weep and sob out her betrayal, which hurt far more than the lash. But at the sight of him her throat closed; she said nothing at all.

Fenna had gone; alone, the two of them regarded one another in the glow from the rush light. The first of the two blows Taloc took had bitten deep and curled around his side to leave a livid welt across his ribs. He looked filthy and exhausted, and she could not read what lay in his eyes.

For the best, mayhap.

"Alanna, why did you do that?" he asked softly. "You should have let me take the punishment."

She examined her heart, and all the things she wanted to say. Honesty won out. "I could not. My every instinct was to protect you. If you do no' ken why…"

Taloc said nothing.

Alanna's anger—or perhaps it was the hurt—rose up then and fairly choked her. "What made you run from me? How could you? Did I no' treat you well? Give you all I could? Even…"

Even her body, her passion, and her heart. But pride would not let her add that.

She heard him draw a breath. "You were good to me, yes. But that did not make me less a slave."

"I did no' treat you like one, did I? I bowed to your dignity, to your wishes. You were never locked up. I trusted you." The last came out in a wail that shamed her.

He dropped his head so his hair covered his face, and said nothing.

"I sensed from the start there was a fineness about you—a dignity. I would no' steal that from you. I—"

"You but purchased me, and kept me as your possession."

"I did no' think of you so. I cared so much—"

He lifted his gaze to hers, eyes smoky and burning with pain. "If you cared about me, about my dignity, you would have sent me home."

"I could not." For a thousand reasons. Because it was forbidden—her father would never allow it. Even more because she did not begin to know how she might live without his smile, the magic that seemed to dance around him when he moved, and the agility of his mind. The sheer thrill of it when she touched him, when he touched her. The heat when his mouth found her breast.

She voiced the least of the reasons. "There are laws in Dal Riada, and they do no' include freeing a slave."

"Your father's laws, are they? You seem to have no difficulty in defying him."

"Aye, that is so, in small ways. But this is no small thing. As you ha' just seen."

She wanted to say far more. She wanted to cry out her sense of betrayal, her disappointment in what she'd believed they shared. Perhaps, as Fenna said, she'd been a fool. For she believed she'd come to mean something to this man.

As he'd come to mean everything to her.

"Rest," he told her gently, in that warm, compassionate voice, the one that had served to deceive her so well. "We will speak again when you feel stronger."

"Nay, Taloc." Alanna swallowed hard, wishing she could hold back the words, and unable to. "You also need tending."

"I will do well enough."

"You think those stripes hurt now? It will be twice as painful once they stiffen. At least let me cleanse them—some of the salve we use on the ponies…"

"Alanna, stop."

She drew a deep, ragged breath. "I canno' stop caring about you." Moving painfully, she assumed a sitting position. "My feelings ha' passed beyond my control. I thought, given all we had shared, you could see that. I thought"—here she gulped desperately—"I meant something to you too."

She heard the ache in her own voice and it should have hurt her pride. She was a proud woman, but when it came to this man it didn't seem to matter.

"You do mean something to me." He spoke the words softly.

Not enough. Not enough to keep him with her.

"Then why leave me wi'out a backward look?"

"For the same reason a trapped bird beats its wings and flies when it sees a chance. I do not belong here, Alanna. And I vowed to return to the place where I've left my heart."

His heart. And here had she been, thinking she had at least some claim on it.

She reached out and gently touched the welt on his side. "I had hoped you might belong here now. With me."

He said nothing.

"I had thought," her voice grated in her throat, "perhaps you had begun a new life."

"I never will."

"Do not say so! Taloc, you maun promise me you will never try to run again. You heard what Father said—next time the punishment will be more severe, and I will no' be able to protect you."

Taloc gazed at her steadily and remained silent.

"Taloc, I will ha' your promise!"

"I cannot give it to you. I will not lie to you; I respect you far too much."

Respect. Alanna took it like the blow it was. She wanted this man's love, lived for him to feel for her as she felt for him—beyond the bounds of status, origin or, indeed, reason. She wanted him to toss away every other consideration for her sake, as she had for his.

And she bore the stripes to prove it.

But she could not change him. From the first Taloc had set foot in Dal Riada, he'd been his own man, had kept the tatters of both his magic and his old life gathered about him. Would she want to change that?

Only if it meant he might love her—love her as she instinctively knew he could, as she'd never been loved.

"Rest," he told her again. "One promise I can make you: I will not leave this day, or tomorrow."

And the day after that? On through the summer, the fall, the winter—Alanna closed her eyes against the pain of it. She could not possibly live with that fear.

She could never endure such uncertainty and pain.

Chapter Twenty-Two

Alanna had spoken truly; Tally's stripes did hurt more fiercely once they stiffened. His back burned like it had been branded, and the welts pulled each time he moved.

As he worked among the ponies, performing simple tasks and leaving Alanna alone in the hut, he spared thought for how Agarex must fare. Fifteen of these—how would he ever endure it?

At least he'd managed to spare Tamia. But she'd been sent back to the terrible existence from whence she'd fled. True, her master remained away campaigning with Donhal, but Tally had managed to improve her lot not at all.

A lesson to be learned, there. He should not have included others in his own risk. Yet, he thought as he stroked Banna's warm neck, he'd involved Alanna, had he not?

Nay, but she'd involved herself, foolish, rash, and courageous woman that she was.

He could not quite reconcile the why of it. Ah, clearly she had feelings for him, but he could not decide what feelings. She wanted to keep him with her, and that argued desire. To be sure, the nights they'd spent together had contained a heat and depth of passion such as he'd never imagined. When they joined, it was total—no slave or mistress, no separation between

Caledonian and Gael.

Her act in throwing herself between him and the lash argued more, though, than desire. Might she truly be in love with him?

Ah, and were Alanna's feelings his responsibility? He had not asked for her love, had not invited it.

And he could not abandon his vow to the goddess for the sake of it.

Standing beside the pony in the morning sunshine, he closed his eyes against a rush of pain. He did not want to hurt anyone, he never had. But Alanna did not understand him if she thought he would settle down here meekly with her.

He heard a call from down the hill and opened his eyes. Labhan approached at a determined lope, an ugly expression on his face and anger in his eyes.

He vaulted the wall and came on; reading the young man's demeanor, Tally braced himself for attack.

Breathing hard, Labhan paused in front of him. "Where is Mistress Alanna?"

"Inside the hut, resting."

"Just as well. I wish to speak to you, slave, and I do no' need her interference. How dare you tak' advantage of her the way you have? Did you ha' to humiliate her in front o' all the clan?"

"I did not intend it."

"Did no' intend?" Labhan echoed him with harsh mockery. "But 'tis exactly what you ha' done. Despite how good she's been to you, far better than any savage deserves. You should be sold to the quarry and worked there until you drop, just like your friend."

"Agarex."

"Is that his name? 'Tis Shite, now. You think his

punishment has ended? His master will work him day and night, while you get off lightly here, once again."

"I did not want—"

"Be silent! Did I give you permission to speak?" Labhan stepped closer, and Banna danced aside uneasily. "Everyone saw what happened last night, and everyone knows what has been going on between the two o' you. You think you can charm her into protecting you? All you ha' done is mak' of her the laughingstock."

"I would have taken my punishment."

"Then tak' it now!" Labhan struck out so suddenly, Tally had no chance to defend himself. Labhan's fist connected with Tally's cheekbone, and Tally went down hard, sprawling on his back and striking his head against the ground. The pain flared so bright that for an instant it blotted out the sunlight.

Labhan followed with a kick and then another. Banna reared and tried to interpose her body between the two men, much as Alanna had last night.

"What goes on here?" Alanna's voice sounded surprisingly strong. Labhan backed off, and Tally got a glimpse of Alanna approaching, her every movement a declaration of pain.

But her gaze remained fierce when it swept over Tally and fastened on Labhan. Tally scrambled to his feet and stood ready to defend himself.

"Do not," Alanna warned, and scorched him with another look. Tally wondered what the reprisal might be for attacking a Gaelic clansman. Quite possibly, it would be worth paying, just to knock Labhan flat.

But he could see Alanna's distress in her posture and imagined what it had cost her to walk out here. For her sake, he stilled.

Precisely like an unruly pony, Labhan tossed his head. "I am but giving him what he deserves, and what he did no' receive last night."

"Get out," Alanna said.

"What?" Labhan's voice rose sharply.

"You heard me." Iron tinged Alanna's voice. "Go. You no longer ha' a place here."

"What?" Labhan gasped once more.

"I do no' want to see you here again."

"But—but I am in training. I ha' worked hard for more than a year."

"I will no' ha' one of my workers raising his hand against another."

Labhan spat into the grass. "You fool o' a woman, he is no' a worker but a slave. Do you no' ken everyone below is laughing at you? Laughing! I would no' sooner work wi' you than for him. Indeed, I begin to think," Labhan sneered, "'tis but one and the same."

"Then go."

The young man did, in as great a huff as he'd arrived. When he'd left, Alanna and Tally stood in silence until she seized his wrist and hauled him around so she could examine his back.

"Let me see. You ha' opened up those welts. You'll have to let me tend that, now."

"Alanna, you have lost yourself a good worker, there."

"He was no' a good worker. He was frequently insolent and secretly thought he knew more than me."

"You have damaged your status with your clan."

Her eyes, pale blue and clear in the strong sunlight, met his then. What did he see there? Rueful acknowledgement? Regret? "Quite possibly so. But that will no' keep them from seeking out my ponies, which are the best in all Alba. Now come, let me bathe that back. We want it to heal clean, aye?"

Tally went with her, an agony of confusion in his heart.

****

"Daughter, there must be some show of retaliation. If you want it to come from your hand rather than mine, so be it. But it must be visible and appropriate. Folk are sneering at you behind your back, and to my face."

Atholl stalked the space around his hearth, clearly beside himself. He'd called Alanna to him on this stormy afternoon, not three days after the floggings—ordered her like an errant slave.

She gave a shrug of disconcern and wished she hadn't. The lashes she'd taken on Taloc's behalf hurt more than she could have dreamed, and seemed slow to heal.

Like her heart. Now, every time she looked at Taloc, she felt a sense of betrayal mingled so tightly with the love she could scarcely tell them apart. It hurt far more than the stripes.

And she looked at him often. Since his attempted escape, she'd stayed each night at the hut. She didn't want to admit it was because she feared he'd run again. But even now while she answered her father's command, she worried Taloc might flee before she got back.

Quite aside from that, her every pleasure came in looking at Taloc—running her gaze over his mane of hair, mentally caressing every tattoo. They had, of course, not made love since the floggings, but she wanted him so much she ached.

She told her father, "I care little what folk say or think of me."

"Well, you should. Status is everything. Why do you think we work so hard to stand foremost among the clans here in Dal Riada? Why do you suppose your brothers compete to conquer this land? And yet you toss our good name awa' for the sake o' a blue man. By the holy light, Daughter, they are thick on the ground and one just like another." He drew an enraged breath through his nostrils. "I do no' approve of your tastes. But if you will indulge them, go back to that other slave wi' whom you dallied."

Alanna stared. She'd not dreamed her father knew about Nenian.

"Do no' look at me that way." Atholl glared back at her. "Did you think it would no' reach my ears? Folk see—and hear—things. And they love to gossip."

"Men ha' relations wi' slaves all the time. Why, Father, should it be different for me?"

"A dalliance is a dalliance and means naught. No man ever took stripes for the sake o' a slave."

"One canno' help what the heart chooses."

"One's heart does no' choose a slave! A savage from the eastern forest… Are you mad?"

"Father, Taloc is no savage. I believe he was a man of importance there, born to a chief's house—"

"It matters little. If you want a mate out o' a chief's house, I ha' allies wi' sons. But I warn you, Alanna, you ha' embarrassed me. Do no' embarrass me again."

"No, Father."

"I ha' perhaps been too indulgent wi' you. You've run wild wi' those ponies when you should ha' made a valuable union long ago. This is what comes o' it. I advise you to trade that slave to someone who will no' spare him as you ha' done, and will use him properly. To the quarry, perhaps."

Alanna's heart fell; she said nothing.

Atholl stormed on, "By your lenience, you ha' made him feel he is entitled to defy you. 'Tis a grave mistake."

Consternation kept Alanna silent. Perhaps thinking her suitably chastened, Atholl went on, "And what is this I hear about you dismissing young Labhan?"

"I did no' dismiss him, Father. He proved uncooperative and, when I charged him wi' it, chose to go."

"Oh, aye?"

Alanna paused. "Clearly you ha' heard an account of it already. From Labhan?"

"From his father, who came to me."

"Labhan attacked Taloc—I could no' keep him after that."

"Taloc, again. I tell you, Daughter, you canno' afford to keep him. I dare say if you got rid o' him, Labhan would return to train wi' you again."

"I do no' want him back. He has proved defiant."

"Not so defiant as your slave, who fled you. Deal wi' it, Daughter. Either discipline that slave or get rid o' him." Atholl sneered. "I never thought you soft."

"So I am not, Father."

"Then prove it to me." A glint entered Atholl's eye. "I imagine those stripes you carry mak' a good reminder o' your folly."

"Aye, Father."

"Then do no' let it happen again."

Chapter Twenty-Three

Tally looked round as Alanna came up the hill, moving like she hurt. He imagined she did—his own stripes had closed over cleanly yet still stung and hampered every movement. He'd not looked at hers in several days. Perhaps he should.

Yet the pain he saw in her face as she hopped the stone wall and walked toward him did not appear entirely physical. For, in contrast to her usual buoyant step, her shoulders drooped and her feet dragged.

What had happened to the brash, confident woman he'd first met? Had she died? Had he killed her?

Emotions rose in him at that thought. He cared for Alanna. It would be as impossible not to care for her as to not desire her. He ached at this change he saw.

He wondered if he'd put that look in her eyes— guarded, hesitant—or her father, the Chief, had. She'd been to see him, summoned without notice, and it appeared the meeting had not gone well.

She crossed directly to Tally and said, "We need to speak together. Leave the ponies to Marc and come sit wi' me."

The old man, at work on the far side of the field, cast a curious eye on them. Without protest, Tally led the pony with which he'd been working over to him.

The rain arriving with the dawn had now ceased, but a strong wind blew inland from the sea. They sat in the shelter of Tally's sleeping hut, side by side but not touching.

Without preamble, Alanna said, "My father wishes me to be rid of you."

"Rid of me?" And what, just, did that mean? Might she release him? Send him home? But no, that would never happen.

Alanna looked at him, her gaze bleak. "He thinks I should trade you to the quarry."

"With Agarex?" Tally had been alive with worry for the lad, beaten so severely. What care might he receive in his master's hands?

"Aye. Father grows weary of the gossip he hears about us, about how I favor and indulge you. It seems everyone knows that we…"

"I see."

"He wants an end to it. And believes you should be traded to someone who will provide the discipline I ha' not."

Tally drew a breath. The cost of his attempted flight, it seemed, went far beyond Agarex's pain, Tamia's despair, and his own loss of faith. For he'd barely been able to summon a prayer since that night. Had his magic died? Had his goddess abandoned him? If so, it made a harsh cost, even more than his liberty.

He engaged Alanna with his eyes. "And so, what will you do? Trade me away?"

Miserably, she shook her head. "I would no' like to. Do you ha' any notion how much worse your life would be if you belonged to someone like Raedh?"

Tally could well imagine. It was why he'd taken Agarex and Tamia with him, and what a disastrous decision that had proved.

Alanna laced her fingers together. "Yet Father believes discipline to be the cure for your defiance, a just return for the way you ha' taken advantage o' me."

"I have not taken advantage."

Her lips twisted ruefully. "Och, you have. And I allow it because…" Her voice trailed away.

"Because?" Tally prompted.

"I believe you to be something more than a slave. From the first, I sensed that; I ha' no wish to see your—your nobility beaten or starved from you."

Tally swallowed hard.

She went on, "That is quite apart from my own feelings for you, which you may well guess."

"You have," Tally spoke with difficulty, "formed an attachment to me."

She gave an unsteady laugh and said, with the frankness that marked her, "I am in love wi' you. Och, I never expected it to happen, not for me. I was too wise, too independent. I never wished to surrender my will or my freedom to any man. 'Tis why I rejected match after match my father offered—good matches, some o' them—and chose for mysel' a living, so I could mak' my own way. And then, what do I do?" She swept Tally with a glance. "Surrender my well-being to you. Compromise my conscience. Kneel at your feet."

Tally did not know what to say. Did she truly love him or was she merely inexplicably fascinated with him, as so many of the young Epidii women had been? The punishment she'd taken on his behalf argued the former, but Tally possessed no conceit. He saw little about himself to admire. Yet so it had been, ever since he was fourteen.

Gently he asked her, "Are you certain what you

feel for me is love, and not just desire? The desire between us is…consuming. And not what I ever thought to find for myself, either. I supposed I was a man of reason and immune to the kind of passion that forces all else from the mind."

"When it comes to me and you, Taloc, the love and passion are so tangled together, I can scarcely tell them apart. But I doubt passion ever made anyone willing to take twenty lashes for another." Again her gaze met his, full of so much honesty it shook him. "At that moment, I cared far more for you than for mysel' and would ha' done aught I must to protect you. Tell me, Taloc, is that no' love?"

"It is," he acknowledged, and lifted his hands in a helpless gesture. "But why me?"

"The gods alone know. Back when I indulged in such things as girlish gossip, my friends said there is no accounting for the choices of the heart. I suppose this proves it true."

"Yes."

"So what is to be done? I ken fine you do no' love me in return."

Her words hung in the misty air, begging Tally to refute them.

Again he shook his head. "Alanna, I do have strong feelings for you. Respect and affection. As for love— you must try and understand: I have lost so much, too much of who I was. My heart. My faith. I think that died there in the forest where we were recaptured."

"Do no' say that." She touched his face softly. "'Tis your faith makes you the man you are."

"Yet the goddess, in whom I have placed so much belief all my life, has abandoned me. What am I to feel, then, save empty?"

"She abandoned you. As you abandoned me."

Again their eyes met. Tally protested, "It is not the same."

"How is it different?"

"I believed the goddess and I had a relationship of long standing. I trusted her—"

"Just as I trusted you."

"Ah." Tally strangled on the word. Yet still, still she had defended him, made a barrier of her own flesh between him and harm.

"Perhaps, Taloc, your goddess has no' forsaken you, as you believe. Perhaps she is challenging you to keep faith wi' her under the very worst circumstances."

Tally thought about it and acknowledged, "If so, then I have failed."

"Not yet you ha' not. You are still here, and there is still time."

"True." But to live the balance of his life here, apart from all he loved, all he was—a challenge, indeed, and one he did not know if he could meet.

Hesitantly, Alanna asked, "Ha' you considered your goddess might yet be watching out for you? That she might ha' caused you to find your way to me for that purpose? Taloc, I can protect you to a certain extent. I can gi' you room to practice your faith and be the man you are meant to be. But you maun, in return, act in good faith wi' me. Else the price will be too high."

"It has already been high."

"It has, aye. I do no' grudge paying my share o' it. But listen to me, Taloc. I ha' put Nenian aside for you, defied my father for you, dismissed Labhan. I ha' attracted the scorn and disrespect o' my clan. In return, I maun ha' your promise you will no' run from me again."

Tally closed his eyes. "Ask of me anything else, Alanna. Anything but that."

"Is it so impossible, this one thing?"

The question told Tally she did not understand what she asked of him. Such a promise meant surrendering all hope of ever seeing his family or his friends again. It meant releasing from his heart the last threads of his past life. No more quiet mornings alone in the forest. No freedom, no calling himself his own man. It meant breaking a sacred vow.

Did he owe Alanna for her protection of him? Yes. He owed her gratitude, kindness, and perhaps a measure of loyalty. Not a promise given under duress.

He opened his eyes again and looked at her. She awaited his answer, wearing an expression of hard caution.

"I would be honest with you, Alanna, above all else. Any such promise given, I fear I might not keep. And so I refuse to speak the words."

Grief flooded her eyes. "If you do run again, I will no' be able to protect you."

"I know that."

"You walk a terrible, dangerous path, Taloc."

"I understand that also. Just as I will understand it if you wish to cast me off now, distance yourself, and so gain back a measure of your clan's respect."

"I could do that," she acknowledged. "But I will no'. Do you ken why? Because the truth is, any time spent wi' you is better than none."

Chapter Twenty-Four

Alanna stood beside the stone wall of the pony field and gazed out to sea, contemplating the emotions at war in her heart. On a clear day such as this, in the kindness of midsummer, it seemed as if she could see forever, or at least most the way to Erin—the land from whence her ancestors had come to claim this kingdom. And they had been bent upon claiming more and more, ever since.

Not a woman prone to nostalgia, she could at least find it in her to sympathize with Taloc's longing for the land from whence he, in turn, had come. The land called, as to a certain extent did family.

Taloc. For the very life of her, she did not know what to make of him, or of these feelings he prompted in her heart. Nearly a week had passed since what she privately called their night of honesty, when he'd refused to promise he would stay here with her.

Nay, he was not a man to lie, and she appreciated that. Yet the very idea of him leaving her again, without a pang or a backward look, made her go hot and cold in turns. Taloc made her vulnerable; he rendered her helpless—something she'd worked hard most of her life not to be.

Yet she could no more change her feelings for him than she could alter the tides. She lived for his smile— she, who had in truth never lived for anyone but herself—for a certain expression in his eyes when he looked at her, and for the thrill of his touch. Last night she'd slept in his arms, and her feelings had nigh overwhelmed her. Still both healing, they'd not yet made love, but her body craved him more than it wanted food. She could not wait much longer.

Mayhap tonight.

A jolt went through her at the thought. Aye, tonight she would lose herself and all her doubts in the scent and taste of him. Because her desire had passed from choice to need, and the future held no assurances.

Old Marc had been after her to take on more help. They needed it, with Labhan gone. And yet doing so would eliminate such mornings as this, when Marc had not yet arrived and the two of them, she and Taloc, worked here alone.

What might she not trade in return for time alone with him?

Even now she could feel him working in the field behind her, a part of her awareness even though she did not look 'round. So deep did the connection between them reach.

Why wouldn't he acknowledge that connection? Why, why could he not love her enough to stay?

Her lips curved wryly. He had spoken no words of love. Which only meant she needed to change what lay in his heart…

Her eyes caught movement on the slope below. Someone approached, climbing the rise toward them—a woman. When she drew closer, Alanna recognized Fenna. Alanna waited until Fenna reached the wall, breathless and red-faced.

"Have you heard?" she gasped.

"Heard what?"

Fenna glanced past Alanna to where Taloc led a pony called Dubh through his paces. "No one has come to tell you, then?"

"Tell me, what? Speak, lass."

"That blue man who ran wi' your slave—what was his name?"

Alanna fished for it in her mind. "Agarex?"

Fenna, still breathing hard, lowered her voice. "He is dead."

"Dead?" Swiftly, Alanna contemplated it. "Raedh never killed him in retaliation?"

"Nay, but he did put this Agarex back to work some days since, for the first time since he took his punishment."

"Working in the quarry, so soon?" Alanna still hurt, and Agarex had taken a far higher number of stripes than she.

"Aye."

"That is hard."

Fenna made a face. "Not everyone pampers his slaves as you do, and Raedh is no' known for his kindness."

"But surely Agarex did no' perish from the work?"

"Nay. But neither did he wish to tolerate it longer. He took his own life during the night."

"Och, by Lugh's spear!" Not good news to hear. And how was she to tell Taloc? He would take the guilt onto himself and suffer for it, if she knew him at all.

She breathed, "How?"

"He got hold o' a sharp piece of metal and cut himself deep. They found him this morning, blood everywhere."

Alanna swore bitterly.

"But that is no' all of it." Fenna laid her hand on Alanna's wrist. "Raedh is furious and calling for justice."

"Justice?"

"For the loss o' his man. He blames you." Fenna jerked her head at Taloc. "He claims naught would ha' happened and his man would no' ha' run, if you'd kept that one in line. He says he will ha' your man in place o' his."

"Taloc? Never. 'Tis absurd."

"None the less, he's telling everyone he means to tak' the matter to the Chief. If Atholl dictates recompense must be made, you may lose your slave after all."

"I will no' let that happen." Raedh would work Taloc to death in the quarry as he eventually did all too many of his slaves. Overwork combined with insufficient food or rest—she could not allow it.

She said, "Raedh has no right to make the claim. Taloc did not force Agarex to run off wi' him."

"That maun be your father's decision."

"Then I will speak wi' my father."

"I wish you joy of it. Folk say he is no' best pleased wi' you just now."

Alanna glanced over her shoulder at Taloc. He had paused with the pony at his side and stared in their direction, as if he sensed they spoke of him.

Alanna smiled grimly. Taloc might try and deny they had a connection; she, at least, knew better.

She turned back to Fenna. "Thank you for telling me. I do appreciate the warning."

"Aye, well, I think I understand wha' he means to

you, though I certainly do no' approve." Fenna rolled her eyes. "I will leave you to it, then."

By the time Fenna was half way down the slope, Taloc had joined Alanna.

"What is it? What has happened?"

"My friend, Fenna, brought ill news. That young man with whom you fled, Agarex—"

"Yes?" Taloc's attention quickened.

"It seems he took his own life, last night."

She felt shock wash over him, swiftly followed by dismay. The lines of his face tightened impossibly and grief flared in his eyes. "Ah, no." An instant's contemplation brought him to the rest of it. "This is my fault."

"Nay. Nay, Taloc. I knew you would say that, but 'tis no' true." She seized his wrists.

"I never should have asked him, not either of them, to come away with me. It caused all this. Had I but gone by myself—"

"You did no' force him to go wi' you. He made his own choice, both then and now."

"His life must have been unbearable, for him to make such a choice."

"His master, Raedh, works his slaves hard and had already put him back to laboring in the quarry."

Taloc's gaze clung to hers. "Then perhaps I do understand. His spirit longed for freedom; the goddess willing, he has found it."

"There is more. Fenna says Raedh may try to make a claim for the loss o' his worker. He blames me for not guarding you well enough and may approach my father for reparation."

"Reparation?"

Alanna forced herself to speak the words. "He might ask to be given you, in Agarex's place."

"I see."

Speaking against what she saw on his face, Alanna hurried on. "I will do all in my power to keep that from happening. I do so promise you."

The expression in his eyes changed, deepened and at the same time softened. He touched her cheek lightly. Alanna promptly lost all the breath in her body. Seldom did Taloc make such a gesture toward her. Oh, he caressed her when they coupled and she offered herself to him. When lying together they became equals, and he always employed great gentleness. But this felt like something more. Tenderness? Affection?

"I am grateful," he said. "Never think, because I made a bid for freedom, I am not grateful."

"Taloc…" She gazed deep into his eyes as she spoke. "I maun confess, I no longer ken how I could go on wi'out you. I will defend you, aye, for your sake—and also my own."

"I understand."

Did he? Alanna hoped so.

"If Raedh goes to my father, I will negotiate, offer some other payment in exchange for his man."

"Do you think he will be satisfied with that?"

"Who can say? But I vow to act in good faith in this, if you will keep faith wi' me, in turn."

Slowly, Taloc nodded, and Alanna breathed again. Not a promise, no, but, Alanna suspected, the best she might win from him.

Chapter Twenty-Five

The night lay deep and quiet, so silent Tally could hear the *shush, shush, shush* of the waves far below the hut, yet he could not sleep. Alanna lay in his arms breathing deeply and clearly exhausted from the work of the day just passed.

Even in slumber she clung to him, arms looped around his body and fingers clenched tight. She could not make her feelings more evident if she tried.

Indeed, she had no need to declare them; her actions spoke loudly enough. For tomorrow she would go to her father's house and answer Raedh's claim upon him.

Agarex's former master had not waited long to make his demand—Agarex had been dead but two days. And from what Marc said, for Alanna spoke little of it, the clan remained in an uproar over the matter, the Chief angry and impatient.

Alanna had said no more about it to Tally, but looked pale and resolute. Marc it was who had filled Tally in, making it clear Tally's very fate hung in the balance, dangling from the fingers of a woman who—

Who loved him.

Tally could no longer doubt that. Nor could he deny the lengths to which she'd go in order to keep him with her.

She'd said nothing more about that either, nor

indicated by word or look just how fearful she might be about keeping him out of Raedh's hands. The extent of his own worry shocked him. He dreaded not only the prospect of life beneath Raedh's merciless control but that of being denied Alanna's company.

To be sure, as he lay staring into the depths of the night, listening to Alanna breathe, it was no longer her emotions he questioned but his own.

What did he feel for this woman? She insisted they had forged a deep connection, and perhaps so. When she was near him, and even when she wasn't, he could sense her emotions with astonishing ease. Her presence brought him a measure of comfort even as her absence prompted a feeling of need, and that alarmed him. For she remained his enemy, and one day he would have to leave this place—and her.

What did he owe her? Gratitude, for certain. She had not said, but old Marc made sure to let him know it might well require a large part of her wealth to repay Raedh for Agarex's life and keep him, Tally, safe.

Their relationship had progressed to the point where Tally did not doubt Alanna would pay that price on his behalf. Had she not offered her very flesh in place of his? And, an honest man, he had to admit he felt more than gratitude for her. Desire, most certainly. A measure of respect, affection.

He dared not admit to more. Home called him every waking moment. The prospect of living the balance of his life here, even with Alanna, hurt like a physical wound.

He touched her cheek very gently, and she stirred in her sleep, turning her face into his hand. He drew her still closer so her head tucked into his neck; she gave a sigh and her eyelids fluttered open.

"Taloc?"

"Hush, I did not mean to wake you."

"I dreamed of you," she said in a voice still more than half drowsy with sleep. "The two of us flew together like birds. We flew east and there was this place…"

"Place?"

With a measure of wonder, she confided, "There was a tower built of pale stone. It shone like a jewel in the morning light."

Tally's throat promptly closed. The tower, his tower that he'd first seen in a Vision and declared should be built as a symbol of his people's resistance. For ten years it had stood, defiant, till the Gaels gutted it with fire.

But how was it Alanna should see it in her sleep?

Slowly he said, "Perhaps you saw the tower because I have described it to you."

She lay still, breathing quietly.

"But it is perfect no more. Your warriors burnt it the night I and the others were taken captive."

"Yet I saw it undamaged."

"Impossible." It still stood, yes, but gutted—like him. It felt as if his faith had been seared away, even as had the inner part of the structure. Would the rest crumble also? Not, perhaps, if he held tight to Alanna, to her belief in him.

"Tell me," she begged, speaking into the night's silence. "Tell me more about your life there before you were seized, about who and what you were." With her finger, she traced one of the tattoos on his chest. "I never tire of hearing."

"Do you not?"

"Nay."

"Well, so," he began, "my life there was one of magic." She'd asked these questions before, and he'd given her bits and pieces of who he was. Now, though, perhaps in return for all she had given him, he confided as never before, opened his heart to her, and told the tale of his mother's grace and his father's courage, his sister Barta's daring and his brother Wick's return along a hard path. He described how it felt to receive a Vision, to be the keeper of an entire tribe's faith. Could he give her any less, in return for her love?

And as he spoke, a curious thing happened. His barriers lowered—he distinctly felt them go down—and as he entrusted that most inner part of himself to her, he seemed to take her somehow inside of him, in exchange.

Spiritual bonding—and far more significant to Tally than the physical kind.

Alanna listened quietly, as one spellbound, her hand resting against his chest and her eyes closed.

When at last he wound down, she said, "I can envision it all, and 'tis so beautiful. You are your mother's son, are you no'? She was full of magic, just like you."

"But I feel it slipping away from me, Alanna, killed off by the ugliness and the distance." Again he caressed her cheek. "That is why I went from you, not because I do not care for you. I feel I will perish if I don't reclaim that part of me."

"And you believe it lies in your own lands. But, Taloc, surely it is inside you—it always has been. I think I saw that from the first, when I beheld you outside my father's hall. It—it called to something inside me, a call such as I'd never heard before."

"The flame is inside me, yes. But, Alanna, I can feel it snuffing out."

"We will keep it alive. Together, we will."

She kissed him. Alanna, as he had learned, was a physical creature who expressed herself best in actions. She demonstrated her feelings for him through the conduit of her desire and could not speak more clearly than now.

"I will heal you," she promised between desperate kisses. "Mend and restore you. I—"

The kisses grew still hungrier, and Tally's own desire rose in response. She could do that to him—call his want and his spirit with her need. She fused her lips to his, slid her tongue into his mouth, and caressed him in a rhythm that set him aflame.

He broke the kiss to say, "Alanna, we should not."

"I am well enough healed. And I cannot live if I don't have you. Cannot live without you, Taloc. I will do whatever I can, tomorrow, to spare you. Do you hear me?"

"Yes." He heard, and felt. Best of all, along with his desire, he experienced a sudden shower of magic— the first since the night he'd fled with Agarex and Tamia. Could this woman truly bring that back to him?

Perhaps, if he entrusted all of himself to her.

They were opposites, two halves of one whole, so it seemed when he slipped inside her, felt her quivering with life and need for him. He could taste her strength and certainty. Could she, his enemy, truly be the one to put his spirit back together?

No chance to contemplate it now because she

wrapped herself around him—arms, legs, spirit. He felt her essence slip inside him even as he took her comfort and heat—question and answer. When the waves of pleasure seized her, he surrendered and gave her all he was, unstinting.

After, they lay together gasping, their hearts hammering in unison. The first time they'd coupled, she'd wept—this woman who he guessed rarely cried. This time, he also felt tears on her cheeks.

"Why do you weep?" he asked gently.

"I do no' ken. Just that when you are inside me, I feel everything so deeply. And it is so beautiful. You are so beautiful."

Tally closed his eyes on a wave of understanding. And so it did not matter that she was mistress and he slave, she Gael and he Caledonian. His spirit spoke to hers; her spirit upheld his.

In this place of pain and suffering, he had found something so perfect it made him breathless.

Tenderly, he drew her still closer, cradled her in his arms, and brushed his lips across her cheek. The silence of the night wrapped around them, and magic tingled through his veins like his life's blood.

Ah, what to do? For he could not surrender his promise to the goddess and stay with Alanna. But he very much feared he could not go from her, either.

One thing he knew: when they made love, his spirit, buoyed by hers, escaped the chains of this place and soared. Perhaps the goddess had not abandoned him after all. Maybe, somehow, she resided in this woman, in her love.

"Taloc." Alanna spoke his name and he opened his eyes. She pressed her palm to his chest just above his heart and gazed at him earnestly. "I love you. I do no' expect you to love me in return. I do no' even expect you to stay wi' me forever. But if I can buy your safety, tell me you will stay wi' me for a time—else I do no' ken how I can endure it."

Tally answered her, but not with words, and they flew together through the dark Dal Riada night.

Chapter Twenty-Six

Alanna stood at the center of her father's hall with her head high and her arms crossed on her breast. Raedh, the quarry master, stood opposite her wearing a deep scowl on his face and carrying an aggrieved expression in his eyes. He'd spent the last many minutes filling Alanna's ears, and the Chief's, with an account of the damage caused by Agarex's death, and why he believed it to be Alanna's fault.

Chief Atholl looked impatient, which Alanna took as a good sign. He'd been embarrassed by the escape and did not like being reminded of it, or having to listen to Raedh's list of complaints. He might privately blame Alanna for what he termed her indulgence of her slave, but she hoped pride might keep him from admitting it to the quarry master.

"So, my chief, you see I am down a worker, and a strong worker, even if he was defiant. I traded in good faith with Master Donhal for him. I still need to supply the final payment in stone, yet ha' lost the means. I demand recompense."

Atholl, a sour look on his face, held up a hand and shot one speaking look at his daughter.

"Enough."

"By your leave, Chief Atholl, it is no' enough. She has overindulged her slave—everyone in this settlement kens that. By the goddess, we all witnessed it when she took his punishment. This is her fault!"

Alanna lifted her chin a notch, thinking how intensely she despised this man. In a clear voice, she said, "It is no'. Did my man force yours to run awa' wi' him? Did he drag him off under threat? Perhaps if you treated your workers better, they would not be so eager to escape you. I would no' treat a pony so."

Raedh sneered at her. "Is that why your pampered slave ran, taking mine wi' him? You are a woman, and soft. Of course he will tak' advantage o' you."

"Soft?" Alanna repeated, on a rising wave of ire. "Me?"

"Enough," Atholl pronounced again. "It does no' matter why the slaves ran. Alanna might ha' guarded hers better—so, Raedh, might you. That is done. The question at hand is whether, Raedh, your claim for a slave to replace yours is valid."

"It is no'," Alanna spoke swiftly, fear replacing the anger in her heart. "The slave, Agarex, made the decision to flee and then to tak' his own life."

"True," Atholl said.

"Aye, and I should ha' expected you to tak' your daughter's side," Raedh spat angrily.

Atholl lit with anger. Alanna knew him to be, for the most part, an even-tempered man. But he could strike out swiftly if he thought his reputation had been impugned.

"Do you, Raedh, accuse me of bias? Why, then, do you come seeking a hearing wi' me?"

Insolently, the man answered, "I ha' no other recourse."

Was it the insolence that turned Atholl's mind? He glared at the man and appeared to make a swift decision.

"You will no' ha' Alanna's man. She needs his labor just as you do, and she speaks true when she says 'twas your slave's choice to tak' his own life. But," Atholl paused even as Raedh began to protest, "you shall ha' a measure of recompense from Mistress Alanna. What do you ask?"

Now Raedh eyed Alanna speculatively. "She is a wealthy woman."

"I am no'." Alanna survived mainly on trade of property or services. She had managed to amass a modest store of silver, and some Erin gold.

"Your ponies are worth a bit."

"Strike a bargain," Atholl ordered, "or I will declare this matter closed."

"My man was worth the equivalent of a pony," Raedh announced quickly.

"He was no'. My ponies are groomed and trained—"

"My man was trained also. And he worked well, when I beat him."

"Perhaps," Alanna said bitterly, "if you had no' put him to work so soon after a lashing—"

"These blue men are like beasts and feel very little pain."

Alanna thought of Taloc wincing when she bathed the stripes on his back, or gasping with delight when she took him into her mouth. "They feel both pain and pleasure just like us."

"You should know, you being a blue man's whore."

Alanna jumped at him quicker than thought, and closed her hands on his throat. She knew she courted a higher fine with such a display but did not care.

Chief Atholl separated them and gave Alanna a hard shake. Staring into her eyes, he said with a measure of disgust, "Truth is truth."

She flinched as if struck, and her cheeks burned. That her father should think such of her! She pulled herself free of his restraining touch.

"Name your price," she spat at Raedh.

A cunning look twisted his features. "One half o' your fortune."

She laughed in disbelief. "You jest."

"I do no'. Half of all you own, or I swear I will ha' your man after all."

Was her vulnerability so obvious as that? Did all the clan know she would far rather trade the bulk of her wealth than see Taloc go from her?

She supposed the stripes on her back had declared that.

Not quite steadily, she offered, "I will pay you five pieces of silver."

Greed sharpened Raedh's gaze. "No' enough."

"'Tis more than generous."

"And not a patch on what you likely have in store."

"Eight pieces, then." Alanna had begun to sweat, and felt dizzy.

"I want gold."

"Gold is rare, and I ha' little."

"Ah, but I think you would no' like to see your pet laboring in my quarry."

She would not. "How much gold?" Her eyes glittered dangerously.

"I am a fair man," Raedh lied. "One piece o' gold for one man."

Alanna considered it. She had but two pieces of gold, in addition to some small pieces of jewelry, in all her possession. She swallowed hard and gave a nod. "Done. Father, you are witness? He is fully paid."

"I am witness, Daughter. It is done."

Alanna drew a breath. A piece of gold could buy ten trained ponies. It would take time and labor to regain that wealth. But she did not care, so long as it kept Taloc safe. And, in turn, kept her heart whole.

****

Tally had been watching for Alanna's return the whole time he and Marc worked together exercising the ponies. He understood what was at stake; she'd confided that much to him when she lay in his arms last night. And when he at last saw her climbing the slope, the discouraged slump of her shoulders did not bode well.

He swore under his breath in his own tongue.

Marc gave him a sharp look. "There now, 'twould appear either she's lost you or you ha' cost her much. I, and half the clan, would gi' a great deal to know what magic you ha' worked on the woman, to win her favor to such an extent."

"No magic," Tally muttered. But he lied; there was magic when he touched Alanna, when she touched him, when they so much as looked at each other. She'd brought that back to him.

And now he might be forced to go from her into the charge of another. The powerful protest prompted by that thought shocked him. He broke from Marc's side and jogged to meet her at the stone wall.

"Well?" he asked, striving to conceal the extent of his dread.

But she heard; a rueful smile quirked her lips even as she laid a hand on his arm. "'Tis well, Taloc. I ha' been given leave to keep you."

"Ah." He closed his eyes for an instant, too relieved to say more.

"But," demanded Marc, who had followed Taloc, "what did it cost you?"

Alanna tossed her head. "Does it matter?"

"I should think so. He's already cost you in skin off your back and in the respect of your clan. What, in wealth?"

"But one piece. Of gold."

Marc's eyebrows flew up and he grunted in disgust. "You fool o' a woman. He will be the ruin o' you, and no mistake." He stomped off back to the waiting ponies.

Tally gazed into Alanna's eyes. "Is it worth so much, this gold?"

"Aye. Bright and beautiful it is, and we trade for it back in Erin, from whence we came so long ago." Her eyes, wide and clear, inspected him briefly from the head downward, and she lifted her hand to his cheek. She whispered, "Trust me, you are worth it. Had he demanded my entire fortune as price for you, you would still be worth it."

How could he keep from loving such a woman? Tally wondered. Yet how give his heart to her when he could not stay?

She leaned across the wall to kiss him softly and he felt her need, reaching for him, claiming him.

For the first time, Tally wondered what it would be like to spend the rest of his life with her here in Dal Riada.

Chapter Twenty-Seven

"I know you."

The words, spoken softly yet with an edge, and in Caledonian, spun Tally around. Not often did Alanna send him away from the pony sheds. That place had become his world—that place, and her love. It should have felt narrow and restricting; sometimes it did. But when he and Alanna were alone together, he found himself lacking for little.

On this afternoon, dealing with a recalcitrant pony and needing the services of the smith, she'd given him an errand, and so he found himself addressed in his own tongue.

Nearly two months had passed since the day Alanna traded a large part of her wealth to keep him. During that time, their connection had deepened impossibly. Though he'd not yet told her he loved her, she must be able to feel what he felt when they kissed, when they coupled—even when he so much as looked at her. Quite possibly, he did not need to speak the words, though she had, over and over again, whispering them to him fervently.

Now the summer waned. They'd had messages from the east, and Tally had started wondering when the bulk of Donhal's warriors would return.

He knew if he meant to keep his promise to the goddess, he must do it while yet they remained away.

If, indeed, he meant to keep it.

"I know you, also," he returned softly. "Nenian, yes?" He eyed the young Caledonian slave thoughtfully. Surely no older than Tally, at twenty-four, the fellow had a slender build and a body full of whipcord strength, with skin marked by tattoos, though not so many in number as Tally's. He wore his reddish brown hair tightly braided, and his bright hazel eyes held a wealth of banked emotion. He sported the rough garb common to a slave.

So this was the fellow with whom Alanna had sated herself before Tally arrived in Dal Riada. Tally had seen him before, yes, but only from a distance. Astonishing, truly, it had taken them so long to meet.

Nenian said, "You are the man upon whom Mistress Alanna spills her favor." He took a step closer where they stood among the others waiting for the smithy's attention. "Her kept slave, her pet."

Was that how folk described him? Tally did not like it much; no man with any self-respect would.

He glanced around at the crowd; no one there appeared to pay them much heed, yet as he well knew, avid ears might hide behind seeming disinterest. He lowered his voice when he said, "What is it to you, friend?"

"It used to be me."

"Yes."

A smile twisted the Caledonian's lips. "Ah, so you knew? Did it disappoint you, learning you weren't her first? She used to take me to her bed, before you came."

"Alanna told me." Alanna, along with Marc and Labhan. So why did he dislike hearing it now? Surely this was not jealousy. Alanna had every right to spend herself anywhere she wished. And he supposed this fellow might appeal to her as well as anyone. But he'd wondered before…did this argue a penchant for Caledonian slaves, rather than for him in particular?

"She amuses herself with you for a time, as she amused herself with me. No, you do not like hearing that, do you?" the man challenged. "But it is true. We used to slip away together. I would receive her kisses, and all that heat."

All that heat, yes—it washed over Tally each time Alanna touched him, drew him down to a place where sensation overwhelmed reason, a rarity for him.

The Caledonian stepped closer and lowered his voice to a mere thread, even though they spoke in their own tongue and few nearby likely understood much of what they said.

"If you were gone, she would probably return to me. Why do you not try and escape again? Now is the time, before those bastards come back from the east." Cunning moved in the fellow's eyes. "I could help you," Nenian hurried on before Tally could speak. "My master is in charge of the stores. I could get you goods for your journey, mark for you the routes of the guards, and help you choose the best time to go. But this time, for the love of the goddess, do not take anyone with you. It will only slow you down and allow them to catch you again."

"Why should I trust you?"

Nenian's eyes met Tally's, and held his gaze. "We are the same, are we not? Fellow Caledonii. Do you truly think I would betray you?"

"If it's possible to get away from here safely, why do you not run?" Tally challenged.

Nenian shrugged. "I've lived here since I was eleven, and have a life here. There's no life left for me back east. My tribe was murdered, all, in a raid long ago. I scarcely know aught but this place."

Tally considered it and asked carefully, "And should I, so, betray Alanna?"

"Betray her?"

"She has protected me. She took punishment for me."

"You think you are that important to her that she will care more than a day or two? I will make it up to her, so I do promise."

Tally liked that idea even less than the prospect of what this man and Alanna had done together in the past. Was it so? Would Alanna forget him if he left? And what of him? If he never saw Alanna again, what would happen to his heart?

Briskly now, Nenian asked, "Do you see those buildings over yon? Those are the stores. My master trusts me, and I sleep alone there. If you decide to run, friend, let me know and I will lend you what aid I can."

Tally nodded cautiously. "And you claim you ask no reward for taking such a risk?"

The fellow grinned nervously. "Only deep kisses, breasts like honey, and all that fire. I want her back, man. And I believe I will have her, with you out of the way."

Tally nodded noncommittally, trying to disguise how much Nenian's words bothered him. Never in his life had he been prone to jealousy. Then again, he'd never before had cause to feel jealous. As it was, even after the Caledonian stepped away, after Tally had spoken with the smith and brought his assistant away to the pony field, he found himself wondering. Was it him Alanna wanted? Or just any likely Caledonii?

****

"So give me all your news," Fenna invited. "'Tis an age since we had a good gossip."

"Gossip." Alanna made a face and took a seat at Fenna's fire. One of Fenna's bairns played there. The other, little more than a year old, clung to Fenna's breast. "I suppose 'tis all you hear of me."

"Aye, to be honest." Fenna also seated herself. "Aside from the usual talk and discussion of the feud between your brothers, 'tis mostly what I hear. Ah, well, folk must ha' somewhat to keep them entertained."

Alanna gazed out through the door standing open to the warm summer's afternoon, and contemplated that. She was not sure she enjoyed serving as others' entertainment.

"Och, come." Fenna juggled the bairn in her arms. "Were it anyone else sleeping in a barren hut in order to be near her slave, you too would gossip about it."

"I suppose so." Alanna focused on her friend and braced herself. "And they are about to ha' even more about which to whisper. Fenna, I think I'm carrying his child."

"What?" Fenna's eyes stared until Alanna could see the white all around the blue. "Say, never!"

"I am no' certain. 'Tis why I came to you. But I ha' missed my last two monthlies. And he—"

Fenna swore with feeling. "Do no' tell me you've been letting him give you his seed. Why, you insisted when you lay wi' that other one—Nenian—you always made him withdraw before—"

"So I did." Alanna bit her lip. "It is different wi' Taloc, Fenna."

Fenna stared. "Ha' you lost your wits, lass? He is a slave! How can you bear his bairn?"

"But, Fenna!" Alanna shook her head. "You do no' understand. When we are alone together, he is no' slave and I no' mistress. And to tell the truth, I could no' bear having him withdraw. I need him inside me. I need all o' him."

Fenna looked flummoxed. From her expression, Alanna guessed she wanted to cry the word *fool*. Only friendship kept her from it.

Aye, and perhaps she was a fool when it came to Taloc.

"Well," Fenna huffed at last, "you are in a fix. Carrying the child of a slave. Given, it happens the other way 'round often enough." She shook her finger under Alanna's nose. "This is why we women should no' dally wi' our servants."

"Aye, you are right."

"Ha' you told him?"

Alanna shook her head. "Not yet. I was no' certain."

"If you ha' missed two o' your monthlies, you are certain," Fenna pronounced. "And anyway, 'twill become plain in a month or so more, will it no'? What will your father say?"

"I shudder to think."

Fenna fretted and, juggling the child in her arms, offered him the other breast. "You ha' already proved yourself weak over this blue man, taking those stripes for him, and sleeping in his quarters. Now this."

"I ken. And I am in no position to raise a child. The

life I live, training ponies and working all day, scarce allows for it."

Fenna met her gaze. "Mayhap you should get rid of it."

"How?"

"There are ways. You might go and see old Luah."

"But she's a midwife."

"And kens much about carrying—and losing—a bairn. But go soon. I ha' heard the 'getting rid' only becomes harder and more painful the longer you wait."

Alanna nodded miserably.

"And having endured that," Fenna said with a touch of asperity, "mayhap you'll learn to keep well awa' from your slave."

Chapter Twenty-Eight

All that night and for the next three days Alanna contemplated it—telling herself over and over again how impossible it would be for her to bear her slave's bairn. She thought of little else as she and Taloc worked the ponies together in the bright sunshine, when they took their meals beside the hearth, and when they lay in one another's arms.

Not a particularly imaginative woman, she nevertheless began picturing what such a child might be like. A lad or a lass? Either way, would the child have its father's fine features? His smoke-gray eyes, a mane of dark-red hair, and a beautiful smile?

Loving Taloc as she did, could she bear putting his child to the death?

Unable to answer that question, she somehow never made the trip to old Luah's hut. She kept hoping her monthly might make its appearance after all, or that she might suffer a fall from one of the ponies. That would take care of the matter.

Distracted as she was, she barely noticed there was something bothering Taloc, also. He seemed distant with her, smiled less frequently and spoke less often, even when they were alone.

Yet he still made love to her, still gave her those deep, drugging kisses that tasted of magic.

"The summer is nearly gone," he mused one night

when, just having pleasured one another, they lay listening to the rain beat upon the roof of the hut. "Already the mornings grow cool and the light changes."

"Aye," Alanna returned, focused on the fact that his hand rested on her naked belly, just above their child—his child.

"When do you expect your brothers and their warriors to return?"

"As I ha' said, they will no' all return. Some will stay the winter to occupy whatever land they ha' taken."

"My home."

She felt it then, the yearning that filled him, and sudden fear seized her. Had his heart not changed? Longing for his land, she understood. But would he still be able to leave her so easily? Was there naught she could give him, from kisses to a child, that would make him want to stay with her?

But he did not know about the child.

She drew a sharp breath. "Taloc, tell me you will not—you would not try and escape again? You will be caught, if you do. And nothing I can do or say will protect you next time."

He met the question with a long moment of silence. When he did speak, he seemed to muse rather than give her an answer. "My mother used to say we were all part of the land—our bones akin to the rock and our blood the waters. When she gathered magic, she did so from the air—she would reach with her spirit and draw it in."

"I ha' seen you do that. When you are working wi' the ponies and…and at other times."

Disregarding her words, he murmured, "So it is

possible, even if I never again see my home, I am there still."

"Aye," she whispered, aching with longing for him and her need for him to want her as much as he wanted his homeland.

"But, Alanna, it torments me that I do not even know who survived that attack, and who died. I remember how fiercely we battled, and seeing Barta and True fighting together. I—I saw her fall and him standing over her, raving like any battle hound.

"But I lost track of my brother, Wick—our chief. Once the tower caught fire, people fled, and all was confusion. The chariots came rolling in, and I do not know what happened after. I may be the only one of my family still alive."

"Aye well, there is another way o' looking at it. You are safe here. Wi' you being captured, at least one of your blood endures."

"A slave." He moved restlessly on the pallet. "The son of chiefs, conquered."

"Not here, Taloc. I ha' told you and told you, when the two of us are alone, we are equals."

"All too often, it does not feel that way."

"It should, for it is true."

Again, he mused. "Am I not just another slave?"

"You are not." She slewed around on the pallet so she could gaze into his face. "I love you, Taloc. I ha' told you that over and over again, also."

"So you have." He touched her face with the gentleness that never failed to seduce her. "But for all that, I am not the first of the Caledonii with whom you have shared yourself."

"Nenian." The name passed her lips before she

could prevent it. "But that is in the past."

"Is it? You would not return to him, if I were gone?"

"What makes you ask such a thing?"

"It is what Nenian believes."

Alanna gasped in consternation. "And what do you ken o' what Nenian believes?"

"He told me so himself."

"Nenian came here?"

"No. I met him at the smithy."

"Taloc," Alanna struggled to think. Was this what had been bothering Taloc for so many days? "He means nothing to me."

"Just as someday I will mean nothing?"

She stiffened in horror. All at once, she felt herself balancing on a knife's keen edge. "Do no' say that. What I had wi' Nenian was naught like to what exists between you and me. That was just…just attraction and release. A—a woman needs what she needs—"

"No doubt."

"I did no' mean it that way! I do no' want you wi' me just because you meet—more than meet—my hunger. Taloc, my need for you stretches far beyond that and is never sated. It never will be. Do no', I pray, be jealous of Nenian."

"No?"

"No. I could no' live without you, could not exist, if ever you went from me." She kissed him, putting all her passion and belief into it, and felt the magic unfurl between them. She coaxed his tongue into her mouth, persuaded his body to cover hers, and felt the fire take light, ever new. Would the heat, the urgency of it be enough to keep him with her?

****

"Taloc, there is somewhat I must tell you."

Early morning on a chilly day that promised rain, the two of them had just risen and gone out to tend the ponies. The soft air, full of moisture, washed over Tally's skin like a caress. But he could feel Alanna's uneasiness and—could it be a trace of fear?

He shot her a sidewise look. "What is it?"

She paused with her hands on the neck of the pony that stood between them and gazed away from Tally. "I scarcely know how to say."

That was not like Alanna; in Tally's experience, she willingly vocalized anything from her displeasure with her father to exactly where, on her body, she preferred Tally to place his mouth.

"It must be something dire, then."

Her pale eyes met his. "Dire is one word—"

A sudden furor broke out below, cries and loud shouting. Alanna and Tally exchanged looks before she hurried to the wall.

Tally followed her more slowly. "What is all this?"

"I do no' ken." She frowned. "Trouble."

They watched, side by side, as figures scrambled below, and a group formed. Slowly, the group moved through the settlement.

Alanna vaulted the wall. "You mind the ponies. I will go see."

Tally, remaining where he stood and watching her, sent out soothing thoughts to the animals on the far side of the field. They came to join him, so a crowd awaited Alanna when she returned.

She looked unhappy, and shot a single look at Tally before she said, "There has been another escape."

Tally came to attention. "A Caledonian?"

"Two of them." She jumped the wall and jerked her head below. "They organize the pursuit. The slaves—both from the quarry—must have gone sometime during the night. Raedh woke to find them gone."

"The quarry?" Where Agarex had labored, and suffered. Yet those workers must have seen how Agarex had paid for his disobedience. What courage would it take for them to flee, in spite of it?

"The quarry," he said, "must be a terrible place."

Their eyes met. Alanna had saved him from being traded into a life there, at the cost of gold for which she'd worked full hard. Gratitude and affection for her both filled him. Ah, but surely he felt more than affection.

"What will happen to them if they're caught?"

Alanna grimaced. "Naught good. And they will be caught, Taloc. Slaves most often are."

They returned to work, uneasy enough that the ponies picked up on their moods and acted up. They paused again when the band of pursuers passed the field with hounds and weapons. Tally could sense their anger and outrage from where he stood.

All that day they waited for word. At nightfall the search party returned, empty-handed and vowing to go out once more at sunrise.

For three days, they searched the surrounding country, but the two Caledonii from the quarry were not found.

A bad precedent, so old Marc declared when he came to work on the third day. The Chief would not be pleased. Atholl liked to make an example of disobedient slaves; this would just encourage others to run.

Alanna looked at Tally then, and the fear in her eyes shone bright. This woman with the courage and determination of a man, who would attempt almost anything, was terrified of losing him. It made him want to reassure her, to vow he would stay. Yet at the same time, news of the Caledonii's successful escape lit a flame inside him that would not be extinguished.

In all the furor he never did learn what Alanna had wanted to tell him, that first morning.

Chapter Twenty-Nine

Tally stood at the door of the hut with the night spread wide before him. In the field, the rough turf glittered with evening dew, soft darkness hiding every hoofprint. Overhead, a hundred thousand stars stretched in patterns as familiar to him as those on his skin. The settlement had quieted, and behind him Alanna slept.

She had felt unwell today—she'd striven to disguise it from him, but Tally could tell. Perhaps, he thought now, given the intensity of their connection she'd somehow sensed and been affected by the decision he'd made.

To leave this place for home. To once more endanger himself—and her.

His feelings for Alanna were real and ran deep. But he'd made a vow to the goddess that he would return home. If he meant to keep that promise, he must do it while most the clan's warriors remained away, and before autumn arrived in earnest.

And if he stayed here, would his spirit not die bit by bit, like a flower touched by the frost? Already, captivity had strangled his spiritual life; prayers that had once come as readily as breathing now eluded him. And when he did speak to the goddess, he heard few answers.

For the past ten years, since his tribe came together with others and he received the Vision of the tower, he'd lived for his faith. Indeed, his love for Rekka had been secondary to it; his every thought rested upon being the man to spiritually guide his tribe.

Since his capture, he'd turned into someone else. First a mere beast, driven across the land. Next a slave, Alanna's possession. Most recently a corporal being who lived for her touch and thrived on her heat.

That was not *him*, Taloc map Radoc. He needed to return to the man he'd once been. Even if that meant leaving the woman he loved—and yes, he did love her. That he could no longer deny.

He glanced at her over his shoulder where she slept in his bed. Their bed, for she'd been living here with him for many and many a night. She had sacrificed for him, suffered for him, and would be devastated when he left her. Part of him would share in that devastation.

But part of him would, so he hoped, return to life. The most important part of him, so he believed.

And what made him think an escape now—tonight—would be any more successful than his last attempt? For one thing, he knew the settlement far better, had memorized the movements of the guards, knew who slept where and when. For another, he had the offer of Nenian's help, and meant to avail himself of it. He did not think the young Caledonian would betray him, not so much because they were both Caledonii—Nenian seemed to have lost touch with his heritage in his time here—but because if Nenian wanted Alanna back, seeing Tally safe away was in his best interest.

Tally cast another long look at Alanna; he longed to go to the pallet, to lean down and kiss her, but did not dare risk waking her. Instead, he slipped soundlessly from the door of the hut and closed it softly behind him. Cool night air washed over his skin like a blessing. When he passed the sheds, several of the ponies stirred restlessly, as if they felt his presence.

Just as he still felt Alanna's.

He paused after vaulting the stone wall. Ah, but could he bear to leave her? There, beneath the starlight, he whispered a prayer for strength, for wisdom.

Goddess, guide me. If this be the right thing for me to do, give me a sign.

The night remained quiet; no voice sounded in his head or in his heart. But far overhead, in the dome of the sky, a star shot like a signal toward the east. Home.

Chance, or guidance? His head declared one thing and his heart another. If he took this step, away from the safety of the wall, and succeeded, he would never see Alanna again. Failing to succeed would bring far more terrible consequences.

For one endless moment he stood, wracked by indecision. The vow he had made to the goddess pulled him forward—down into the settlement he went, a shadow keeping to the walls, avoiding the notice of the guards. Nenian's storehouse stood to one side, so quiet it might have been uninhabited. But when Tally scratched on the door he heard movement inside.

A moment later, Nenian peered out, hair disheveled and obviously risen straight from his bed. He stared at Tally for a full moment before he blinked and whispered, "Come in."

The interior of the place lay dark. Cautiously, Nenian lit a rush light and looked at Tally again. "What is this?"

"I have decided to leave here—now, tonight."

Nenian's eyebrows soared. "You are leaving Mistress Alanna?"

"I must go home. Does your offer of help still stand?" Tally asked impulsively. Nenian could undo him now with a single call or whistle, piercing the quiet night.

But Nenian nodded readily. "Indeed, I will help you, friend—give you supplies for your journey, and say I saw you heading north along the coast. It is not a bad route, that—far more open than going through the forest, and I think that is the way the two from the quarry took, when they got clean away. But you must head due east from the settlement before turning up into the trees. Your only chance is to move quickly before they get after you with the hounds."

"Yes," Tally agreed. Even now, he feared Alanna would wake and find him gone, that their connection might pull at her and so draw her from sleep. Yet everything remained quiet, the very night a blessed hush.

"Here." Nenian turned to the rows and stacks of goods that lined the long hut. Taking up a pack, he began shoving in food items, a waterskin, and even a thin blanket. He must, Tally thought, enjoy a position of considerable trust with no one here to watch him.

Nenian thrust the loaded pack at Tally. "Go swiftly, friend, and as fast as you can. Travel for a ways eastward along the water, as I say, and between the rocks. The presence of the guard, there, is thin. Do not look back."

An easy thing to say, not so easy to put into practice. Already, part of Tally's heart longed for Alanna. Or was that merely his flesh?

"Thank you," he began to tell Nenian, but the Caledonian pushed him outside.

"Go," he bade again. "Fly like a bird."

****

Like a bird. Those words curled through Tally's mind again and again, echoing one of his mother's songs. The song blended with the *shush, shush* of the waves when he pelted alongside the wide, limitless ocean and, in a trice, slipped past the guard. It increased when he climbed high above the settlement and into the trees, where he set as swift a course as he dared. He found he could move much more swiftly alone than with Tamia and Agarex on his heels, and his heart rose, indeed, very like that wild hawk he'd once seen. In the dark beneath the trees, he moved like a flickering shadow and behind him the night remained quiet.

Or did it?

Suddenly, his every instinct pounded at him, and the song disappeared from his mind. He paused, breath caught, and looked back even though he could see nothing. Stretching his other senses—hearing and inner awareness—he reached back, and back.

Alarm flooded him like a drench of cold water. Flinging the loaded pack over his shoulder, he ran.

How far and how long he ran, he never later knew. Pursuit came swiftly when it came, and not at all quietly: instead it chased him down with voices shouting, the clatter of weapons, and the unmistakable crying of hounds.

Tally, no mean runner, cast his pack aside and ran full out, dodging trees and getting whipped by branches, his every breath now a prayer. The hounds ran faster still, trailing him far ahead of their masters.

He tried to think—how had they discovered his absence so quickly? He knew he hadn't been sighted by any of the guards. Had Alanna awakened? But if she had, she would never betray him.

Betrayal.

An image of Nenian rose into his mind. But why? If Nenian wanted a return to Alanna's favor, his best chance lay in Tally's escape.

Bitterness twisted his features even as he gasped for more breath. The reason did not matter, not now. He'd been betrayed both by his fellow Caledonian and by the goddess who once more failed to protect him…he had no choice now but to run until he dropped.

The foremost of the hounds caught him before that happened. A great, tall beast, it leaped and snagged Tally's bare shoulder, bent on pulling him down.

Too desperate to heed the pain, and far too spent to employ any magic, Tally tore himself free and stumbled on. But the stumble allowed the second hound to reach them. He felt its teeth penetrate his forearm as he fell. Groping frantically for his ability to communicate with such beasts, he asked them both to back off.

They did, panting and gazing at him with wise yellow eyes. But he had no chance to get up and resume his headlong flight before a band of Gaels burst through the trees, weapons drawn.

Tally recognized the foremost of them—the chief's man, Belloch, the same who had come after him before. Belloch leveled his sword point at Tally's throat and glared.

"Accursed slave! I should spit you where you lie."

Tally almost wished he would. It must prove a swifter and less painful death than what would now follow from the Chief, in retaliation.

Yet he wanted, still, to live. And he refused to take the course Agarex had chosen. Breathless, he reached for his courage and braced himself.

****

Alanna doubled over and vomited onto the forest floor. A fine time for the babe in her belly to make its presence known and turn her sick, though it happened frequently enough. She had heard of illness in the morning, but Taloc's child seemed apt to render her weak at any moment of the day or night.

Good thing his pursuers had outdistanced her so they did not witness this shameful scene. Had they caught up with him yet?

Did she want them to?

She did not know the answer to that question, which pounded through her with each footfall and every heartbeat. A successful escape meant she would never see him again, this man who now made up the better part of her world. She needed him the way she needed breath. Yet recapture—that was unthinkable. She whispered a fervent prayer for his escape—what did her happiness matter in comparison with his?—and forced her body on.

She heard them before she saw them, heard Belloch shouting above the restless movements of the hounds, and her heart sank so violently she thought she'd collapse. Was there anything she could do? Might she fight her fellow clansmen so Taloc could run off?

But how could she fight them? She'd come straight from her bed and neglected to so much as bring a weapon.

She burst onto the lurid scene and stopped again,

frozen by dismay. Two of the pursuers carried torches, which allowed her to see far too much.

Taloc lay sprawled on his back, on the ground, bleeding from both his forearm and his shoulder. The hounds, restless, still circled him, and Belloch's sword hovered just above his throat.

When Alanna appeared, the men turned to stare, all save Belloch, and Taloc's eyes met hers with an intensity she felt through her whole body. In them she saw—

Regret. A measure of panic and resignation. Love? Och, she could not tell.

Even now, she did not know if he truly loved her.

Belloch, still breathless from the chase, snarled at her, "Mistress Alanna, your slave proves more trouble than he is worth."

Nay, but he was worth any price, any cost. The balance of her riches, the skin of her back. The entire world—the life of his child?

Ah, that she might not be willing to give.

She said, "He has been recaptured. Let me take him home."

"You ken fine I canno' do that. He will ha' to go before your father for punishment."

Suddenly, Alanna feared her legs would give way, that she would vomit again. Her father would not be open to bribery or, at this point, persuasion.

"And," Belloch added heavily, "given the escape o' those last two, I doubt the Chief will be inclined to mercy."

The men hauled Taloc up, bleeding heavily where the hounds had torn his skin. His gaze still clung to Alanna's and, drawn irresistibly, she stepped forward to seize his hand. As soon as they touched, she could feel everything he felt.

All his exhaustion, his desperation, his regret. And his clear knowledge that there would be no escape from the consequences of what he'd just done.

Chapter Thirty

Alanna's father did not appreciate being hauled from his bed in the middle of the night. When Belloch and the returned party invaded his hall, he looked impatient and angry enough to spit.

Alanna, who'd struggled all the way back to marshal her thoughts and her arguments, wondered how best to placate him. She might plead on Taloc's behalf, but she doubted he would escape punishment, and in this instance, she dared not take that punishment for him.

It would be severe, very severe. A second offense—unheard of from a slave—warranted the harshest answer. And had Atholl not promised as much?

Such punishment, even if Atholl would allow Alanna to accept it, which he would not, might well cost the life of her child.

Taloc's child.

The first possibility might not deter her—she thought far more of Taloc than a child of her own. The second did. She'd already fallen in love with the idea of bearing his bairn, one that might have eyes like his and, hopefully, a measure of his spirit.

But it meant she would have to stand by and watch him endure what must come.

"Daughter," Atholl bawled, "stand awa' from

him."

She moved away from Taloc, releasing her grip on his elbow for the first time. All the way back she'd kept her hold on him. Now she felt the separation like a blow from a sword, sharp and damaging.

All the things she wanted to say trembled on her lips. *Father, I need him. I cannot live without him. I carry his child.*

She could express none of that. Och, the last would eventually become evident, and she might argue it to her father privately but would not air it here before these other men—this thing even Taloc did not know.

"Spare him," she asked instead. "I am certain he has learned his lesson—"

"Spare him?" Atholl repeated as if she spoke some other, incomprehensible tongue. "He is conspicuously slow in learning his lessons, this one. A slave so disobedient should be put to the death."

"Nay, Father." Alanna took a step toward Atholl. "You do no' understand. In his own land, this man is of noble birth, the son of a chief just like my brothers, like yoursel'. Should such a man bend easily to the will of others?"

Atholl eyed Taloc without favor. "Not easily, nay. But he maun bend."

"Allow me to buy his freedom."

Atholl scoffed. "Would you truly be such a fool over again?"

"I will trade the rest o' my wealth in exchange for your leniency."

"I do no' need your wealth. One day I will own all this great land." Atholl sneered. "Including any *noble* savages who might remain alive. Nay, he maun be put to the death."

Alanna trembled where she stood. "Father, let me at least buy his life. You may punish him as you choose, but please do no' put him to the death."

"Do you ken how heavy the punishment would ha' to be?"

Alanna cast a look at Taloc before she said, "Father, I beg you allow me to speak wi' you alone."

"Do no' think you can talk me round, lass."

"I do not. Only—I beg a word, please."

They went to his inner chamber, where he'd been sleeping. There Alanna drew a breath and, not wasting the precious chance she'd been given, said, "Father—you need to know I carry Taloc's child. If you agree to spare him, I will handfast wi' him and—"

She got no farther. Atholl's expression changed, his face hardening into a mask of outrage. He struck Alanna across the face with force that knocked her off her feet and onto the floor. "Slut," he hissed, glaring at her through narrowed eyes. "'Twas bad enough when you took not one but two o' those savages to your bed. Aye, did you suppose I would no' ken? But to get his filthy brat inside you—you should be beaten until it comes clean away."

Alanna dabbed blood from the corner of her mouth and scrambled to her feet. She shook from head to foot and found all words had deserted her, save *no, no, no*.

Atholl pushed past her and out to the hall, where he faced Taloc, still flanked by his guards.

"My daughter insists you are *noble*. Your punishment will, therefore, be an unusual one, fitting such an elevated state. I order for you thirty lashes and hanging in the wicker cage for three days."

"No." Alanna said it aloud this time.

Taloc looked at her. Clearly, he did not understand what this meant. Young and strong he might be, but this ordeal could kill a man.

"The punishment," Atholl concluded, "to be carried out at once."

****

Alanna had blood on her mouth; Tally saw that at once when she and her father emerged from the inner chamber. It did not take anyone much above a fool to realize Atholl had struck her.

He, Tally, was a fool, though. He'd read the goddess's sign wrong. And Nenian had betrayed him.

He still did not understand why, when the man could have been rid of him and free to try and win back Alanna's good favor. Now, however, that reason did not matter. All that mattered was his, Tally's, own actions had put that shattered, terrified look in Alanna's eyes. And he must face the consequences.

For when her father pronounced the sentence, this time she did not offer to take it for him. Not that he would allow her to. But last time, she'd rushed to put herself between him and the lash; now she stood silent, staring at him in agony.

He could draw but one conclusion: by leaving her, by running a second time, he must have killed whatever love she had for him. And only now that he'd lost that love did he realize in truth what it meant to him.

That thought, and not the promised punishment, filled his head as he was dragged away by Atholl's men, back outside into the night that had already begun lightening to dawn. He was held by three men at the cleared place out front, even though he did not struggle, and Alanna stood by, refusing to look at him. A woman changed, she had lost her proud stance and instead drooped where she stood.

The settlement came awake around them. To the sound of Atholl's bellowing and of running feet, the clansfolk tumbled from their beds to find a spectacle unfolding before their eyes.

Tally would not let himself think about being at the center of that spectacle, or the pain that must ensue. Even when a curious, large structure made an appearance, dragged out by half a score of men, he focused only on the woman beside him who, he now saw, had given and given to him, asking little enough in return.

As for the rest of it, the goddess had brought him to this.

He must endure.

****

As before, he was forced down onto the stones in front of the Chief's hall. As before, a whip was presented to the Chief's hand. A crowd—still steadily increasing in size—stood all around, hushed and avid.

At the first blow, Tally's body reacted, bowed, and stiffened without his leave. He turned his head and sought, with difficulty, Alanna's gaze. She returned his look now, but for once—for once—he could not sense her emotions.

One blow, two, three. He ordered himself not to cry out—could he not muster some pride, here before these Gaels? Son of a chief, a man of courage. His father, Radoc, would not have made a sound, above a grunt.

But the whip flayed him, set him afire, and he lost

count of the blows which all tumbled into one in a blaze of pain. Screams filled his mind and his heart until a merciful blackness rose and overwhelmed him.

Even in the darkness, he rode the waves of pain. His senses came and went—a glimpse of a staring face here, the Chief's voice still shouting, and hard hands pulling at him, prompting further agony.

He groaned. Then he tumbled deeper into elsewhere, a far different place and time.

A boy again, he could not be more than six, for he sat beside the hearthstones of the hut in which he'd been raised, with the rest of his family around him. And his father, Radoc, looked hale and hearty. Tally had been slammed back though time to days before his father took the crippling injury dealt him by a Gael's chariot.

A rare enough moment, this, with everyone together around the hearth. Usually Wick was out in the company of his friends and Barta off running with Father's hounds. Indeed, two hounds, both of them Father's, sat close by now, as much a part of the family circle as the rest of them.

Mother spoke, and Tally heard joy in her words. "This, my beloved family, is a holy night. The end of summer, it marks an important point in the turning of the year. Winter is hard upon us, but we will remain strong."

She wove a complicated pattern above the fire with nimble fingers, and the flames danced, lighting the faces all around: Father, gazing at Mother with so much love in his eyes it made the breath catch in Tally's throat. Wick, watching her also in fascination, his lips parted. Barta had her fingers tangled in the coat of the hound Valor. He, Tally…

He could feel what Mother felt so clearly it almost hurt. This, then, had created the core of his life—the spiritual existence and what lay within.

Faith. Beauty. Belief.

Mother shed all these upon them when she smiled and said, "Let us break this bread together and pledge our loyalty and gratitude to the god and goddess, who have given us so much. Strength and health, bonds uniting us to one another and to this land that exists forever in us. All hearts and spirits come home this season. Let us always remember to return home."

Essa turned a shining look upon each of them, warmer than sunlight and more enchanting than stardust. "And, my darlings, no matter what happens to us in the future, always, always remember that we are blessed."

Chapter Thirty-One

"Father, please—I beg you cut him down. The rest of the punishment has been carried out, and it is enough. He is beaten bloody and raw." Alanna wound her fingers into her father's tunic in desperation. Not a woman who ever begged for anything—she had far too much pride—she would go on her knees now, and readily, if she thought it might turn her father's heart.

Atholl shot her a look of disfavor. Following the terrible scene outside, she had trailed him to his inner chamber, where he dressed for the day as if the unthinkable had not just happened. Now he drew his tunic from her grasp with a touch of disdain. "Your slave's sentence has been pronounced, and the rest of it will be carried out. In full."

Outside, Taloc hung by his wrists inside the wicker cage, which had in turn been hauled aloft by half a score of strong men. His back still ran freely with blood, and he appeared to be unconscious.

"But—" she said in a voice that did not sound like her own.

"Three days in the cage. Daughter, he does not learn, this one. What good did it do for you to tak' his punishment last time, eh? He merely fled you again—made a fool o' you again."

Alanna could not argue that. The hurt of Taloc's abandonment mingled with and intensified the agony she now felt on his behalf. She'd experienced every blow right along with him.

It did not seem fair for her to care so very much, and he so very little. Yet it changed nothing in her heart, or in her need to defend him. Nothing could—or would—ever change her feelings for Taloc. She would go to her grave loving him.

But what could she say to her father that would make a difference?

"Surely now, Father, you see how fine and noble he is?"

"Fine?" Atholl stared, echoing the word incredulously.

"From an elevated house among his kind, as I told you before. You witnessed his courage! He did no' utter a sound throughout that punishment—and you laid it on hard."

Atholl spat into the fire. "I do no' ken, Daughter, what he has done to enchant you. But you maun get over this penchant for savages. Go out and look at him hanging there—see him for what he is."

Alanna swallowed convulsively. "But, before this punishment ends, he may well die."

"I only hope he does, and mayhap cure you of your sickness. Och, and Daughter"—here Atholl shot Alanna a stern look—"go see one of the midwives. Get yoursel' a potion to rid you o' his dirty whelp. Understand?"

Alanna understood, and turned sick inside. Yet she hadn't finished bargaining. "Father, only cut him down and let me tak' him home to tend his wounds. In exchange, I will gi' you all my obedience, including what remains o' my wealth and all my ponies—"

"Get out o' my sight."

"What?"

"Are your ears addled as well as your wits? I do no' wish to look at you."

Alanna ducked her head and went, knowing she had nothing more to offer and little else to give. But the sight that met her outside turned her hot and desperate all over again.

The punishment of the wicker cage was not leveled often. Only upon a few occasions in Alanna's lifetime had she seen it used, and with good reason. For it held the sentenced up to ridicule as well as physical harm.

At the moment, mercifully, Taloc remained senseless and unaware of what happened to and around him. It was, Alanna knew, the only mercy he could expect. If—when—he came to, he'd find himself suspended some two lengths off the ground, dangling both from stout ropes and manacles anchored to the top of the cage. His feet did not reach the woven floor below him. The agony would be excruciating.

Passersby could spit at him, rock the cage, perhaps even poke things between the narrow bars. For the moment, most spectators had cleared off, though a few remained, watching solemnly to see if Taloc would waken.

Alanna prayed he would not, at least not soon. His back still ran with blood, which dripped down and had spattered the stones beneath the cage. His head drooped between his bunched shoulders and his hair—that glorious mane through which she'd run her fingers time after time—covered his face.

The sun rose on what looked to be a warm day. For three days and nights Taloc would receive no care, no food or water. His stripes would scab over and stiffen, insects would swarm him. His position would make it difficult for him to breathe.

Alanna did not want to stay and witness any of this. Love kept her where she stood.

****

We are blessed.

The words, spoken in his mother's voice, accompanied Tally out of the darkness. With a breath that seared his lungs and with blinding light against his eyelids, he returned to—

Pain.

A thousand agonies assaulted his senses all at once, making him gasp and reach for the darkness once more.

It would not come. He found himself caught in a brutal wakefulness, with his mother's voice still in his ears.

Blessed?

His back was afire, making it hard to breathe, and agony had seized his arms and shoulders, by which he seemed to hang, suspended. Peeling his eyelids open, he assessed his position.

Hanging, yes. Out in the bright, hot sunshine. His mind shied from those facts even as he struggled to draw air into his lungs. His heart beat in such shuddering thuds it hurt the rest of him.

His toes reached helplessly for the ground, and his every sense screamed at him. He could not endure it.

Blessed, his mother insisted.

Madness. Through the bars of the cage—a narrow thing with space at both foot and head—he could see people watching him. Atholl's clansfolk. His mind flinched at the thought of Atholl, and a wall of black hatred arose, but he fought it back desperately. He had no energy for hate, not if he wanted to stay alive.

Did he want to stay alive?

He saw her then, standing to one side of his prison, much as if guarding him. No need for a guard; he hadn't any hope of escaping this, not with his wrists in metal hoops and suspended here helplessly. She held herself tight, arms wrapped around her upper body, and when he moved feebly, her attention quickened.

Tally shook the hair out of his face in an effort to see her better. She stepped forward and grasped the bars of the cage.

"Taloc—" Tears flooded her eyes and spilled over. She paid them no heed. "I ha' pled wi' my father. He refuses to release you before times."

Then he must serve his sentence. He did not know how, could not conceive of enduring three days so, through each day, through each night.

Alanna must be able to read that truth in his eyes. Passionately, she said, "You are strong. You can survive this. Then, after, you will heal. We can be together—"

Tally had to struggle for words against the pain. "If you can forgive me."

"There is naught to forgive."

"I left you…"

Her fingers gripped the bars still harder. "There is naught to forgive! You are who you are—a holy man, a shaman—and should be free, not—not fettered." She stumbled over that word, and her eyes flew to the shackles. "I would set you free today if I could, send you home as you deserve." Her tears streamed down. "'Tis I who is sorry, Taloc, sorry for keeping you. You should fly free, like a wild bird."

He groaned. "The goddess has abandoned me. I shall never again fly."

"You will. And she has no' abandoned you. You maun believe!"

A crowd of young boys came by. They jeered at Tally and rocked his cage, laughing as he swung inside its narrow confines.

Alanna beat them off, waving her fists and screaming like a madwoman, and then set herself with her back to him. He realized she did indeed mean to guard him from all comers.

We are grateful.

A haze rose and claimed Tally's mind. He wished he might travel back to that glad scene in his parents' hut and escape the agony, but that did not happen. He merely drifted, eyes half open, consumed by pain.

All he saw was a pale yellow head, turned determinedly away from him. But it did not matter which way she faced, for her love wrapped around him, sure and strong.

Chapter Thirty-Two

"Come awa' from there, Alanna. 'Tis no' good for you." Fenna stepped closer and whispered so none but Alanna could hear. "Nor for your bairn."

"Hush!" Alanna snapped from her half-stupor and clawed her way back to determined awareness. How long had she been standing here? Nearly a day now—just as long as Taloc had been hanging in the cage at her back.

If he could endure, so could she. But—did he still endure?

She spun to look at him, and her heart sank anew at the gruesome sight. He sagged from his ropes, arms stretched impossibly, teeth bared in a grimace of pain. The blood that had run over his tattoos had dried in patches and created new, far more terrible patterns.

He looked dead, but she could see him struggling to breathe, gasp by gasp.

Fenna asked softly, with a hard nod in Taloc's direction, "He does not ken about the bairn? You ne'er told him?"

"Nay."

"Do you mean, then, to get rid of it?"

"Nay!"

Fenna eyed her, not unkindly. "If you stand here two more days, lass, the matter may well tak' care o' itsel'."

"I dare no' leave. When I do, folk come and torment him." Alanna gripped her friend's arm. "Fenna, will you stay, just while I go to relieve mysel'?"

"And earn your father's displeasure?"

Alanna grimaced. "Will you at least take a message to Marc for me? Tell him to get up to the sheds early tomorrow and make sure the ponies are well guarded tonight."

"That I will. But you do no' mean to stay here all night?"

"I will sleep beneath that cage if I ha' to."

"You are mad."

"Fenna, I love him."

Fenna inspected Taloc frankly before turning her gaze back on Alanna. "Not much left to love, is there? Besides, Alanna, he does no' love you. If he did, he would no' ha' left you wi'out a backward glance. Ah, look. Your father is coming. I will speak to Marc for you."

And Fenna fled with alacrity.

Atholl had, indeed, emerged from his dwelling, a frown clouding his face. He approached Alanna swiftly, a big man comfortable in his power but, at the moment, appearing confounded.

His words echoed Fenna's, though he delivered them in a roar. "Daughter, come awa' from there."

At the sound of his voice, Taloc twitched. Alanna felt him return to awareness and felt the shudder that wracked his body. But she did not budge from where she stood and met her father's one-eyed glare full on.

He looked furious, and she braced herself against the possibility he might lash out in his anger.

She lifted her chin. "I am a free woman, Father,

and can surely stand where I wish."

"In defense of a disobedient slave? You are an embarrassment to me. And you are interfering wi' his punishment."

Alanna glanced at Taloc. He'd lifted his head and his eyes were open. "I am no'."

"You ha' attacked your own people in defense o' him, a filthy slave. I will no' tolerate it."

"He has suffered enough."

"No' by half." And, with an ugly look, Atholl reached out with both hands, gripped the bars of the cage and shook it violently.

****

Tally's world rocked. Pain exploded through his body and for an instant the blue sky beyond the bars of the cage seemed to flip upside down. His stomach turned—from the motion and the pain—and hot vomit rose to the back of his throat.

His senses flickered like sunlight when the shadow of a bird passes overhead.

He wanted to fall back again into the cavern of darkness wherein the pain muted to a drum that kept time with his heartbeat. But movement—any movement—shattered that refuge, and now his world swung from side to side. Through the bars he could see…

The Chief, Atholl, Alanna's father, looking enraged. At the sight of him, at the sound of his voice, Tally heard again the whine of the whip rising and falling, and felt the pain of it flaying his skin.

He saw Alanna also, facing off with the Chief, staunch as any warrior. She had been there as long as he had been here—an eternity—standing strong.

You are blessed, blessed to have earned such love.

He wanted to laugh at his mother's words. He wanted to spit, but his mouth was too dry.

Let me die, he begged the goddess, begged his mother because, clearly, the goddess no longer listened. *It is my only hope.*

Son, you cannot surrender. Did your father give up when he was sore injured?

I am not my father.

No; you are beloved of the gods and gifted with magic. Call upon that magic now.

The edges of his vision dimmed. He could see only the brightness of Alanna's fair hair and hear only her voice.

"He needs tending. He needs water, if he is to live."

"You understand the punishment. No water before he is released. If he lives, he lives. If he dies there, so be it."

"If he dies there, Father, I will never forgive you."

There came a flurry and a thump. Tally realized Atholl had knocked his daughter to the ground.

"Go home. And let fate take its course."

"I will no'." Alanna scrambled up again. Tally once more felt her love wrap around him like a protective blanket.

"Then, Alanna, I am ashamed to call you my daughter."

****

"Water." The word broke harsh from Tally's lips. Alanna's face, pale as milk and striped by the shadows of the bars, gazed up at him. The agony in her eyes reflected his own.

"Taloc, my love, there is no way—I would if I could. The bars are too narrow."

She swayed on her feet. How long had she been there? How long had he been here? Forever.

"I am dying." He did not mean to speak the words aloud, but they escaped him. The pain had sent him repeatedly into a well of darkness. Now, though, his strength failed him. He possessed little with which to battle.

"I ken, my love, I ken." Tears streaked her face, and made paths through the sweat and grime. She tried to wiggle her hand between the bars in order to touch him but could not. Behind her head, light faded from the sky. Another endless day faded to night.

For most of this day she'd paced around his cage, chasing away those folk who would torment him, shooing away the insects that swarmed. Now she, too, appeared at the end of her strength.

Tally's head spun in a slow circle. It felt as if the cage moved even though Alanna held the bars tight.

"Not much longer," she lied, desperate to encourage him. "Just a day and a night. You maun hang on, Taloc. Promise me you will."

He could not; he had nothing left for which to reach.

"Turn to your faith," she urged, her gaze holding his. "I ken fine how strong that is."

His faith?

Alanna bit her lip. "And if you maun fly away from me, if that is the only relief you can find, know I love you enough to offer you even that peace—"

"Daughter!" The bellow came from behind her. Atholl had once more emerged from his hall. "It is enough. Awa' out o' there! I will no' tell you again."

The Chief seized Alanna from behind. Hard hands spun her around; a fist delivered the first blow, the second. Alanna fell to her knees. The chief drew her up and smacked her across the face. She fell once more and, this time, did not stir.

Atholl glared at Taloc where he hung and aimed a high kick at the cage, sending it swinging.

Tally fell into the familiar darkness, lit by pain.

Chapter Thirty-Three

The bird rose from Tally's feet and struck upward on strong wings. A hawk it was, tawny brown with soft speckled feathers. The very picture of vigor, it soared and caught the warm air current of the dying day, where it hovered, looking down at him.

Free—even as Tally was not—it should fly away. Instead, it met Tally's gaze with wild, smoke-gray eyes.

He recognized the truth in that moment, just as if he gazed into a polished shield, or a quiet stream. His spirit, bowed by exhaustion and pain, stirred and reached out feebly. Oh, by the goddess, the hawk was him and he was the bird! Released, just as Alanna had said—able to fly.

The notion lent him strength, enough so that his spirit rose from his mangled body and, drifting upward from the blood and the agony, abandoned it. He filtered between the narrow bars of the cage and, floating like mist, seeped into the mind of the bird. From there he spread his awareness throughout its body, each feather and every limb.

Once there, all pain fell away. Instead he could feel the bird's life force, the fire in its blood and bone. The hawk circled, continuing to rise upward, and Tally spoke to it, the words like thoughts in his own mind.

I have seen you before. You caught my attention during our march here, and you flew up from my feet.

I have always been with you, my son.

I could not feel you. I thought you had abandoned me.

I cannot abandon you. I am inside you, flesh of your flesh, spirit of your spirit. You but closed your heart to me.

Why return to me now? Tally asked.

She who loves you far more than herself has prayed for your release.

Tally looked down. He saw himself still hanging inside the cage, a shocking sight with long, filthy hair covering his face and a body contorted by pain, split, and stained with blood.

How can she love that? There is little left of me.

The bird did not reply. Tally looked again and saw Alanna lying in a heap beneath the cage, blood on the stone under her head.

Emotion exploded in his heart—compassion so deep it could only be the true expression of love.

Come, said the bird, *fly free as she bade you.*

He did not want to go, could not bear to leave Alanna. At the same time he wanted it, more than anything. He heard her voice again: *If you maun go from me, know I love you enough to offer you even that peace.*

They flew. Up into the darkening sky they streamed until the cage and the woman became distant. Tally saw the land—beloved, blessed land—spread out beneath him. He saw the sea, endless and holding the light to its bosom. Never had he felt so strong or so free.

The bird gave a victorious cry, and it resounded through Tally's spirit. All pain, all thirst and weakness fell away from him.

In the sky, time lost meaning. There was just the wind rushing past, the air buoying them from beneath, and the boundless sense of release.

Who are you? Tally asked eventually, without words. *Are you my goddess?*

No answer came, but he felt warmth and laughter fill the hawk's heart. He persisted. *Are you the great god?*

I am neither. I am both. I am Caledonia, and I am with you always.

With a flash of wonder, Tally knew that to be true. The love of this land filled him. Whether ruled by Caledonii or Gaels, its magic and the beauty of its forests and glens would endure forever. Just like his spirit.

He felt immeasurably strong. He felt wondrously blessed.

Where will you go? asked the bird.

Home.

They soared away, eastward.

****

"Here, Alanna, lass, sit up. Up wi' you." Kind hands urged Alanna into a sitting position; a cool, wet cloth pressed to her head. She sat, struggling for an instant to recall where she was, and why.

Dark surrounded her. The air had cooled and now struck against her skin like a balm. Somewhere close at hand a torch flared and—

Taloc.

Memory hit her with a thump akin to those her father had delivered.

He had knocked her down, left her lying on the

ground. Off guard.

It was Fenna who'd once more come to her and helped her up, the soothing cloth in her hands.

"By all that is holy—I should ha' been standing guard. They will torment him."

Fenna huffed. "They will no'. Not now."

"Why not?"

For a long moment, Fenna did not speak. With reluctance she finally admitted, "I believe he is dead."

That got Alanna to her feet on a surge of panic. She spun to face the cage. The man inside, filthy and bloodied, hung motionless like so much meat. He did, in truth, look dead.

Her poor, battered heart faltered within her. She moaned a single word. "No."

"I canno' see him breathing, Alanna. Since I got here, he has no' moved. We canno' touch him and make sure, but I fear 'tis so."

Alanna wailed, "Get him out o' there! We maun get him out."

"You ken fine we canno'. Your father will no' allow the cage to be opened until the sentence is served. Let me help you awa' home. You hit your head when you fell, and need rest."

"I care no' about me." Alanna clawed at the bars of the cage, her reason flown. "I maun touch him. I maun hold him."

"Hush. Would you anger your father all over again?"

"I do no' care. I care for nothing—"

Alanna threw herself on the hasp that secured the door of the cage. The structure rocked and the man inside flopped lifelessly. She managed to work the hasp and lift the bar before her father's men came, refastenend it, and dragged her away by force. The cage, behind her, slowly settled into motionlessness once more. The man inside, face covered by his hair, did not lift his head.

The men released Alanna when she was violently sick all over the ground, and allowed Fenna to lead her home. There being almost nothing in her stomach—she'd not eaten since taking up her position beside the cage—the bout was short, but it shook her. She wept wildly as Fenna helped her over the stone wall.

Old Marc came out of the shed when he heard them. "What has happened. Is the Caledonian slave dead?"

"Aye," Fenna replied shortly.

Dead, dead, dead. Aye, Alanna had prayed to the gods for Taloc's release, anything that would end his pain. But what of her? How was she to live without him?

Marc grunted. "'Twas foolishness anyway," he pronounced, just as if Alanna could not hear. "A lass taking a slave to her bed."

Alanna vomited—or tried to—again.

Marc backed off. "What is the matter wi' her?"

Fenna bit her lip and said nothing of the child. "Help me get her inside. Then run and get one o' the healers."

They half dragged, half carried Alanna into the hut and laid her on the pallet, where she and Taloc had twined and loved together, where his child had been conceived.

How could she endure, now he'd left her? How, when she loved him with every breath?

Marc went out, and Alanna seized Fenna's hands. "Am I going to lose the child?"

"I do no' ken."

"I cannot! 'Tis all I ha' left o' him."

"Then garner your strength, my lass, and fight."

****

Tally flew. At one with the hawk and the night sky, with each of the stars that pricked through to shine above him and all the land below, he streamed like part of the air itself and hurried home. Home.

That word sang through his mind again and again. All the longing he'd kept clamped down through a fierce act of will throughout his captivity arose and now possessed him.

We are grateful.

Yes, Mother, we are.

When was the last time he'd felt like this, smiled like this? Oh, he'd smiled at some of Alanna's clever quips, her teasing.

Alanna.

The joy burgeoning inside him, uplifting him, died a rapid death. He saw her again, lying in a heap beneath the cage where his body hung, and it pulled at him, pulled, pulled... But he was free. Nearly home, soon to be with those he loved.

Yet—he loved Alanna.

He did, yes? Or had she but been his warm hearth in a storm, his refuge, his defender?

He could not deny that she loved him. He'd seen that in her eyes, in every fiber of her when she stood on guard for him. She'd felt his pain, shared his agony.

Made it her own.

Have you ever been loved so? his mother asked.

You loved me. Father did.

And still do, she assured him.

Rekka loved me.

So she did. That was a gentle love, was it not? Alanna would tear down the world for you if she could.

She is the enemy.

Son, look below you. What do you see?

Tally looked. He saw trees, endless forest, rocky peaks, broad swales of heather and gorse.

The land I love.

Do you see any boundaries? Any theirs and ours? From up here, from where we are, it is all one. One heart beating for the world. One great love.

Tally looked. The ground blurred before his eyes.

Son, this land has a heartbeat. Call it what you will, it shall endure so long as those born here are able to love—love the land itself and love one another.

Mother, I want to go home.

But what about the pull from behind him, the cord that seemed to connect him to that woman lying on the ground? She with the clear blue eyes and the fierce, heedless love…

Tally turned his back on that pull, and flew on into the sunrise.

Chapter Thirty-Four

"Chief Atholl, she will no' take so much as a sip of water. She will no' rise. I fear for her."

Alanna's father sighed. Alanna, lying flat on her back upon Taloc's pallet, where she could still catch his scent, heard that sigh even though he and Fenna stood outside the door of the hut.

He asked, "Has the healer seen her?"

"Aye, Chief."

"Has my daughter lost the brat?"

"Not yet, but I do fear—"

"'Twill be for the best."

Tears seeped from the corners of Alanna's eyes— she who until she met Taloc had wept so seldom. Perhaps, she thought, in the past she hadn't refrained from weeping because she was strong but because she'd never cared enough to mourn for anything.

She folded her arms across her belly. She cared now. She wanted this child with a desire so fierce it shocked her.

"Chief Atholl, I am afraid we may lose her along wi' the child, if it does come awa'. Should she weaken any further—"

Alanna's father grunted.

"Perhaps, Chief Atholl, if you were to cut down the cage—"

"He is dead."

"Aye, so I ken. But if his body might be brought here, if she could tend it…"

"The sentence is the sentence. He will hang there until tonight."

His verdict spoken, Atholl left. Fenna came into the hut softly and crossed to the pallet. Alanna felt a hand on her brow.

"Come, lass. You maun tak' a drink for the sake of the bairn, if naught else."

Alanna nodded. She struggled up, and Fenna brought the cup.

"There, now. This grieving will do you no good, nor the child."

"I ken." Taloc's child, with a smile full of light and eyes full of magic—all Alanna had left of him.

She seized Fenna's arm. "Fenna, I want this child."

"Then as I ha' told you, fight for it. Eat and drink for it, live for it."

Alanna nodded again. But she felt broken inside, and the darkness that filled that broken place frightened her so she could barely breathe.

"What have I done? Fenna, 'twas I who bade him go. I gave him leave to take his release—and he went. He went!"

"Aye, and now, lamb, you maun carry on."

****

They flew steadily out of the night and into the sunrise. When the light gathered golden around them, spreading from the pale rim of the world, the hawk still had not tired or alit anywhere.

Tally could feel its heart beating, the life rushing through its veins even as the wind ruffled its feathers. And then up ahead he saw—

But mayhap he felt it before he saw it, the tower shining white through the dawning, the one he'd first Seen in a Vision more than ten years ago. But it could not be shining now; it lay gutted and broken, a beacon for the Caledonii no more.

Yet, as his mother would say, the beacon, ruined or not, would continue to shine as long as one Caledonian believed.

He caught his breath, or the hawk did.

He believed.

Take me, he told the bird, and it gave a wild cry that echoed over the hills, over the rock.

The light rushed toward them, enfolded them. Beneath the hawk's wings, Tally saw…

A Gaelic settlement carved from the trees like a scar on the land. Trees surrounding it as far as the eye could reach, like a furry green pelt, and to the north a great inlet of water—the Moray. Beyond, the eastern sea. And there, there not so very far, not far enough from the Gaels' encampment—

The tower and home.

It claimed him even as his heart reached out to it. In that glorious moment, all else—his pain, his torment, even the love—was forgotten in sheer joy. The land, the place to which his spirit belonged. Peace.

Circle, he bade the hawk. Let me see what remains.

Little enough, it seemed—the settlement he'd left only months ago looked unrecognizable. The tower stood like a broken tooth; Tally realized its magic shone only for him.

He longed to know if any of his family had survived the battle wherein he'd been captured. He saw again his sister, Barta, falling and her husband, True, standing and fighting above her like a ravening beast. But he'd lost track of his brother, Wick, after his final glimpse of him, and Wick's wife—

Upon that thought, the door of a half-ruined hut, below, opened. The hut had seen fire and recently been repaired; it stood in worse case even than the tower. The man who emerged from it wore a set of well-worn leather skins and bore an ugly scar across his brow, below a crop of wild, reddish-brown hair.

Wick. Gladness seized Tally and sent the hawk spinning upward. The bird circled the clearing even as someone below called his brother's name. Wick turned.

A figure hurried out from another of the huts. Clad like a man, she had long brown hair, hanging loose, and leaned heavily on a stick.

Tally knew her also. If he'd had any doubt, it would be laid to rest by the tall, lithe man who came loping after her—Barta's husband, True. She rarely took two steps that True did not follow.

They lived. All three of them.

The land, the spirit of Caledonia endured…

Tally wished then he could descend to the ground. Let them know he'd come home, ask them what had happened following that terrible battle, ascertain how they'd survived.

Tell them that back in Dal Riada, in the narrow, blood-splashed cage, he hung dead.

His spirit might fly free, but his body, now far distant from him, had surrendered its fight. Was it not so? Surely only death could part spirit from flesh.

The hawk gave a restless cry. The three standing below looked up. Barta merely stared, but Wick's expression transformed to one of wonder. True made a sign, one acknowledging enchantment.

Tally ached to speak to them, these folk he loved so well. Yet the bird's tongue would not serve. And—

And another love pulled at him.

The hawk circled once more, catching the buoyant currents of the air. Tally strained to look back the way he had come—so far, such a terrible distance.

But he could feel her, still. And even as the hawk circled the place Tally had loved all his life, where he would have sworn his heart lay, he realized he'd left a large part of that heart behind.

He had made a promise to the goddess, yes—to return to this place, to keep faith with the land and what remained of his family. But now grief mingled with joy at his homecoming. Much as he longed to be with those standing below, he longed to be with Alanna also. Working in the sunny field with the ponies. Sitting beside the fire with her in the clear evenings. Sharing kisses and laughter. Alanna had spoken for him, battled for him, and in the end—

She had bidden him take the path to freedom, an act of pure love.

Nay, no one had ever loved him so. No one ever would. As for that freedom—he wanted to be here more than almost anything, but perhaps not at the cost of Alanna's sacrifice.

The way he had once ached for home, he ached for her—the woman who made up the other half of him, who held his being in the palm of her hand. Ah, he'd supposed his heart rested here. It had, once; it did no more.

Yet how could he possibly go back? His body hung in the gory cage, broken. Returning to Alanna meant returning also to the pain, weakness, and blood. Could he withstand that?

For Alanna's sake, and only for her sake, perhaps he could.

He knew then, still riding a current of air high above the Epidii settlement, what it meant to love—to be willing to trade anything, endure anything, for the beloved. When had he lost so much of himself to Alanna? At what moment had he gifted her the better part of his being, his spirit?

Please, goddess. He prayed then, as he had not in weeks—with intensity and belief. *Grant me the grace and this bird the strength to return.*

There would, he knew, be unbearable pain. But Alanna would be there also, and in her love he would endure.

The hawk gave one final cry of victory. The three figures on the ground all still watched it, startled. Keep this place for me, Tally thought as the bird whirled and streaked away westward. And he fancied he felt his mother smiling.

Chapter Thirty-Five

"'Tis time, Alanna. The men have begun cutting the cage down. I thought you would want to be there so they do not—so you can take charge of the corpse."

"Aye." Alanna struggled up from the pallet, moving like an aged woman. She felt ill unto death, had felt so since the moment her father's men put Taloc inside the cage. But aye, she would be there. She wanted no one harming him any further.

"Fenna, you ha' been a good friend to me."

"It does no' mean I think you are right in this, lass, just that I can see how much you are hurting."

"Wait. Let me fetch Banna. She will carry him back for me."

Alanna ran to bring the pony from its box. All around her the day died, light once more bleeding from the sky and, overhead, stars began to prick through. At dusk, Taloc's sentence would be served.

Horror and eagerness filled her in equal measures as she hurried ahead of Fenna down the hill. When she reached the space in front of the Chief's hall, she saw no sign of her father, but his man, Belloch, was already at work, along with a small crew. They had the cage cut down and, even as Alanna ran up, worked to unbar the door.

Belloch nodded at the pony and asked, "What's that for, Mistress? He will no' be riding up to yon field."

Alanna looked at Taloc. He sprawled against the inside of the cage, his arms still secured inside the shackles.

With her best note of command, she ordered, "Get him out o' those."

They sneered but unfastened the hasps. Two of them dragged Taloc out of the cage and slung him over Banna's back. The pony took a few skittish steps but, when Alanna spoke to her, settled into a firm stance.

Alanna wanted to touch Taloc so much it hurt. She wanted to caress his skin, smooth the tangled hair out of his face, and brush his cheek with her lips. But her father's men still stood by, watching her with avid criticism, and she feared her father would, at any moment, emerge from the hall. Better to get Taloc away home.

She turned the pony, winding her fingers through the lead, and Fenna edged up. "Do you need my help? Only, I maun get home to the bairns. I ha' been awa' far too long."

"Go, Fenna. You ha' done more than enough. I thank you."

"But…what will you do wi' him?"

"Tend him, wash him, prepare him to go to his gods." Where he belonged. A man like Taloc map Radoc was, possibly, not meant for the world. "I will ask Marc to help me."

"Very well so."

Fenna went one way and Alanna the other, back up the hill at a slow and solemn pace. As she walked, she wondered what had become of the woman she'd once been—sure of herself, dauntless and confident.

Now the one thing of which she felt certain was that she'd love this man until she took her very last breath.

Old Marc, who'd been minding the ponies and, Alanna suspected, keeping an eye on her, came out to meet her at the wall and scowled at Banna's load.

"What do ye mean to do wi' that?"

"Help me take him into the hut, Marc."

Marc gave her a long look before heaving Taloc's body from the back of the pony and onto his shoulder. With what sounded like a snarl, he stomped inside with his burden.

"On the pallet?"

"Aye. Face down, please, so I can—can clean his wounds."

"He be dead."

"No matter." She'd longed for three days to soothe Taloc's hurts, to take these terrible marks of torment from him.

"He will no' care, lass."

"But I will."

Marc settled Taloc more gently than he might have, and left. Alanna hunkered down beside the pallet, where she surveyed the damage. Dark stripes, clotted black with blood, scored his back, and the wounds on both wrists, where the shackles had cut deep, showed livid. After all her longing, she found she could not touch him after all—could not bear to feel his flesh turned cold and lifeless that had once held so much warmth and magic.

She lowered her forehead to the edge of the pallet and wept.

And wept.

How long the storm lasted, she never knew. When at last it ended, the air in the hut had grown dark. She rose, lit a couple of rush lights, and went out to fetch a basin of water.

Overhead, the sky shone clear and dark blue, patterned by a thousand stars. But out over the sea a bank of cloud had begun rolling in. They would have rain before morning.

As if it mattered to her. She could not bear to think of the morning, of endless days stretching ahead of her, of years spent yearning for what could not be.

Above her head in the clear sky, something fluttered. Ignoring it, she stooped over the spring that supplied the ponies with water and filled her basin.

As soon as she straightened and turned, a bird swooped at her head. It was a large bird, though she could not see it very clearly in the rapidly gathering gloom.

"Be gone," she told it, and went back inside to her task, leaving the door ajar.

****

Alanna did not know him, in the form of the hawk. That truth surprised Tally, for he'd been able to sense their connection, strong and vital, all the way back to her.

When the hawk settled on the sill above the hut's sole window opening, he saw why. She had lost herself in contemplation of the figure that lay, like so much dead meat, on the pallet.

Could that be him? Poor beleaguered fellow, his flesh bloodied and torn. Did he have the courage to return and inhabit that house of weakness and pain?

It would not be easy.

Many things worth having were not easy.

Through the hawk's keen eyes, he watched the woman kneeling with her back to him, beside the figure on the pallet. Very gently, she sponged the dried blood from his back before smoothing his hair with extreme tenderness. He could feel her grief and love—her need—pulling at him strongly, making nothing of his will to resist.

She leaned forward and touched her lips to his, and he felt that also, like an echo of a beautiful song.

Please, he implored the goddess once more. *I do not care what it costs me. Please, for her sake.*

He opened his eyes and drew a breath.

Alanna knelt just beside him, very near. Her hair, only half braided, tumbled forward to touch his cheek, and her lips hovered but a hair's breadth away from his. When she felt the breath rush into his body, out of her own, she twitched violently. Her eyes widened and sought his, full of disbelief and dawning wonder.

For an instant that lasted forever, they gazed into one another's eyes, and Tally saw the joy seize her, oversetting even the disbelief.

"Alive," she whispered. "You're alive!"

Tally could not answer her, not then, for the pain rushed in on him, hitting everywhere at once—in the joints and muscles of his shoulders and arms, in the ruined flesh of his back, in his mind.

Oh, such a cost to this return! But oh, what he saw in Alanna's eyes had the power, so he believed, to bear him up through it.

She lifted a hand to his cheek. "How? Do I but dream? Is this true?"

Tally groaned.

"Taloc, you were gone from me. Gone."

Calling on the remnants of his strength, he whispered, "I was gone, yes. Love brought me back again."

****

Much later, after Alanna had soothed Tally's back with cooling salve and sponged the grime from his face, after she'd encouraged him to drink fresh water brought from the spring, and the night had deepened to impossible silence, she wove her fingers through his.

She could feel the weight of agony that bore him down, and could almost taste his weakness. Pain shone from his eyes when he looked at her, and a thin sheen of sweat slicked his skin. But he breathed; his heart beat, and warmth had returned to his skin. By whatever means, and however impossibly, he had returned to her.

"Taloc," she whispered, "I need to know how this thing happened. They told me you were dead." So far, no one but she knew anything different. Marc had not returned to the hut, and no one else had come to inquire. For the time being, she wanted to keep the secret between them.

She wiggled her fingers into his hand. "I need to understand this miracle. Are you strong enough, love, to tell me?"

He seemed to contemplate the question. His thick, brown lashes fluttered shut, and he drew another deep breath, one she could tell hurt. From whence, she wondered, could a man gather such strength? And was she selfish, asking him to speak?

Yet he told her, "I am strong enough."

"You said…" She faltered. "You said love brought you back to me. Were you truly dead?"

He pondered that question also before he opened his eyes. In them Alanna saw the magic she'd first glimpsed back at her father's hall, now banked and deepened.

"I think I was. I am not certain. I flew, Alanna, I flew! When you released me, I fled the pain, and I flew."

"How? Where?"

"I rode piggyback on the spirit of a hawk. He carried me and, Alanna, I went home." Dreamy pleasure flooded his eyes.

"Home?" It was all he'd wanted since he'd arrived in Dal Riada. "I saw the hawk, but how could he carry you?"

"I joined with him, my spirit did. I became him, and he me."

Deep magic, indeed.

"And," she repeated yet again, "you made it all the way home."

"I saw those I love. They survived that terrible battle, Alanna! My brother and sister survived. The tower still stands. Ruined, yes, but it can be repaired. It can be restored along with the Vision, the dream for the future. Caledonia, free."

Alanna swallowed a sudden lump in her throat. "Then, why did you no' stay there, awa' from the pain? Wi' those you love."

His fingers tightened on hers till it hurt. He gave a faint smile. "Because, much as I love them, I love you more."

Alanna's throat clenched and her heart bounded alarmingly. A fierce joy filled her, like flame. She whispered, "What did you just say?"

"You heard. Much as I longed for home, I could not bear the distance from you, Alanna. So I returned."

"You returned. To—to all this pain. To being a slave. To—"

"Worth it." His lips moved slowly. "Worth it all, if I am with you."

"Och, Taloc—"

"Do not weep again. You wept the whole time you tended me."

"Your poor body—"

"It will heal. And pray, call me Tally. That is what those I love call me."

"Tally." The name tasted sweet in her mouth. "Noble Tally map Radoc, full of wisdom and grace and belief."

"Not all those things. Just love. But as my mother says, love is the most powerful of all."

"So it must be, if it brought you back to this." Not releasing his fingers, she mopped the tears from her cheeks. "So, 'twas as easy as that? You chose to return and—"

"The bird brought me." His eyes drifted shut.

"You rest." She dropped kisses on both his eyelids. "My beloved, just rest."

"But what will we do…"

"Do not worry about aught now. We can think about the future in the morning."

He sighed like a child, and she thought she heard him whisper under his breath, "All will be well, for I am blessed."

Chapter Thirty-Six

Marc turned up the next morning, much earlier than he usually arrived, with a shovel tucked under his arm.

Alanna who, despite her exhaustion, had done little more than doze beside Tally's pallet and watch him sleep, hurried out to meet the old man.

Rain had come during the night, in a broad sweep from the sea. Now mist cloaked the hillside and moisture fogged the air.

When Marc saw Alanna, he spat into the grass. "I thought you might need me to help bury your slave. Now, whilst no one can watch."

"Why should I need to bury him?"

He shrugged. "I supposed you'd not want to watch him rot. And you'll no' manage it on your own, will ye?"

"I'll no' bury him at all." Alanna drew a breath. "He's alive."

She had the pleasure of seeing Marc's jaw drop. "Eh? But—'e was dead when we brought him up here last night."

"We thought he was dead. We must ha' been mistaken."

"He weren't breathing."

"He was, very low."

"Well, curse me!" Marc glared at the shovel and

looked disappointed. "He's come to his senses, then?"

"He has, though he'll no' be moving under his own power any time soon. But he has both served and survived his punishment. You can tell them that, when you go back down."

"Your father will no' be best pleased."

Alanna no longer cared what pleased her father. Something—perhaps the last remaining ties of loyalty—had broken between them yesterday when he struck her down so brutally.

But she said, "He should be. A slave is valuable and I still ha' the worth of mine."

Marc's eyes narrowed. "If you can keep him in line. He'll no survive your father's displeasure next time."

Too true.

"What will you do?" Marc asked curiously.

A good question. At the moment, Alanna cared only that Tally had come back to her because he loved her. No matter what happened in the future, she could hold that truth close to her heart.

"I mean to tend my slave and get him well." And then they would see.

Marc went off down the slope. He would spread the word, she knew. And what a furor it would likely cause.

She fetched more water and went back inside to find Tally sleeping soundly. She told herself it was what he needed, but knew he needed food and drink also, and could take neither while lost in slumber.

She went off to tend the ponies, but checked on Tally often. By noon, he felt feverish, the skin of his back hot to her touch, and he moaned in his sleep.

She paced and fretted, and worried. She thought about calling for the healer and put the idea away from her. The healer would not come. No one came near them; her father did not send any of his men to inquire, and even Fenna stayed away.

She turned the ponies loose to graze in the field. She tended her man and prayed harder than she had since childhood.

Great goddess, heal him. He is yours, more than mine, and he will be mine till my dying breath. Only tell me what to do for him.

No answer came, just a mild feeling of comfort. The long day ended, Alanna bedded the ponies for the night. She returned and bathed Tally's skin again, gently, to try and cool him down, and tipped water to his lips. Then she sat on the floor beside the pallet and listened as another storm blew in, bringing the night. Rain beat at the hut and rattled the door.

She lowered her chin to her chest and dozed, only to come awake again when she felt fingers stroke her hair. She knew that gentle touch, unlike any other. Turning her head, she gazed into Tally's eyes and caught her breath.

"By all that is holy, you've come awake! How do you feel?"

He appeared to consider it. His lips moved feebly without sound before he forced words through them. "Terrible. But…better. Thirsty."

Alanna scrambled up swiftly, to bring water.

"Here," he bade her, "help me sit up."

The next few moments cost them both in agony. But Tally's skin felt cooler, now, to Alanna's touch, and when she pressed her hand to his chest, his heart beat steady and strong.

He refused food but took all the water she offered. After, they sat side by side on the pallet, fingers entwined.

"You will heal," she told him, against the evidence of what they'd both just endured. "It will hurt less, day by day. 'Twill take time, that is all. And one day—"

She broke off, not knowing what to promise for the future. She must tell him about the child. Would he be glad? Dismayed?

He spoke softly. "While I slept just now, I dreamed. No ordinary dream, this. It was what my mother used to call a true dream, a Vision."

"Aye?"

"I believe I saw what lies ahead."

Alanna's stomach flipped and her fingers tightened on his. "Tell me."

His voice took on a note akin to music. "I have not had such a dream as this since I was captured. I thought I'd lost the magic."

"You will never lose the magic, Tally. You live it, you breathe it. I believe 'tis what I first loved about you. What did you See?"

"The tower all repaired and shining like a beacon fire. I was there with my family all around me. Alanna, the last time I had a Vision of the tower, it had not yet been built, but I knew it must be, that it would become a symbol of strength for the eastern tribes. Now I know it must be rebuilt once more."

Alanna's heart faltered in her breast. "But that means—you need to be there. You wish to leave me, still?"

"No, you do not understand. I said we all were

there—me, my brother, my sister…you. You were with me, Alanna." He looked at her, his eyes filled with the gray mist lent by the Sight. "And we had a child—a wee boy with fair hair." Very gently, he covered her belly with his hand. "Have you something to tell me?"

"I have." Her throat closed; she could say no more. She need say no more, for joy flooded his eyes. He brought her fingers to his lips and kissed them.

Against the great weight of emotion, she managed to speak. "You are no' displeased?" Before he could answer, she rushed on, "'Tis why…that is, I would ha' taken that punishment for you as I did the other, no matter how cruel it was. But I would no' risk the harm to your child."

"I would not have let you take my punishment again. Alanna, this child—well, he makes it clear why I was captured and brought here, made a slave. I believe one day he will be important to Caledonia."

"Alanna!" A roar came from outside the hut, startling them both.

Father? Alanna wondered. But nay, that was not her father's voice.

Tally struggled up and attempted to rise. Without much effort, Alanna pushed him back down.

"Stay here. I will go see who that is." When worry flooded his eyes, she added, "I ha' my knife."

Outside, rain still lashed down, and the afternoon looked dark as night. A figure stood just beyond the stone wall, one trembling with rage.

For an instant, Alanna failed to recognize him. He had his hood up covering his hair, and she could not see his face clearly.

She loped to the wall and stood facing him.

"Is it true?" he demanded. "He lives?"

As soon as he spoke, she knew him. "Nenian," she breathed. "You should no' be here."

He stiffened in outrage, hands clenched into fists. "I want to know if it is true."

"That Taloc lives? Aye."

Nenian swore bitterly and raised a fist. Alanna backed off a step.

"He should have died in that cage, or under your father's whip."

"What is it to you if he lives or dies?"

"Fool!" he spat at her. "You favored me, before he came. Gave me gifts and took me to your bed. I pleased you then. With him gone, I might well please you again."

Pieces fell together in Alanna's mind, making a terrible pattern. "You are the reason he was caught so swiftly, are you not? What ha' you done?"

"I did no more than offer him help. He accepted. A word in Master Belloch's ear did the rest."

Rage swept through Alanna, from her toes upward. "Do you ken wha' you ha' cost him? What you nearly cost me?"

"I regret only that he survived." Nenian lifted both his hands. "I do not understand. What kept him alive all that time?"

"Love," Alanna returned. "Mine for him, and his for me."

"Love?" Nenian repeated it with a sneer. "I comprehend he loves you so much he ran from you twice."

"And came back again, in the end." Alanna's chin jerked up. "Get out of my sight before I answer your vile behavior as it deserves. And do no' let me see you again."

He spat, the spittle hitting the sodden ground at her feet. "You are naught but a bitch in heat, wanting it from any Caledonii that will give it to you. You proved that when you spread your legs for me."

"Aye, curious I should have so lowered mysel'. But now I ha' learned the meaning of nobility and devotion." Of forever, but she did not add that. "You may well throw stones at me, Nenian. But you betrayed one o' your own, who trusted you. May the gods curse you for it."

"They have already cursed me—that happened the first time you looked my way." He bared his teeth. "Keep your filthy tribesman. I wish you joy of him."

Clearly, he wished her anything but. He turned away and stomped off angrily, leaving her at the wall.

"We canno' stay here," she said aloud, to herself.

She spun and returned to the hut. Tally stood in the doorway, supporting himself with both hands on the framework.

She repeated it to him. "We canno' stay here."

Beads of sweat covered his brow and upper lip, evidence of what it had cost him to move from the pallet. But he asked, "No? Then what are we to do?"

Deciding it on the moment, she told him, "We will follow your Vision, Tally, and return to the place where you belong."

Chapter Thirty-Seven

At daybreak, the rain still continued, locked in tight. Alanna, swathed in her short cloak, went out to care for the ponies. Tally lay on his pallet, cheek in hand, and struggled to think.

Alanna carried his child—the wee lad he'd seen in the Vision. The grandson of two chiefs he would be, and born of two warring factions. In his blood would run the ancient water of Caledonia and the bright defiance of Dal Riada. He would become this glorious land, in the flesh.

Tally narrowed his eyes and allowed his spirit to soar. If he tried, could he See the future again, a time when this land he loved so deeply might be united like the blood of his son?

And might he, Taloc map Radoc, have a hand in that, in uniting east and west into one land which embraced magic, peace, and beauty?

He moved on the pallet restlessly, and regretted it. Evidently, his recovery would not be swift. Just as evidently, it would not be easy for Alanna, a woman of property and standing, to abandon her life here.

Had she meant what she said? Would she give up her place and live the rest of her days among strangers—for his sake? It made him feel grateful and humble, unworthy of such sacrifice.

The door of the hut opened, and she came in,

drenched to the skin, hair darkened with the wet and raindrops glittering on her face.

He asked, "Are the ponies well?"

"They are well enough, though as always they seem to pick up on my emotions. And I think they miss seeing you."

"Has no one else come up from the settlement?"

"Not even Marc. Surprising, is it no'?"

"Then come and rest. You have had little sleep, so come lie with me."

"There is no room, and I do no' wish to hurt you."

"You could never hurt me."

She shed her clothing as she crossed the hut and crawled in beside him, naked. He twined an arm around her and heard her sigh. In mere moments, she slept.

And that gave Tally an opportunity to study her, this woman who had—and would—give so much for him. Thick, fair lashes now darkened by rain, a beautiful face honed by exhaustion, and a bare shoulder showing above the edge of the blanket. A single person, who now made up the better part of his life. No—he smiled—two persons now.

He thought back, in wonder, over the events that had occurred since the firing of the tower. All that darkness, fear, and pain had brought him to the greatest blessing of his life.

Yes, Mother, he whispered, *all that while, I should have believed.*

****

Chief Atholl came striding up the hill the next afternoon, once the rain cleared. It left a world turned fresh and clean; when Alanna stepped outside she fancied she caught the first hint of autumn on the wind.

260

Autumn. And when winter came, she'd be far away from here, among strangers.

Would they accept her, Tally's family who had lost so much to her people? What if they treated her as harshly as her clan had treated Tally?

It did not matter. Wherever he went she needed to be, and she'd suffer far worse to remain with him.

Now her father came, with Belloch at his side. She watched the two men approach through the sparkling air. Her long sleep at Tally's side had done her good, and she felt stronger. But this encounter would not be easy.

When the men drew near enough, she saw how impatient her father looked, how serious.

"Daughter," he called, "I hear your slave lives. Talk of it runs rife all over the settlement."

"He lives," Alanna confirmed.

"How is that? He looked dead when we cut him down."

"The powers have spared him."

Atholl grunted in dissatisfaction. "The powers, it seems, exist to confound me. Do you mean to keep him wi' you?"

"Aye."

"Then, Daughter, I am here to warn you—there will be an end to your defiance, and to his disobedience. If I see signs of either again, he will receive what he has already, over again. I hope you ha' learned your lesson."

"I have, and it has been a hard one."

She'd learned that her father, who had knocked her down so easily, cared far more for his reputation than for her welfare. She'd learned to trust no one as she did the man in the hut at her back.

"Sometimes," Atholl said, "it requires a hard lesson."

Alanna lifted her chin. "You need no' worry, Father, about further defiance."

"Good."

"Taloc and I will be leaving here as soon as he is fit to travel."

"Leaving?" Atholl's single, pale eye narrowed.

"Aye. Mysel', the man I love, and our child will remove from your sight."

He exchanged an incredulous look with Belloch. "And go where?"

"That need no' concern you. 'Twill tak' a while. I'm sure you appreciate Taloc will require sufficient time to heal, but as soon as he can sit a pony, we are gone."

"I suppose he has persuaded you to this." Atholl gestured angrily. "He has enchanted you. I am sorry I ever set eyes on him, and if you think you can take these ponies—"

"They are my property," Alanna told him in some satisfaction, "as, in your eyes, is the slave. Did our other clansfolk who moved east to settle the lands we seized from the Caledonii no' take their belongings?"

"So!" He glared. "You mean to go east."

"My child will scarcely be welcome here."

"What makes you think it will be welcome among those savages, either? You are a fool."

"If I am, I will accept the consequences."

"Perhaps you did no' learn your lesson so well after all. Just know, Alanna, if you choose that filthy slave over your own blood, you will remain no daughter to me. I cast you off."

"Do you no' see, Father, more hatred and division will no' heal this land? Only joining together will do that."

"Hark and listen to her!" Atholl said to the silent Belloch. "The lass who has battled since she was born, now suing for peace. I will ha' you know, Alanna, I do no' want to heal this land, but to conquer it."

He spun on his heel and left her standing, even as had Marc and Nenian. Alanna, watching him and Belloch return down the hill, felt nothing. To her mind, Atholl had already cast her off when he knocked her down on the stones in front of his dwelling. She belonged here no more.

****

"Are you sure you're strong enough to ride?" Alanna gazed up at Tally with concern. He looked pale beneath his tattoos and, though he tried to hide it, she knew that weakness still dogged him. Beads of sweat now moistened his skin, but he met her eyes determinedly and nodded his head.

"I am well enough."

A mere fortnight had passed since Alanna's father disowned her. She'd spent those tending Tally, organizing her belongings, and giving away all she could not take with her.

The parting from Fenna had been hard; so had that from Marc, somewhat to her surprise. The old man had become a second father to her, in some ways closer than her own.

Other things, though, told her she did well to leave. Her father's men, or perhaps Nenian, had roused ill feeling toward her and Tally throughout the settlement.

Two nights ago, shadowy figures had crept up and set fire to the pony sheds. She'd got the animals out just in time.

"We will travel slowly, in stages," she told Tally, "for the ponies' sake if not yours."

"Mine as well." He flexed his back and grimaced. He healed steadily but had a long way to go yet. "Do you think we will run into any fighting?"

"Another reason we travel slowly. I will ride ahead each morning and scout the way." Alanna hoped, eventually, to meet up with one of her brothers, with whom she might bargain. But she'd said nothing of that to Tally.

He gazed away eastward; she fancied she saw longing in his eyes. But when he looked down at her from Banna's back, he said, "Alanna, love, are you certain about this? You are giving up everything, and may never return here again."

Love. He called her love.

She smiled at him. "I am taking everything that matters with me. Anyway, I want a better place for our child to grow up, free of all this ugliness and hate."

His gaze sobered. "There is hate among my people, also—they hate the Gaels, and fear them."

"Do you think they will accept me?"

"I hope so, if only for my sake."

A bird appeared on the horizon. It streaked toward them on broad wings, circled them twice, and gave a loud cry.

Alanna caught her breath. "'Tis a hawk."

"So it is."

They watched the bird veer away through the sky and streak away eastward. "A messenger from the gods," Alanna whispered.

Tally laughed, a sound Alanna once feared she'd never hear again.

"Then, my heart, let us follow him."

Chapter Thirty-Eight

The tower came in sight all at once above the tops of the trees. Tally blinked at it, thinking this another Vision, for he could see no signs of burning on the stones. Instead, the structure shone like the beacon he'd first conceived it to be.

Then he realized the truth: the rays of the setting sun, now well behind them, caught the surface of the pale stone from which the tower had been constructed, and hid all wounds.

"Look," he said softly, capturing Alanna's attention.

She looked up slowly. For the last day, she'd ridden in near silence, seeming to have fallen into a stupor. The journey had been hard, given Tally's physical condition; he worried, also, about hers and about the welfare of their child. Weariness had become a heavy weight, and danger hovered at every hand. They'd been forced to veer many times to avoid bands of Gaels and even Gaelic settlements. Her presence might guarantee his safety if they were captured—but he doubted it.

"Ah," she said now, her eyes widening. She turned her head to stare at him. "Have we reached the place?"

"This is the tower of which I spoke. I only hope my family members are truly here." It had occurred to him that the flight on the back of the hawk and what he'd seen during it might have been a dream driven by fever and pain.

Alanna turned to glance behind her. "We are very close to that last Gaelic camp. I believe it may ha' belonged to my brother, Donhal."

"What makes you say that?"

She shrugged. "I thought I recognized one or two of those guards we espied as being his men."

"There may, then, be ongoing battles. For, if what the bird showed me was true, my brother Wick was here but ten days ago, and if he is here he will fight." Impulsively, Tally reached over from Banna's back and touched Alanna's hand. "Two camps, two brothers. Two chiefs. What if we—you and I, Alanna—are to be the bridge between them?"

She bit her lip. "That very thought has been in my mind. How did you know?"

"Because, love, it would make sense of my capture, would it not? Put a meaning to being hauled away from home, and to all the pain. What if it was the goddess's intention all the while that you and I should return here together?"

"And wha' if your fierce tribe will no' accept me?"

"They will."

"So I ha' been telling mysel' all this way. But now I see that," she nodded at the tower, "and I feel uncertain."

Tally gazed into her eyes. "I will defend you and our child, with my life if need be."

"I do no' want for you to lose your life, for that or any reason." Tears flooded her eyes.

"Faith, Alanna. Believe in the goddess. Now, come."

They rode on toward the settlement, the very place where Tally's parents lay buried, the same where Barta's magical mate, True, had proved himself in trial and where Wick had, some ten years ago, returned to them.

They met the guards—who stared at Tally and his train of ponies in disbelief—some hundred paces out. They consisted of two young men, one of them Tally's good friend Omarex, and they made so much racket others soon came running, spears at the ready.

"Tally!" Omarex's face split as he beamed in wonder. "How come you here? We did think you lost forever."

"It is a wonder we did not take your head off," said his companion, Desacan. "We thought the cursed Gaels were on the attack again."

As more tribe members hurried up, Omarex asked, "What of the others who were captured with you? And who is she?" He glared at Alanna. "She looks like a Gael."

"So she is—"

Tally had no chance to explain farther. His sister, Barta, came running up with True close behind. Tally found himself pulled from his pony and crushed—painfully—in a hug.

"By the goddess! Tally!" Barta rarely wept, but her eyes now filled with ready tears, which promptly spilled over. She gulped as she cried, "You have come back! I prayed and prayed you might return to us. Oh, you don't know how I prayed." She cast a look at the man behind her. "Tell him, True."

True beamed a smile and nodded his shaggy head. "So she did."

"Wick?" Tally managed to free himself from Barta's fierce grip. "And Verica? The children?" He'd not seen them in his Vision, through the hawk's eyes. And anyway, this was reality, as Barta's strong embrace proved.

"All survived the attack. Verica was badly wounded, but she recovers, slowly." Barta turned her warlike gaze on Alanna. "But why have you brought a Gael here on our ground?"

Tally sucked in a breath. Here it was, the crucial moment, and come so swiftly after all. "This is Alanna. She helped me survive my captivity and allowed me to get away to you now. I pray you will make her welcome here with us."

Stunned silence met the words. It was True who spoke first, in his deep growl.

"Then you had better bring her along."

****

Tally had rarely known Alanna so silent. All through the glad greetings that followed, the exclamations over Tally's presence and his hurried explanations, she spoke but once and that to Wick, when he moved to clap Tally on the back heartily.

"I pray you, do not. He is still healing."

Wick gave her an inquiring look from his dark eyes before turning again to Tally. "There is a story in it, no doubt, as Mother would have said."

"A long story," Tally agreed. "But we are weary to the bone, and the ponies need tending."

"Gaels' ponies, here." Barta's eyesbrows twitched violently. "We have no facilities for them." She looked at Alanna, and Tally almost heard her thought: *or for her*.

"No matter," Wick declared. "We will manage. First, let us offer you what food we have, drink, and tending for whatever wounds you may carry. You can see we are still rebuilding after the attack that saw you captured, Tally, and all those after. But," he added proudly, "we refused to surrender the tower. Barta, here, kept insisting you would return and wish to rebuild it."

"So I have," Tally smiled at his sister, "and so I do."

They sat together by the chief's fire, out in the open—few of the huts remained whole and those, so Barta assured Tally, housed the wounded, the aged, and the children. Tally, who cared little where he sat, could not stop smiling. This place felt and smelled like home, and the gladness with which he was welcomed warmed him despite his exhaustion.

That welcome, however, did not extend to Alanna. His brother and sister brought her into the circle around the fire for his sake. But when they looked at her, their uncertainty and hostility showed.

It came to him then—as she had protected him in Dal Riada, he might well now need to protect her in turn.

"So what, just, is the situation between you and the Gaels?" he asked at length, when they'd spoken long together and the dark of the evening began to come down. Alanna sat at his right hand, still uncannily silent, while joy and weariness nibbled at him.

Verica, who had come to sit very close at her husband's side, grunted. Wick glanced at her before he answered. Their daughter, Essa, sat between them, and Barta, too, had brought the triplets to sit with her and

True, though like Barta herself they rarely kept still.

"I suppose you would call it a stand-off. Your capture along with the damage to the tower made a hard blow for us. But it also made a strong rallying point. Not only did we pick ourselves up and strike back, we hurt them." Wick glared at Alanna. "We regained this site, and we mean to hold it throughout the winter, and beyond."

Barta said, "Since then, there have been a number of raids, some of them fierce indeed. Between times, we maintain a heavy guard."

Tally nodded soberly. "There is a Gaelic camp not far off—we circled it on the way in."

Bitterly, Barta agreed, "The land to the west of here is full of Gaels, so it seems. So tell me, Brother, why have you brought us another one?"

Tally reached out and clasped Alanna's hand. Her fingers curled into his tightly. He knew, if she had hope of a future here with him, he must persuade these folk to reason, and do it well.

"When I was captured and taken away from here," he began slowly, "I believed my life was over. I had no real hope of seeing this place ever again, or of seeing any of you—I will confess, I lost my faith then. I thought the goddess had turned her back on me."

"You?" Barta's gaze softened. "But apart from Mother, you have the brightest faith of anyone I've ever known."

"I felt betrayed," Tally confessed. "I did not understand that the goddess led me still. To Alanna."

"*To*, not *away*," Wick mused. Who would have supposed, Tally marveled, his strong, grave brother would be the first to understand?

Tally nodded. "I forgot to be grateful. I forgot I was blessed. But the goddess led me straight into Alanna's hands, and when the worst happened, when I thought to leave her behind and return here, she took my punishment. And, in the end, she gave up even her home to come away with me."

The others gazed at Alanna with curious eyes. Little Essa, lying with her head on her mother's knee, smiled.

Alanna spoke. "I did no more than see the man Tally was, in truth—full of dignity and magic. I did no more than give him my heart."

Wick asked, "What happened to the others who were taken captive with you, Tally? How do they fare?"

Tally shook his head. "The word is not so good. Cemedd and Agarex are both dead. Cemedd died during the march, fighting for his freedom, and Agarex took his own life following our attempted escape. Tamia, who also tried to escape with us, avoided punishment but lives in a harsh household, as do most of the others."

Wick pressed, "Is there a chance we might rescue them?"

"'Twould be a dangerous proposition. I wish I could have brought them all away with me. The risk of retaliation against them, though, forbade it."

Barta spoke angrily. "Yet the thought of leaving them there, abandoning them, cuts deep."

Again, Alanna spoke. "You do not ken, Mistress Barta, the ordeal your brother suffered as a result of his second escape attempt. I thought him lost in death. By grace alone did he return to me."

The others were silent a moment, contemplating it.

Then, characteristically, Barta declared, "I am saying only that I would prefer he brought one of our own back to us rather than an acursed Gael."

"And I am saying," Tally returned, "it is time for healing. What do you see, Sister, sitting here around this fire?"

"I see what is left of our family."

"Yes, and the next generation." Tally nodded at the four little ones. "The grandchildren of Essa and Radoc. And," very gently he laid his palm against Alanna's belly, "I bring you another."

His family stared.

Barta drew a sharp breath. "Half Gael? What would Father say?"

"What would Mother say?" Wick interposed. He smiled. "I see, Brother."

"Wick, when you handfasted with Verica, you united two tribes. When Alanna and I join hands, I hope to accomplish even more."

"It is a noble intention." Wick shook his head. "But I doubt one marriage will achieve a peace."

"No, but we can negotiate for it. We have been battling the Gaels all our lives and have achieved only pain and strife. Perhaps it is time to try love."

Chapter Thirty-Nine

"A word, Mistress Alanna, if you do not mind."

The strident call halted Alanna on her way back from the midden, early next morning. Ah, and would it not have to be Tally's fierce sister who intercepted her, wearing a look of mutinous rebellion?

Alanna paused reluctantly and faced the woman. Barta's eyes, like Tally's, were smoke gray, but they held a far different expression, that of a warrior looking for battle.

"Where is my brother?" she demanded.

"Tally still sleeps; he is in dire need of the rest." Alanna raised her chin, determined this forceful woman should not intimidate her. She understood she'd now need to find her way among these strangers. She would fight to do so, for Tally's sake—and that of their child—if not her own. "You ha' not seen the extent of his injuries, and ha' no idea what he has been through."

Barta's antagonism lessened just a whit. "And you would have me believe you care so very much about him?"

Alanna stood firm. "I do care for him, Mistress Barta. It matters not what you believe."

Barta snorted and tossed her head. "The others may accept you, if Tally asks. It will not be so easy with me."

So Alanna imagined.

Barta swept her up and down with a hard look. "For instance, am I expected to accept whatever child you may carry is truly his?"

"It could belong to no one else."

"So you claim."

"Your brother and I both believe this child was meant to be. He will be important to the future of this land."

"He? You know it will be a boy?"

"Tally has Seen so."

That silenced Barta.

"Mistress." Alanna chose her words with great care. "I may not be of your blood, but I was born in this land and belong to it all the same. And, just like you, I want an end to the hostilities. I long for peace."

"Peace for Caledonia? It is a dream."

"Aye, but a good and noble dream, aye? We might not be able to achieve it for all Alba, not in our lifetimes, but here in this wee part of it? Possibly."

Barta's triplets—barely distinguishable from one another—ran up then and threw themselves at her. Two girls and a boy, they looked about eight years old, and had their father's oddly-colored eyes and long limbs.

Alanna asked, "Do you no' want that for your children?" And mine, she added silently.

"To be sure." Barta drew the children closer, managing to encircle all three of them with her arms.

"Then give me a chance to help achieve it. Let me prove myself to you."

Barta glanced over her shoulder. Her husband, True, approached at an easy jog. Alanna could sense the connection between them, almost as if they communicated without speaking.

"Good morn, Mistress," True bade Alanna in his husky voice. "How fares Master Tally this day?"

"Gaining some of the rest he so desperately needs."

"He has not told us all of what befell him," Barta spoke again. "What are these dire injuries of his?"

"I will let him share that wi' you."

"Oh? Why can you not tell me?

"Because the story is his to tell, and he will do it much better than I."

One of the triplets looked up at Alanna. "Ma says you are an accursed enemy Gael in our mist."

"Midst," Barta corrected and had the grace to look abashed.

"Yes, pup." True tossed the child's wild hair. "But enemies do not always remain enemies, as I know full well. I was given a chance when first I came here. We will offer Mistress Alanna the same."

****

"So," Barta challenged when they once more sat around the fire, "how do you mean to prove yourself, Mistress Alanna, and attain this elusive peace?"

The adults—all six of them—had gathered to speak together without the children present, but not before Tally had been cornered by both his siblings, Barta demanding to view his injuries.

The extent of them had struck Wick silent. Barta swore bitterly, and tears flooded her eyes.

"Oh, what have they done to you? There, so far away from us, all alone—and how, Tally, can you claim to love *her*, in the face of this?"

"Do you not see, Barta?" he'd returned. "Love is the only thing that can save us."

Yet Barta still seemed ready to battle with Alanna.

"Sister," Tally began, only to have Barta interrupt him.

"Nay—she told me she will prove herself and achieve a peace. I swear to you, naught less will make me accept her here among us."

"Barta!" Wick chastised her this time.

"Nay, Wick. After all our seasons of battling, all we have suffered and lost, will you just welcome her in?"

"Yes," Wick returned steadily. "If Tally tells me he trusts her."

"I do," Tally avowed.

Verica leaned forward from her place at Wick's side and laid her fingers on Barta's arm. The most badly wounded of them all in the fight that had seen Tally captured, Tally could sense what it still cost her to be there with them. Yet he welcomed her cool head and her wisdom.

"Barta, from what Tally has shared with us, he was led through this ordeal to find Alanna and deepen his faith. There are, indeed, such times in life when we cannot turn away from our fate, however painful it may seem. I say, give her a chance."

"As do I," Wick averred.

True shot an apologetic look at his mate. "And I. Were we not all given such chances, in the past? And did we not make the most of them?"

Barta did not look pleased.

"Sister," Tally said, speaking to her from his heart, "this endless battling will not be halted by separation, but by union."

She spat, "Try convincing the Gaels of that."

"It is precisely what we mean to do." Tally glanced

at Alanna. "We spoke much of this, near the end of our journey, and have birthed a plan, one that will not work without Alanna on our side."

"If she *is* on our side," Barta muttered.

"Do not take it personally," Wick told Alanna. "She is like this with everyone."

"Tell them, love," Tally bade Alanna, "about the politics of your clan."

"I ha' two older brothers, Donhal and Graedh, who have long contested for our father, Atholl's, favor. Graedh, the elder, would be all things to him and was first to move east, to claim land and extend Da's holdings."

"Donhal MacAtholl—I know that name," Wick murmured, and shot a look at Verica.

Alanna went on, "The trouble is, Dal Riada is actually three kingdoms, and all with the same intention. My father competes with other high chiefs even as my brothers compete wi' each other. It is, so I believe, why your tribes ha' been pushed so hard in recent years—everyone wants his own piece of eastern Alba."

"So," True asked, "what can you hope to do about it?"

Alanna lifted her eyes to each of them in turn. "I mean to negotiate with whichever of my brothers presses you here. I do no' ken who it may be—they have been awa' from Dal Riada most the season, and we ha' had little word these past weeks. And, for Tally's sake, we dared no' get close enough to see, when we passed them by on our way here. But..." She glanced at Tally. "I mean to present mysel' as soon as ever I can, and make a bid for some kind of truce."

"A truce?" Verica echoed.

"A measure of peace, as I say. I think 'twill be my brother, Donhal, since on our way in I caught a glimpse of some men I know to be his. I hope it is, for he will be far more reasonable than Graedh, who has as hard a head as—" Her gaze strayed to Barta, and she broke off.

"Donhal MacAtholl." Wick repeated the name again. "Remember, Verica, it was he we met in the forest, after we left the Diminii, he who allowed me to battle for your freedom."

Verica leaned her head against Wick's shoulder. "My valiant husband, how could I ever forget?"

"Donhal likes to bargain," Alanna declared, "and I will challenge him to another such. I can no' promise he will accept, but I do vow to do my level best to persuade him."

"I will go with you," Wick decided. "I do not doubt he will remember me."

"If 'tis himsel' and no' Graedh," Alanna cautioned.

"We had best pray on it, all of us," Tally said. "But I have Seen a Vision of the tower standing tall and strong again, a shining beacon. And I believe, with Alanna on our side, we may endure."

"A Gael to save us!" Barta lamented. "Now, there is true irony."

Chapter Forty

"Beautiful woman, come awake to me."

Tally whispered the words into Alanna's ear and watched the pale lashes flutter on her cheeks. He supposed he should let her sleep. Yesterday had been difficult for her and had taken its toll, both the journey to and from the Gaels' encampment and the ordeal of facing her brother there.

She'd returned looking ashen with weariness, but with victory shining in her eyes. Her first words still echoed in Tally's mind.

My brother, Donhal, sends his greetings.

"He remembered me," Wick told Tally later, "and favorably, despite the way our last encounter ended. I think we will be able to deal honorably together. He tires of trying to please his father, just as we all tire of the dying." Wick had clasped Tally on the shoulder. "We have tentatively agreed on a boundary, with your tower standing as the marker. And, Brother, Alanna was our means to his ear."

Alanna's eyelids flicked open and her clear, blue eyes met Tally's. She smiled.

I am blessed.

Oh, by all that was holy, how could he ever have doubted it?

I am grateful.

Great Goddess, thank you for leading me to her,

despite all the fear and pain. This love Alanna offers me is worth it all.

"Good morn," she bade him.

"Good morn," he returned, and kissed her. When he did, he felt the warmth of her passion, like a wild current just waiting to rise. He felt the strength of her love for him and the magic of the ties that bound them so securely together. He wanted to lose himself completely in her.

But first...

He abandoned her lips to trail his way down her body and plant the most tender of kisses on her belly. "Tell me my child is well and strong."

"He is certainly strong." Her eyes caressed him. "Strong in spirit, no doubt, just like his father."

"And in determination, like his mother?"

"Och, Tally, how will we ever be able to harness him?"

"I doubt we will. Alanna, he will be the new Caledonia—half of the east and half of the west, a forerunner of the future."

"I do no' doubt he will be a wee imp." She laughed. "And raising him will take every shred of our wit and patience. Och, I forgot to tell you, Donhal said he is willing to negotiate for the release of the others who were captured wi' you."

"Indeed?" Tally contemplated it, almost afraid to believe. "At what price?"

"I think I could persuade him to trade for a pony or two." She sobered abruptly. "Now if only I could be as persuasive wi' your sister, Barta, and convince her to accept me. If she does, I do no' doubt the rest of the tribe will follow."

"Do not worry about Barta."

"Why not? She has a great deal of influence, and she detests me."

"So has Wick a great deal of influence, and I could see from his expression when you returned last night he is disposed to hold you in great favor."

"I would no' wish to start a feud between them."

Tally laughed. "They have been feuding most their lives, being so very different from one another. But it comes to me, beautiful Alanna, that we need to accept our differences. After all the warring, there will be peace only if we can allow one another to be the men, and women, we truly are."

She touched his cheek lovingly. "You sound very certain."

"I am certain."

"How?"

"There is magic in it."

"Ah, just like when that brown hawk carried you from the land of the dead back to me."

"It was love did that," he assured her. "And it is love that will set this land free in the end, that will cause those who come after us to cherish it as we do. Neither war nor distance nor any other changes can prevent that, because Caledonian hearts are—"

She caught the words on his lips with her kiss, and finished the thought for him.

"Aye, my love, Caledonian hearts are noble, and blessed."

A word about the author…

Award-winning author Laura Strickland delights in time-traveling to the past and searching out settings for her books, be they historical romance, steampunk, or something in between.

Born and raised in Western New York, she has pursued lifelong interests in lore, legend, magic, and music, all reflected in her writing. Although she enjoys travel, she's usually happiest at home not far from Lake Ontario, with her husband and her "fur" child, a rescue dog.

Author of numerous historical and contemporary romances, she is the creator of the Buffalo Steampunk Adventure series set in her native city. *Noble and Blessed* is the third book in her new historical Hearts of Caledonia series.